P9-CCX-541

DISCARDED BY THE
LEVI HEYWOOD MEMORIAL LIBRARY

PRESSED TO KILL

Other MANDY DYER MYSTERIES

PRESSED TO
KILL

DOLORES JOHNSON

F
JOHN
MYST

THOMAS DUNNE BOOKS
ST. MARTIN'S MINOTAUR ⚑ NEW YORK

This is a work of fiction. All of the characters, organizations, and events portrayed in this novel are either products of the author's imagination or are used fictitiously.

THOMAS DUNNE BOOKS.
An imprint of St. Martin's Press.

PRESSED TO KILL. Copyright © 2007 by Dolores Johnson. All rights reserved. Printed in the United States of America. No part of this book may be used or reproduced in any manner whatsoever without written permission except in the case of brief quotations embodied in critical articles or reviews. For information, address St. Martin's Press, 175 Fifth Avenue, New York, N.Y. 10010.

www.thomasdunnebooks.com
www.minotaurbooks.com

Library of Congress Cataloging-in-Publication Data
Johnson, Dolores.
    Pressed to kill : a Mandy Dyer mystery / Dolores Johnson.—1st ed.
        p. cm.
    ISBN-13: 978-0-312-34785-7
    ISBN-10: 0-312-34785-5
    1. Dyer, Mandy (Fictitious character)—Fiction.   2. Women detectives—Colorado—Denver—Fiction.   3. Dry cleaning indusry—Fiction. Denver (Colo.)—Fiction.   I. Title.
    PS3560.O3748 P73 2007
    813'.6—dc22

                                                            2006046950

First Edition: January 2007

10 9 8 7 6 5 4 3 2 1

To my long-time friends, Doris Bennett and Virginia Murphy, and as always, to my family—Dale, Jeff, Mindy, and Aaron Johnson—with love.

ACKNOWLEDGMENTS

I wish to thank Steven E. Weil of Rochmont Ranch Wear in Denver who, with co-author G. Daniel DeWeese, wrote *Western Shirts,* which provided me with information for one of the characters in this book. Additional information came from two books, *Chasing the Rodeo* by W. K. Stratton and *Ranch Dressing* by M. Jean Greenlaw.

Special thanks to Johnna and Mike Van Why for introducing me to country bars, even though the Last Roundup in my book is entirely my own creation. Other thanks go to Taleen Vick at Lancaster Western Wear, Jacki Tallman, public information director at the Jefferson County Sheriff's Office, and as always, to Joe and Kaye Cannata of Belaire Cleaners.

I couldn't have finished the book without help from my two critique groups—Thora Chinnery, Cindy Goff, Donna Schaper, Rebecca Bates, Barbara Snook, and Diane Coffelt, and to Lee Karr, Kay Bergstrom, Carol Caverly, Christine Jorgensen, Cheryl McGonigle, Leslie O'Kane, and Peggy Swager, as well as my agents, Meg Ruley and Annelise Robey.

These acknowledgments would not be complete without a thanks to Steven Weil's grandfather, Jack A. Weil, who is credited with being the first person to put snaps on commercially made cowboy shirts. He turned 105 years old on March 28, 2006, and is still working four hours a day, five days a week at Rockmont, a company he founded in 1946.

PRESSED TO
kiLL

CHAPTER

ONE

I'd noticed some subtle and not so subtle changes in Ardith Brewster's appearance in the last few months.

She came in to Dyer's Cleaners every week with a load of cleaning to be done, and until recently, her suits had always been in neutral tones—beige, black, or gray. Her blouses had been tailored, and she never had any slacks or pantsuits in the orders.

I sometimes wondered what she wore around home on the weekends. The only thing I could conclude was that she thought her wardrobe befitted her job as a loan officer at a bank here in the Cherry Creek area of Denver, where the cleaners is located. In keeping with her no-nonsense approach to life, she also wore her chestnut-colored hair in a tight little bun on top of her head.

But suddenly she began to show up with drop-off orders of brighter clothes—a sleeveless red dress with a jacket, a peach-colored suit with a frilly floral-patterned blouse, and even an embroidered full-skirted dress in purple. She said she couldn't resist the purple dress because it reminded her of the lilacs that were in bloom around the city now that it was May.

I'm Mandy Dyer, the thirty-something owner of Dyer's Cleaners, and I try to keep my opinions to myself about customers' wearing apparel. Maybe that's why I never ventured a comment until one

Friday when Ardith showed up in a lemon yellow outfit, with her hair suddenly loose and curled around her face. If my own short, dark hair looked half that good, I would let it grow out to shoulder length.

"I like your new hairstyle," I said. "It's really attractive."

She blushed at the compliment. Then she glanced around the call office, which is what we call the customer area of the cleaners, as if she were trying to make sure no one would overhear her.

"The man I've been dating likes my hair this way," she said, bending over toward me as if she were revealing a big secret about how to launder money through her bank.

"Well, he's right," I said, somewhat surprised that she'd share even that much of her personal life with me. "It's very becoming."

"And I have to tell you, I never would have met him if it hadn't been for Dyer's Cleaners. I owe it all to you, Mandy."

I was stunned. Not only am I opposed to people who try to set up their friends with dates but also the idea of playing matchmaker reminded me of my mother. God forbid that I might turn into Mom, whose goal in life seemed to be to find a suitable husband for every single woman she knew, especially me.

"Why do you say that?" I asked, drawing back from Ardith as if she'd accused me of robbing the bank. After all, we never even traveled in the same social circles, so how could I have had anything to do with the new man in her life?

"Do you remember back in March when you had that open house here at the cleaners?" she asked. "I believe it was the fiftieth anniversary of the day your uncle opened his first store in Denver."

I certainly did remember, and boy, had that been a mistake. Who knew that so many people would show up for a piece of cake, a cup of coffee, and a glass of champagne? Maybe it was the coupon for 50 percent off, good for a month, which we offered to the many people who dropped by that afternoon. The call office had been woefully inadequate to hold the crowd, and I'd finally allowed people to spread out into the plant.

In fact, we gave some impromptu tours of the presses and cleaning equipment that day. I've known owners of dry cleaners who actually have big windows in the back shops of their plants so that passersby can watch employees at work on the equipment. People seem to be fascinated by the huge pieces of machinery that belch steam like prehistoric monsters or look like modern-day robots with mechanical body parts, but the day of the open house, I came to wish there was a pane of glass between the visitors and my crew. The tours disrupted work, and there were even a few items of clothing that had to be recleaned.

"I met him here," Ardith said, interrupting my musings about the horror of that day. "He was such a nice dresser that I was immediately attracted to him."

Not necessarily the best criteria for selecting a man, I thought, but being a dry cleaner, I let it go.

She smiled. "I guess you're responsible for that, too, come to think of it. I mean for the sharp creases in his pants and the brightness of his freshly pressed shirt. So different from most of the men I know."

I couldn't help wondering about that comment. After all, she worked with bankers. Weren't they supposed to be good dressers, always in suits and ties?

My morning counter manager, Julia, had come out of the back of the plant, and she must have overheard the conversation.

"So who is this man who swept you off your feet?" she asked.

I frowned at Julia, and Ardith's face paled at the realization that we hadn't been alone. "Oh, I can't say. We want to keep our relationship quiet for now."

That sent up a red flag with me. The guy must be married, I figured, and probably his wife was the one who kept him so well dressed. But surely Ardith was astute enough to avoid falling in love with a married man. After all, she had to analyze loan applications and be smart enough to decide whether or not someone was a good risk and would repay the loan.

Okay, maybe that wasn't the best analogy. How could you compare love to money, unless, of course, you were my mother who was convinced that you shouldn't consider one without the other?

Ardith may have realized what I was thinking. She seemed to want to justify herself. "We want to have time to get to know each other before we go public with our relationship. In fact, we're planning to spend the whole weekend at home together—just the two of us."

I didn't know what to say to that, so I busied myself with placing her cleaning in a bag, along with a ticket I'd just printed out for her on our computer. I handed her a copy of the invoice. "I'll be right back."

I went through the door into the plant and found her pickup order on our conveyor. I was amazed to see that the invoice stapled to the garment bag indicated that the current work even had a pair of jeans. Lucille, who does our mark-in, had also identified a red-and-white dirndl skirt and a matching blouse in the order. Definitely not the type of clothes Ardith would wear to work. Maybe this mysterious new man in her life was going to be good for her after all.

I returned to the call office with the order and hung it over a hook on a rail at the end of the counter before I tallied up her bill. By then, Ann Marie had arrived for work, late as usual. She's twenty going on fifteen, but the customers seem to like her rather ditzy personality, and at least she hasn't quit on me. There's a big turnover in this business, and just staying the course is a plus.

While I was retrieving the clothes from our conveyor, Julia must have told Ann Marie that Ardith had found a boyfriend here at the cleaners.

"That's cool," Ann Marie said. "I wish I'd meet someone here, but everyone is either *sooo* old or *sooo* married."

Ardith, who must be about forty, seemed to get increasingly embarrassed. I wondered if it was because of the reference to "old" guys or if maybe it was because she was thinking about her married lover. Anyway, she couldn't seem to get out the front door fast enough. She grabbed her clothes and handed me several bills as she left, telling me to keep the change, as if she were giving me a tip. I applied what was left over as a credit to her next order.

"That's really nice," Julia said as the door swung shut, "having a romance bloom right here in the cleaners."

Perhaps she was comparing it to the unromantic way she'd met her husband and the father of her three children. She said he'd picked her up when she was walking down the street. If that marriage could last, I guessed I could be hopeful that Ardith's romance would work out, too.

"What's the guy's name?" Ann Marie asked. "Maybe we can check him out on the computer."

"She wouldn't tell us," Julia said.

"And don't bug her about it the next time she comes in," I warned.

I was looking at Ann Marie, but she had moved on to another subject by that time.

"You know," she said, "maybe we should start a dating service. We could have a bulletin board where singles could, you know, put up notices that they were looking for a date."

"Absolutely not," I said. "This is a dry cleaners, not a dating service."

I didn't tell her that I actually knew the owner of one dry cleaner who had done just that. He also had another bulletin board where people could post notices for lost pets and people who would do lawn work. It seemed tacky, although I would rather someone found a missing dog or cat through my cleaners than a lover.

I also knew dry cleaners who had shoe-repair services, ran gift shops adjoining their plants, and had all manner of side businesses. It didn't mean I was going to start any of those, either. I wanted customers to know that dry cleaning was our one and only business.

"There's a Laundromat over by where I live," Ann Marie said, "that has singles nights, where you can go and wash your clothes and meet someone at the same time."

I shook my head. "That might be okay for a coin laundry, but not for a dry cleaner."

She shrugged as I started to leave for the back of the plant. Julia was already waiting on another customer, and a second person had just entered the call office.

Ann Marie followed me through the door into the plant. "I still think we should have a bulletin board," she said. "I could handle it for you if you want."

I stopped in my path. "No. What I do want is for you to go back out front and wait on the customer who just came in."

"Okeydoke," she said, her blond ponytail bouncing as she swung around toward the call office. "It was just a suggestion."

The next Tuesday, I stopped for breakfast on my way to work. I didn't do that often, but this week was my plant manager's turn to open up the cleaners, so I was meeting Travis Kincaid for breakfast.

Travis is a private investigator, and I'd nursed him back to health in January, after he took a bullet in the leg. I'm not a natural born caregiver, but I'd felt responsible for him getting shot.

We had a history that went back to high school, although I'd known him primarily by reputation, a reputation so dark that I once stood him up because, frankly, he scared me to death. In fact, if we'd had a category back then called "Most Likely to Go into a Life of Crime," he would have won hands down.

That's why I'd been shocked to find him on the other side of the law when I needed the services of a PI the previous year. He'd even told me that the mysterious scar on his cheek, rumored to have been from a gang fight back in junior high, was actually the result of falling off his bike. The scar gave him a dangerous look to go with his slightly cynical features, dark hair, and piercing eyes, and no matter how much he denied it, he seemed to attract women like a magnet. When I was taking him meals, women with sexy voices seemed to call him with the same frequency that telemarketers call me.

Is it any wonder I was a little skittish about committing to a serious relationship, even though he said that's what he wanted? Never mind that we were even having trouble seeing each other now that he was back on his feet.

I worked days, and he'd been tied up at nights recently, working undercover at a loading dock, where he'd been hired to find out who was stealing electronic equipment off the trucks.

I'd been thinking about Travis and my trust issues, when I realized the restaurant's only waitress, a plump blonde in her twenties, seemed to be ignoring me. In fact, she started to make an end run around me with a coffeepot after offering up refills to a bunch of construction workers at a back table.

I toyed with the idea of tripping her. Instead, I settled for yelling "Excuse me" as she went by.

She gave me an annoyed look.

"May I have some coffee while you're here?"

She turned up a cup on the table, slopped coffee in it, and said hopefully, "That all you want?"

"I'm expecting someone else. I'll wait to order until he gets here."

"Suit yourself," she said, and headed toward the kitchen. I opened a copy of the *Denver Tribune* that I'd purchased at a rack outside the door. I started through the paper, scanning the headlines.

I don't even know what made me notice a small article on page ten, "Woman Murdered in Denver Home Identified." Maybe it was because I lived alone, despite the fact that Travis kept making suggestions about us moving in together.

At any rate, I'd even turned the page before I went back to read the article. Any hope I'd had of enjoying breakfast was gone as soon as I glanced at the first sentence. It read: "A woman found strangled in her home in South Denver has been identified as Ardith Brewster."

It couldn't be Ardith from the cleaners. It had to be someone with the same name. I kept reading. "Police were called to the house Monday morning by a coworker at the Fulton Bank in Cherry Creek after Brewster, a loan officer at the bank, failed to show up for an important early-morning meeting."

I still couldn't believe it. I kept remembering how happy she'd been just days before, when she'd told us about the new man in her life, and now some bastard had taken all that away from her. Had it been a botched robbery, or someone intent on rape? It was all I could do to force myself to finish the article, but I had to find out. "It is estimated she'd been dead for at least twenty-four hours, and according to a police spokesperson, she was believed to have known her assailant. There was no sign of forced entry, and she appeared to be entertaining someone at the time of her death."

Oh dear God. My heart felt as if it were about to pound out of my chest. I couldn't breathe. Her words flashed in my mind like a blinking neon sign: "In fact, we're planning to spend the whole weekend at home together—just the two of us." As much as I wanted to deny it, I had to admit that the killer could actually be the man she'd met at the cleaners. Now I couldn't stop reading. "The spokesperson said detectives are looking into a connection between Brewster's death and three other homicides in the Denver area within the last few years. In all the cases, the women lived alone, appeared to have known their assailants, and were killed in similar ways."

My hands were trembling, and I was near tears by the time I finished the article. I was already in shock about Ardith and her mystery man, but now I had this gnawing fear deep in my gut that one of our customers could be a serial killer.

TWO

I slammed the paper shut and stared into space. Why couldn't it be like that old TV show *Early Edition,* where the hero gets an issue of the next day's paper and can change events before they happen? I wanted to make this article go away, make the murder disappear.

How could I have done anything about what happened? Okay, I could have pushed Ardith harder for the name of her lover, but that had seemed too intrusive at the time. What good would it have done? It wouldn't have prevented her death, but at least it might have pointed to her killer. It might have prevented future murders.

"We really need to move in together. Then we wouldn't have to meet at such god-awful hours."

I jumped as Travis slipped into the seat across from me. I hadn't seen him coming.

He took one look at me, and I could hear the concern in his voice. "Are you okay? What happened?"

The waitress who'd been ignoring me was at our table the moment Travis sat down. What did I say about women falling all over him?

She glanced at me. "He's right. You don't look so good." She didn't give me time to respond, not that I would have answered in front of her. Besides, her attention was back on him. "What would you like? We have a great ham and egg special for six-ninety-nine."

Travis said that would be fine. I didn't know if she was planning to take my order, but just in case she was, I said, "I'll just have some more coffee when you bring his food."

Travis didn't argue with me about it, and I was grateful for that. I didn't think I could eat anything if my life depended on it.

He waited until the woman left. "What's the matter? Want to tell me about it?"

I shook my head. I couldn't bring myself to talk about it. Not right then. "It's just a problem at work," I said finally. "I have to think about it for a while and figure out what to do."

He didn't push me. Instead, he told me about his job on the loading dock. "I think we're about to wind it up sometime this week. I have a pretty good idea who's stealing the merchandise." He went on to explain about it, but I wasn't really listening, except that I saw him eying me every few minutes, as if he knew I was lying about the reason I was upset. It was probably because I was beginning to itch. That's a problem I usually have when I lie.

"Now I just have to wait until another trailer comes in, then bring the cops into it," he said.

The cops. I figured I should probably call the police and be done with it, but I didn't want to call them. I'd had far too many experiences with them, and I didn't want any more, at least until I figured out who Ardith's mystery man could be.

The waitress returned with Travis's order. "Here you are, honey." She slipped the plate on the table, filled his coffee cup, then apparently decided my half-filled cup didn't need topping off. "Anything else you want, just whistle."

"At least have some of my toast," Travis said when the waitress left.

He handed me a slice, and I took a bite. It stuck in my throat, and I had to call it quits. In fact, I had to get out of there.

I stood up. "I'm really sorry, Travis. I have to get to work. I'll talk to you later."

He started to get up, then stopped.

"Yeah," he said. "Give me a call." I wasn't sure from his expression if he was angry or hurt.

Things didn't get any better when I arrived at work. Julia and Ann Marie were waiting for me when I got to the front of the cleaners.

"My God, did you hear about Ardith Brewster?" Julia asked as soon as I appeared.

I nodded.

"If she'd just told us the name of the guy . . ." Her voice trailed off.

"I'm sure glad I never met someone here," Ann Marie said, as if all our customers had homicidal tendencies. One was way too many, and I knew I had to do something to make sure the bastard was caught.

I had a more urgent problem, however. "Please don't mention this to any of our customers or the other employees," I said.

"I won't," Julia said, but I could tell by the way Ann Marie dropped her eyes that she'd probably told at least a few other people.

"Ann Marie?" I asked, waiting for her answer.

"Okay," she said finally.

People began to come in the cleaners on their way to work, and it was several hours before there was a lull in the traffic. At that point, I asked Julia if she'd had any thoughts about what Ardith said that might be a clue to the killer.

"I remember thinking that the guy must be married if he wanted to keep their relationship hush-hush."

I nodded. "Do you recall how she mentioned his sharply creased pants and his freshly ironed shirts?"

Ann Marie said, "Yeah, he must have been a real snazzy dresser, huh?"

"But then Ardith said he was so different from the other men she knew," I continued.

Julia shook her head. "I guess I didn't pick up on that."

"What doesn't make sense to me is that she worked with bankers, and they all wear suits and ties," I said.

"Yeah, but they're so stodgy," Ann Marie replied. "I went out one time with a guy who worked in a bank, and he was *really* boring."

Actually, Ann Marie tended to favor guys who had a lot of body piercings and tattoos, so her comment didn't surprise me. However, maybe she had a point. "Snazzy" versus "stodgy." I'd have to give it some thought.

I needed to talk to Mack Rivers, my plant manager, who was like a father to me and could keep a confidence better than anyone I knew. Before I headed back to his station in the dry-cleaning department, I told Julia and Ann Marie that I would return to help cover the noon hour so they could take turns going to lunch.

Ann Marie followed me through the door into the plant. "Maybe we should still think about having that bulletin board for people who want to find dates," she whispered. "This guy might put up a notice to meet someone else, and then we could catch him."

That's all I needed—to hook up some other woman with a killer. "No way," I said. "Absolutely not."

"Okeydoke," she said. I never thought she sounded sincere when she said "Okeydoke." At least when she'd said she wouldn't tell anyone, she'd said "Okay." "But I still think it might work." She did a little pirouette and headed back to the call office.

I continued to the rear of the plant, where Mack was at his usual place at the spotting board. He was in the midst of treating what looked like salt at the bottom of a formal gown. The owner of the dress must have been caught out on icy streets in one of our spring storms after someone had put salt on the sidewalk.

"When you're through with that, I'd like to talk to you," I said.

He nodded and said he'd be in my office in a few minutes. Before I could even find the article in the newspaper, he had come inside and taken a seat opposite my desk in one of the two chairs I have for visitors.

I handed him the paper and pointed to the article.

When he finished, he looked up. "She's one of our customers, isn't she?"

"Yes, she's a loan officer at a bank, but it's worse than that." My voice began to shake despite my effort to control it. "She was in last week and said she'd met someone here at the cleaners. She even told me I was the one responsible for this new man in her life."

"Christ," Mack said, "Who'd she say it was?"

I shook my head, trying to get my vocal cords under control. When I thought I'd recovered, I explained that she'd refused to give his name. "But she said she met him during that open house we had in March." I went through the rest of the conversation, including the strange remark she'd made about his clothes. By the time I got to the end, my voice was shaking again.

Mack pointed to the article. "But doesn't she see that kind of attire every day in her job at the bank?"

"That's what puzzled me, too," I said, but then I launched into Ann Marie's snazzy-versus-stodgy theory about the man.

Mack stared off into space. "I was just thinking—didn't you have a guest book for people to sign that day?"

That's what I liked about talking to him. He was more than just my sounding board.

I jumped up and went to the filing cabinet where I'd stored the guest book. "Bless you, Mack. That's a great idea."

I'd intended to use the book as a way to get new customers. If a person who'd ventured into the cleaners that day wasn't already a customer, I'd planned to send a reminder to him or her to try our services. However, the whole open house had left such a bitter taste in my mouth that I hadn't gotten around to doing the mailing yet.

I already knew one thing. Only a small percentage of people who'd tromped through the plant that day had signed the guest book. If I were ever foolish enough to try such an event again, I would name an employee to be in charge of the book, just like at a wedding.

I pulled the other visitor's chair over to Mack and opened the book. Together, we examined the names in it, looking for men who wore something a little different from the standard suit and tie.

I tapped my finger on one of the entries. "That's Bill Merrick. He's the owner of that high-fashion men's store here in Cherry Creek. He's always in Armani suits, but unfortunately, he's old enough to have been Ardith's father."

Mack frowned at me. "What does that matter? A lot of women are attracted to older men."

Touché. I couldn't help wondering if Mack, a black man in his sixties, had ever dated a woman who was a lot younger than he was, but I didn't ask.

Instead, I said, "I would hate it to be Bill. He's kind of a stuffed shirt, but he's such a good customer." That made me sound awfully greedy, so I added, "Of course, I don't want to believe that it's any of our customers. I want it to be a complete stranger."

I knew that was unrealistic. How could it be a stranger when Ardith had credited me with keeping the man's clothes in such good shape?

"Are there any names here that you don't recognize?" Mack asked.

I pointed to one signature. "I don't know this one—Dennis Jacobson. I'll check him out."

Mack pointed to another name. "What about him—Lieutenant Joe Erickson?"

"He's an air force officer attached to the Buckley Air Force Base, and he always brings us his uniforms to be cleaned."

"Hmmm," Mack said. "Maybe she went for guys in uniform. Besides, aren't military officers always the epitome of sharp dressers? You know, spit-and-polish and all that."

"I think *spit-and-polish* refers to their shoes," I said, smiling for the first time all morning.

Most of the people who'd signed the book had been women, but Mack went down the list until he found the name of another man. "How about him—Mel Sutton?"

"Oh, yes, I remember he was here that day. He's a Denver police officer. He said I should have hired an off-duty cop for crowd control. But as I recall, he wasn't in uniform that day."

Mack shook his head. "Maybe she saw him carrying one of the uniforms we'd just cleaned and had a thing for the police."

I didn't offer a comment, since I'd once had an interest in a plainclothes detective, but now I shied away from them like the plague.

Except for a few men whose names didn't ring a bell, there were no more signatures in the guest book. I made a note to check the names I was unfamiliar with on our computer. Maybe something would jog my memory about them—for instance, a notation that they were "dandies" who were fanatically sharp dressers. I should be so lucky.

Mack seemed reluctant to leave, but he finally got out of his chair. "I guess I should get back out there and check on the machines."

"And I suppose I should call the police." It was the last thing I wanted to do. I always try to do my civic duty, but I've developed this reputation for getting too involved in murder cases. I didn't want to be involved in another one, and I sure didn't want to give the police the names of my customers. I didn't think the authorities had any right to the names, any more than they'd had the right, when the Patriot Act was passed, to see what books a customer had checked out of a library or purchased at a bookstore.

Mack probably knew what I was thinking. "Why don't we think about it until tomorrow—see if we come up with any more ideas that might narrow the field."

That was what I wanted to hear. Besides, I'd had another idea—something I needed to find out.

As soon as Mack left, I called my longtime friend Nat Wilcox at the *Tribune*. Since he was a police reporter, he would probably be able to give me the information I wanted. That is, if he weren't out on a long lunch hour with his current lady love, who just happened to be my stepcousin, Laura.

I'd been against the idea of Nat and Laura dating, mainly because I had this awful feeling that when they broke up, they'd expect me to take sides.

I caught him at his desk. "Yo, Mandy," he said as soon as I spoke. "You must have been reading my mind. I was planning to call you in a few minutes. I've got stupendous news. It's going to blow your mind."

Well, it couldn't be the thing I'd feared. I expected to hear any day now that Laura had broken up with him because of benign neglect on his part. After all, Nat had a habit of standing up every woman he ever dated or abandoning her in the middle of dinner, all in pursuit of the almighty scoop.

"So are you going to tell me or not?" I asked, anxious to get to my request. Maybe he'd won the Pulitzer Prize for crime reporting, if there was such a thing, and was bursting to let me know.

"Can't say right now. What if we get together for dinner tonight?"

"Okay," I said, but I wasn't willing to wait that long to ask my question.

"Great," he said.

We set up a time to meet at one of those yuppie places in LoDo, short for Lower Downtown Denver. It was known mainly for the level of noise of its diners and drinkers, but if that's where he wanted to meet, it was okay with me.

"So now, what can I do you for?" he asked.

"I read about the murder of a woman named Ardith Brewster, who was killed over the weekend. It said the case was similar to several other murders in the Denver area in the last few years. It said all the women had been—"

"Uh-huh, uh-huh." I could tell Nat was anxious for me to get to the point.

"I wonder if you can find out the other three names."

"Why do you want to know?"

Since he was all wrapped up in his big surprise, I'd hoped maybe I could slip the request by him without any nosy questions.

No such luck. But I certainly wasn't ready to tell him I was looking for connections to my place of business.

"Well, I thought I remembered one case in my neighborhood, and I wondered if any of the others were from Capitol Hill." I began to itch the way I always do when I try to lie. "Could you check and let me know?"

Apparently, the answer satisfied him, and fortunately, he couldn't see me scratching my nose. "Hey, I can do better than that. I've got the info right here. Hold on."

Unfortunately, I'd phrased the request the wrong way. I was afraid he would give me addresses only. I was right.

"Not to worry, Mandy," he said when he came back on the phone and reeled off the addresses to me. "See, they all happened miles away from you, even though you live in one of the high crime areas in the city."

"Thanks for reminding me of that," I said. "So what are the names?"

I was surprised Nat didn't inquire as to why I needed the names, too, but I heard someone yelling for him in the background. Apparently, that saved me from further questioning.

He gave me the names, along with the dates of the murders: Marla Adamson, Sandra Ryan, and Lorraine Lovell. After giving me the address for Ardith, too, he said, "Look, I gotta go, and you can rest easy. Like I said, none of the victims lived in your neighborhood."

If none of them had ever been customers, it would be even better. "Thanks, Nat. I'll see you tonight." I hung up before he realized that my request for the names hadn't made a lot of sense.

My other line had been blinking, and I hit the button to connect with it. "We're swamped up here in front," Julia said. "Can you send someone up to help us?"

"Better yet, I'll come myself."

I grabbed the list of names I'd written down. As soon as there was a break in business, I could look up the names on the computer at the counter just as easily as on the one back here in my office.

When I got to the call office, it was obvious what the problem was. Julia moved her head in Ann Marie's direction in silent disapproval.

Ann Marie was in the midst of flirting with a customer named Brett Harrison. He always brought us his tuxedos to be cleaned. Brett was a waiter at a fancy restaurant, where he had to dress up in what he called his "penguin suit" to serve the customers.

He didn't fit the profile of what Ann Marie liked in a man. Or maybe he did. Her kind of guy never even used a dry cleaner, but Brett probably wouldn't have, either, if it weren't for the tuxes. He had dark hair, was in his twenties, and usually wore jeans and T-shirts when he dropped off his cleaning.

"Whoops," she said when she saw me. "I better get back to work."

"Okay," Brett said. "I'll give you a call later."

"Okeydoke." Her eyes swept across the waiting area, where customers were beginning to show their irritation at the lack of service. In fact, one woman had turned with her pile of clothes and was exiting the premises.

"Next," Ann Marie said, as if she were completely innocent of creating the boondoggle.

With Ann Marie back at work and me to help with the backlog, we cleared out the place in record time.

"What's going on?" I asked her when the last customer left.

"I was just thinking about that open house," she said. "I remembered that Brett came in that day, so I decided to see if I could find out some more about him. Aren't you proud of me?"

No, I was appalled. "You are not to go checking out customers, much less go on a date with them. Don't you remember what you said earlier about how you're glad you never dated any of our customers? You could be dealing with a killer." I paused. "Not that I think he's a killer, but I do not want you to try to check him out. Do you understand?"

"I guess so." Ann Marie dropped her head.

"Besides," I continued, "he would have been too young for

Ardith." That, of course, was nonsense. If older men could date younger women, why couldn't older women date younger men?

Ann Marie didn't answer, so I added, "If he calls you for a date, I want you to turn him down."

"Okeydoke."

I was shaking by the time I finished my tirade. It was against my principles to interfere in an employee's personal life, but I decided this called for extreme measures.

I took a few deep breaths before I turned to our computer and started typing in the names Nat had given me to see if they matched any of the ones in our database. Marla Adamson: no evidence she'd ever been here. Sandra Ryan: another no. I was beginning to feel as if I were being paranoid. Just one more name to go—Lorraine Lovell.

Her name came up on the computer. Damn, damn, damn. She'd been a onetime customer a year ago, and she'd picked up her dry cleaning the next day. I checked the dates she'd been here against the date of her murder. They were only a few months apart, just the same as Ardith's meeting with her mystery man and her murder had been.

THREE

I wished I'd never looked up Lorraine Lovell's name on our computer, but I hadn't been able to let go of the idea that one of the other victims might have been a customer. Now I needed to talk to Mack again.

As soon as I was sure the Ann Marie–induced rush was over and that she wasn't going to start flirting with another customer, I excused myself and headed for the back of the plant.

This time, I found Mack taking his morning coffee break in our lunchroom. Good. I really needed a strong shot of caffeine, although a straight shot of something else might have been better.

"Got a minute?" I asked as I poured myself a cup of coffee.

He nodded, and I took the coffeepot over to where he was sitting at a yellow Formica-topped table. I refilled his coffee cup, returned the pot to its burner, and glanced around the lunchroom just to make sure we were alone. Since Mack had come in at the crack of dawn to open up the plant, he was taking an early break. None of the other employees was in the room yet.

"Remember how the article I showed you said Ardith's murder bore a resemblance to several other cases in the Denver area?" I said.

Mack nodded.

"Well, I called Nat about it, and he gave me the names of the other victims. One of them, a woman named Lorraine Lovell, had been here twice—to drop off and pick up a single load of cleaning. It was a few months before her death last year."

Mack slammed his coffee cup on the table with a bang. "Damn. You think she might have met someone here, too?"

"That's what I'm afraid of."

"Why don't you go back in the computer and find the names of other customers who were here the same day she was," Mack suggested. "Maybe one of the people will be a match for someone who was here the day of the open house. That might narrow down the field."

I didn't know what I'd do without Mack. "That's a good idea. I'll give it a try."

"Did you ask Nat about the cause of death? The article said the women were all killed in a similar way."

I shook my head. "Frankly, I didn't want Nat to get suspicious about why I was interested. You know how he is. I just said I wanted to know if any of the women were from my neighborhood."

Mack was silent for a few seconds. "I was wondering—maybe you could ask the crew to write down the names of any people they remember who came through the plant the day of the open house," he said.

Just then, I saw a blur of short-cropped gray hair and a bilious green pantsuit out of the corner of my eye. I knew it had to be Betty the Bag Lady, who worked in the laundry. She was always partial to bilious green, a color I characterized as a mix between mustard and avocado.

She was already heading for our table, and I tried to indicate to Mack with a jab to his knee that the conversation was over. Unfortunately, he must have thought I was just exhibiting my normal klutziness, not trying to send him a signal.

"You wouldn't have to tell people why you wanted to know," he added.

Betty never missed a thing, perhaps from her years of living on the street before I gave her a job. "Why do you guys want to know who was at the open house?" she asked, plopping down in a chair between Mack and me.

I fumbled for an answer that would satisfy the nosy ex–bag lady. "We were just discussing the fact that so few people signed our guest book that day and we were trying to find out who else had taken our tour."

I could tell Betty wasn't buying my explanation. It was probably because I began to scratch my nose.

She gave a snort. "Yeah, right. Like I'm going to believe that. I heard Mack say you didn't have to tell us the real reason."

So much for trying to outfox her. I tried a different approach. "It really isn't any of your business, Betty."

"Hmph!" she said. "You think just because I'm stuck over in the laundry, I don't see things. Well, I see plenty. I can tell you that."

I decided to call her bluff. "Okay, what did you see the day of the open house?"

She leaned into the table. "If you must know, I saw a real creepy guy from my neighborhood. He has long hair and a scraggly beard, and sometimes he gets into an old rattletrap of a car and leaves home about the time I come to work. He wears grungy old jeans with holes in them and T-shirts with packs of cigarettes rolled up in the sleeves, and he has an earring and a lot of tattoos."

"And you really saw him here?" I asked, my voice filled with skepticism. Frankly, the description sounded like someone Ann Marie would have been interested in—until she started sleuthing.

Betty nodded. "Yep, and I remember thinking to myself, What the tarnation is he doing in a dry cleaners?" She moved back in the chair and folded her arms. "So there. I did see something."

I couldn't help smiling at how she could come up with such a preposterous story. "Well, thanks for the information, Betty."

Mack got up to go, and I picked up my coffee cup and went with him. I didn't want to be subjected to any more of Betty's tall tales.

"Want me to look into why the guy was here?" she yelled after us. "I thought at the time that he must be up to something fishy. I could try following him around for a while."

"No, Betty," I said. "That won't be necessary, but thanks." When we were out of the room, I shook my head. "Where does she come up with such whoppers?"

Mack glanced over at me with a strange look on his face. "You know, I think I remember the guy she was talking about, and he was kind of creepy-looking."

I asked each of my counter people to write down the names of any of our male customers they remembered being in the cleaners the day of the open house. Maybe that would produce some names that weren't in the guest book.

After that, I spent most of the afternoon on the computer, bringing up the names of customers who'd been here the same days as Lorraine Lovell. Unfortunately, my work was all in vain. There were no matches with men who'd signed the guest book at the open house. Still, I made a list of men from the earlier visits.

One was a married politician, Barry Sampson, who had begun bringing his clothes in separately from his wife. He always insisted that the two orders must never be mixed together when we bagged them. I later learned from a neighbor that the couple, although technically separated, lived in the same house because they thought it might hurt his political career if they got a divorce.

"I've heard they remodeled the house so they can each have separate quarters, including kitchens," the neighbor had told me. "That way, they never have to see each other except at political gatherings and when they run into each other in the yard and start arguing about their dog. I'm sure there'll be a big custody battle over Poopsie if they ever get a divorce."

"Sounds like *The War of the Roses*," I'd said to the woman, referring to the movie where Michael Douglas and Kathleen Turner played a couple who systematically destroyed each other rather than either one moving out of the house. They finally wound up falling from a chandelier, although it was unclear whether they died or not.

I wished at the time that Mack had been at the front counter to hear me, since, as a part-time actor, he was always citing movie plots that reminded him of real-life experiences. He'd have known what I was talking about immediately, but the Sampsons' neighbor gave me a blank look, as if I were talking about the actual war of the same name. I had to explain the whole movie plot to her.

At any rate, the Sampsons' living arrangement seemed so strange, I put Barry at the top of my list of suspects who might have been stalking other women. Besides, bearing in mind that Ardith had said her lover was so different from most of the men she knew, I noted that Barry always wore three-piece suits with plaid vests, not a style particularly popular anymore.

I included some single men on my list. One was Cal Ingalls, a petroleum engineer, whom Julia referred to as the "Marlboro Man," apparently because of his rugged outdoor looks and his propensity to wear jeans and cowboy boots with his sports jackets.

By the time I got through, I had also written down the names of a pro football player who liked to wear leather, a male model who wore sweaters loosely tied around his neck or jackets slung casually over his shoulder, as if he were ready to strike a pose for a photo shoot. I even added the name of a minister with a turned collar, although I felt a little guilty about it.

When it came right down to it, I couldn't believe any of them was a serial killer. I began to focus on Betty's "creepy" guy. I'd had a chill shoot up my spine when Mack said that he might actually have seen the same person. However, as the day wore on, my initial reaction turned to a vague hope that Betty's guy might be the killer instead of one of my customers.

I even began to wonder about how I could check him out. I'd have to figure out a way to learn more about him from Betty without arousing her suspicious. Unfortunately, she was suspicious about everything, and I sure didn't want her to take it upon herself to spy on the guy.

I was glad when seven o'clock came and I could go home, put my feet up, and study my list of suspects. I was already in my car when I remembered I'd promised to meet Nat for dinner. I was on Speer Boulevard, heading in the right direction for LoDo, so I kept going when I got to the street where I would have turned up to my Capitol Hill apartment.

Strange, I thought, that Nat hadn't mentioned bringing Laura along for dinner. Maybe he'd been offered a job in New York City or Washington, D.C., and wanted to discuss it with me before he told her about it. After all, he'd always considered himself the Colorado equivalent of Bob Woodward and Carl Bernstein. He coveted the idea of investigative reporting in one of the major news markets, uncovering either political scandals or Wall Street high jinks.

I had a hard time finding a parking place in LoDo. The diners and drinkers had gotten there ahead of me. I'd also heard on the car radio that the Colorado Rockies were playing a game at nearby Coors Field. That ensured that the bar would be filled with pregame revelers.

I finally settled for putting my car in a parking lot that charged an exorbitant fee and then hiking the two blocks to Alfie's, a sports bar with a reputation for being so loud that its decibel level could shatter glass. Frankly, its name sounded more like an English pub to me.

Nat was waiting for me as soon as I entered the door. "I've got a table in back," he said, and I marveled at his skills at securing a table for us, since the place was teeming with customers.

The huge room was so dark, I could hardly see. I presumed this was so that patrons could better see the large-screen TVs that were showing a variety of sports events, some of them probably reruns of past glories of the Denver Broncos. As a matter of fact, the TVs were about the only decor to speak of.

I nearly tripped over several steps that led to the slightly elevated area at the back of the room. Thanks a lot, Nat, for warning me about it, I growled to myself. When I finally managed to get my footing again, I saw Laura waiting at the table.

She's my friend as well as my stepfather's niece, and she gave me a dazzling smile as we approached the table. I could have sworn she'd had a teeth-whitening treatment recently.

Last winter, she'd broken her leg, and my mother had come up from Phoenix, ostensibly to help out. All Mom actually accomplished was to give Laura a makeover, which had sent Nat into a tailspin. He'd always had a thing for tall, gorgeous blondes, and Laura fit the bill by the time Mom got through with her.

Even though Laura purported to hate her new look, I noticed that she'd kept some of Mom's beauty tricks. Or maybe it was love that made her seem to glow, even in the dim light.

She and Nat had been dating since I'd made the mistake of introducing him to her, and against all odds and my dire predictions, they were still together. Usually, Nat's blond girlfriends dumped him long before this.

"Hi, Laura," I said, stopping just short of saying I hadn't expected to see her here.

Now fully recovered from her broken leg, she jumped out of her chair and gave me a hug. I'm five five, and she's a good five inches taller than I am, plus several inches taller than Nat. The height difference didn't seem to bother her, and Nat saw it as his idea of the perfect woman.

We sat down, and I turned to Nat. "So, what's your big news?"

He seemed to be bursting at the seams, to use an old clothing cliché, but he glanced at Laura. "Should I tell her, or do you want to?"

Suddenly, I had an uneasy feeling about this—since Nat's news was apparently Laura's news, too.

"Let's tell her together," Laura said.

"Okay, on three," Nat said. "One, two, three."

"We're engaged," they said in unison.

"What did you say?" I asked, figuring the din of the other customers would give me time to recover enough to give a polite response.

"We're engaged," Laura repeated in a louder voice.

"Congratulations," I said.

All the time, I was thinking about what I'd say when the two of them got a divorce. You're both my friends, and I don't want to take sides. Nat, I know you've been my friend for a lot longer than Laura has, but after all, she's family. Laura, I warned you that he'd forget all about your birthday and anniversary if he were on the scent of a story. Surely you remember that?

Laura put out her hand so I could admire her ring.

"Wow, it's beautiful," I said.

"We're getting married next month," she continued. "I know it's fast, but I've always dreamed of a June wedding. Anyway, I want you to be my maid of honor."

I hesitated for as long as I felt I dared. "Sure," I said, although my heart wasn't really in it.

A guy at the next table broke out in a yell. For a moment, I thought he was cheering my decision to be a true friend, no matter what the consequences; then I noticed that he was yelling because the Yankees got a home run on the TV. I deduced this because he was wearing a Yankees T-shirt and cap.

"Oh, thank you. You don't know how much this means to me." Laura reached over and hugged me again.

Nat did the same, although he seemed embarrassed about it. A show of affection had never been a part of our relationship, established way back in junior high. "It was either that or you were going to have to be my honorary 'best man,'" he said.

The happy couple already had a pitcher of beer on the table, and Nat poured me a glass. I offered a toast and a silent prayer that they would live happily ever after, thus ensuring that I could remain friends with both.

"We don't want a big fancy wedding—just something simple, with only our closest family and friends in attendance," Laura said.

The moment she said that, I had a scary thought. "Who are you going to ask to give you away?"

"Uncle Herb, of course," she said.

I don't know why I even asked. Her own father had died when she was a child, and Herb was her closest relative. Since he was also my stepfather, that meant my mother would have to be told about the upcoming nuptials, as well. Didn't Laura remember anything about Mom's last trip to Denver?

Simple was not a word that came to mind when I thought of Herb, a boisterous retired used-car dealer who favored plaid pants and white shoes, or Mom, who fancied herself the Scarlett O'Hara of Phoenix in her frilly gowns that looked like lace curtains. *Flamboyant* was more the term that I would use when I thought of them.

"So, have you told Herb about the wedding?" I asked.

Laura had a worried look. Apparently, she did remember Mom's January trip. "No, we wanted to wait until we told you. We're going to call him as soon as we get home, but I wanted to know how you think we should handle it."

Nat seemed amused. He always liked to tease Mom, which had never endeared him to her, and he seemed to be relishing the idea of taking her on again.

"Who knew that we'd eventually become steprelatives, huh, Mandy?" he said.

I ignored him and focused on Laura. "All I can tell you, Laura, is to be very firm that this is *your* wedding, and you're going to make all the decisions."

Laura nodded, but I couldn't help remembering what a wimp she'd been when Mom set out last time to completely remake her.

"Maybe you should wait awhile to tell them," I said as an afterthought. "Either that or tell them all the plans are made already."

Nat hailed a waitress so we could order dinner. Alfie's turned out to have a very limited menu. I ordered a cheeseburger with fries, while Nat and Laura selected steaks. I hated to make it easy on Nat, since he seldom offered to buy my meal, but I decided it was the least I could do to celebrate their engagement.

I spent most of the meal listening to Laura and Nat discuss their wedding plans. They hoped to hold the wedding at a location in the foothills overlooking Denver. I had serious doubts that they could secure the site on such short notice, considering that Laura had her heart set on a June date. Since we dealt with brides all the time at the cleaners and I knew how far ahead they planned their nuptials, I felt I had some degree of expertise.

"I would get right on it," I said finally. "Those wedding places fill up fast."

Laura and Nat both looked at me as if I'd somehow put a hex on their plans.

I cleared my throat. "To change the subject, I was wondering about those murders that I talked to you about earlier, Nat. The article said all the women were killed in a similar manner. Do you know what it was?"

Laura's face paled, and I regretted that I'd brought up such a subject in the midst of the wedding talk.

On the other hand, Nat was immediately on alert, his nose for news suddenly sniffing more than idle curiosity on my part. "Why this sudden interest in the case?" he asked. "You don't usually ask this many questions unless you're somehow involved."

"If you must know, Ardith Brewster was a customer," I said.

"Are you sure that's all?"

I nodded and willed myself not to start itching.

Nat leaned over toward me. I could tell that he was still suspicious, but he apparently decided to wait until later to grill me. "Okay," he said. "The police want to keep the MO hush-hush, so this is strictly off the record. The women were all strangled, and their wrists and ankles were bound with the same cord used to kill them."

I glanced over at Laura. She looked as if she was going to be sick. I felt the same way. I also felt guilty. Talk about putting a pall over the conversation.

CHAPTER

FOUR

The phone was ringing when I got to my third-floor apartment in Capitol Hill. I almost tripped over Spot, my cat, when I rushed into the room. I was hoping the call would be from Travis, on a break from his nighttime surveillance job on the loading dock.

I owed him an explanation for my panicky behavior that morning. Now, at least, I thought I could talk about it and maybe even pay him to give me some help.

I grabbed the phone, but I never should have picked up. It was Mom in Phoenix, and my heart sank. Who said news doesn't travel at the speed of light?

"Laura just called Herb and told us she's going to marry Nat," Mom said. "I have to tell you, Mandy, that I don't really approve."

"I figured as much."

"Herb says I should just keep out of it."

Good for Herb. Maybe he had more backbone than I'd ever given him credit for.

"But you know I can't just sit idly by and see her make the biggest mistake of her life," Mom said.

Why not? I wondered. She'd been married six times, and with

the exception of my father, who died when I was a baby, her other four marriages before Herb had ended in divorce.

"Herb doesn't even really know Nat," Mom said.

I had an uneasy feeling about what was coming next.

"I told him we needed to go up to Denver at once so he can get acquainted with Nat and see for himself. Laura is such a lovely girl, and Nat is so short."

Trust Mom to zero in on some physical attribute.

"Besides, he's so irritating," she said.

Okay, I could accept that as a reason to get annoyed with him, but if Laura could put up with some of Nat's less desirable traits, it wasn't any of Mom's business.

"I agree with Herb that you should keep out of it." By the time I voiced this opinion, I was holding the phone up against one ear and opening a can of cat food at the same time.

I heard Mom sigh. Spot let out a pitiful meow, and I bent over to scoop canned tuna into his bowl. I dropped the phone and missed whatever Mom said next. Fortunately, I missed Spot as well, but my clumsiness sent him streaking to a far corner of the room.

"You almost broke my eardrum," Mom protested when I picked up the receiver.

"I'm sorry. The phone slipped out from under my chin."

"Well, as I was saying," she continued, "I told Herb that, at the very least, we should go up to Denver to help Laura with wedding plans. I could tell from what she said that Laura doesn't have the slightest idea what to do."

Of course, Mom had plenty of experience with that, which is why on my first, only, and, I might add, disastrous attempt at marriage, I exchanged vows with Larry the Law Student before a judge at the Denver City and County Building.

Mom had never forgiven me for that, and she must have read my mind. "You know, if you had taken the marriage ritual more seriously, you might still be married."

The remark hardly seemed worthy of a response, coming as it

did from a woman who'd been married almost as many times as Elizabeth Taylor.

I argued anyway. "No, Mom, I might still be married if Larry hadn't dumped me for another fledgling attorney once he passed the bar."

And that, I thought, is why I'm still skittish about committing to a serious relationship with Travis. I cherished my independence, and besides, I wasn't sure I could trust a guy who'd been a chick magnet back in high school and, from what I could tell, still was.

"Anyway," Mom said, ignoring my remark about Larry, "I think I've convinced Herb that we ought to go up to Denver to help plan the wedding."

I couldn't deal with this right now. I had too many other things to worry about, the main one being that I had to call the police about Ardith Brewster. "I think you're talking to the wrong person," I said. "You need to talk to Laura."

On that note and with the threat of their imminent arrival hanging over my head, I hung up the phone and Spot slunk back to his dish to claim his food.

Within seconds, the phone rang again. Mom must be on speed dial, I thought. I grabbed the receiver. I need to be more forceful with her, I told myself.

"What do you want now?"

This time it *was* Travis.

"Are you all right?" he asked, and I could hear the surprise in his voice at the way I'd answered the phone.

"I'm sorry. It's been a really bad day."

"I was afraid of that. I've been worried about you since break-fast, but I figured I'd give you a chance to get things under control at work before I called."

Oh, yeah, I *had* told him it was a work-related problem, and in a way, I guess it was.

"Want to tell me about it? I have a few minutes before I have to get back to the loading dock."

If that was the case, I decided I might as well unload my problems on him. "I think one of our customers is a serial killer."

"What did you say?"

I repeated the frightening words, and after that, I was off and running. I blurted out everything, my sentences tumbling over one another.

Travis was a good listener, probably from hearing the stories of clients who'd come to him for help. He didn't interrupt until I finally stopped for breath.

"When did Ardith say she'd met this man?" he asked.

I guess I had forgotten to mention that. "At the open house we had back in March. You remember my talking about it, don't you?"

He was silent for so long, I thought we'd been disconnected. "Sorry," he said. "I don't recall."

Okay, so I was wrong about him being a good listener. "Surely, it must ring a bell—the way I carried on about it."

More silence. "Oh, yeah. I guess I do." I wasn't sure I believed him, but I let it go.

"Now I'm trying to figure out the names of any men who were in the vicinity that day. You know, men who don't fit the traditional profile of the well-dressed man."

He didn't say anything for a few seconds, and I wondered if his mind had wandered again, the way it had apparently done when I talked about the open house. At least this time he might have an excuse. Maybe something suspicious was going on at the loading dock. I was about to let him go and tell him we could talk about it later.

"Want me to check out any of the names you've come up with?" he asked finally. "No charge and strictly confidential."

"Could you? But I insist on paying."

He didn't argue. "Let me grab a piece of paper and a pencil." Another pause. "Okay, all set."

I reeled off the names on my suspect list. They were already etched in my mind.

"Anything in particular you want me to be on the lookout for?"

Bless him. This was more than I had any right to expect.

"Well, I guess any police records, particularly for sex offenses." I remembered how Ardith had said the man wanted to keep their relationship secret. "Oh, yes, and whether any of them are married."

"All right, will do. Gotta go now, but I'll get right on this tomorrow."

Before I even had a chance to say good-bye, he cut the connection. Not even an "I miss you" before he hung up. I was disappointed and relieved at the same time. Hopefully, he'd be able to come up with something about one of my suspects that would narrow my list.

I collapsed on my sofa bed, too tired to pull it out into its sleeping mode. I was even too tired to be irritated at Travis's obvious lack of attentiveness back in March. At least he was willing to offer his help now. Maybe tomorrow would be a better day.

Unfortunately, things didn't improve the next morning. I stopped to tell Mack about my computer search for the days Lorraine Lovell had dropped off and picked up her clothes, and how I couldn't find any matches to men who'd signed the guest book at our open house.

When I arrived at the front counter to relieve Ann Marie for her midmorning break, the first person I saw was her prime suspect, Brett Harrison. He was waiting in line to be helped. Julia and Ann Marie were busy with other customers.

"Hi, Brett," I said. "What can I do for you?"

Since he didn't have a pile of clothes in his arms, I knew he was here to pick up the tuxedo he'd dropped off the previous day for his job at the high-class restaurant.

He was wearing a T-shirt and jeans, so tight that they fit like skin. I had a hard time visualizing him as a snooty waiter in a tux, a towel draped over his arm as he asked a customer to sniff the wine when he poured it.

"I'll just wait for her," Brett said, motioning toward Ann Marie, whose flirtation yesterday seemed to have paid off.

Damn. I didn't like this at all.

Julia was between Ann Marie and me, so I couldn't even give Ann Marie a warning look to cool it with the handsome dark-haired waiter-cum-murder suspect.

Ethel Anderson, a heavyset matron of the country club set, was only too happy to move around Brett and head for my station. She was trouble and as tight with her money as Brett was with the cut of his jeans.

Mrs. Anderson was always having us redo work for some invisible spot or wrinkle that only she could see. I hate to admit it, but sometimes we merely held the garment on our conveyor until she returned, which seemed to satisfy her that we'd gone out of our way for her.

"I have a problem," she said. "My maid brought this outfit to you last week, and look what you did to it." She held up a blue knit dress. "It pooches out in the seat, and it simply won't do to wear it this way."

No, what made it pooch out, I thought, was Mrs. Anderson's rather ample derriere, unlike "Brett's cute butt," as Ann Marie had once described it.

I stifled my response and typed her name in our computer. At the same time, I strained to hear what Ann Marie and Brett were saying at the other end of the counter. All I could make out was Ann Marie's giggle.

As my eyes scanned Mrs. Anderson's recent cleaning history, I failed to see a listing for the blue knit dress. Ten to one, she'd worn it once, which accounted for the sprung seat, or else she'd taken the garment to a discount cleaners and now she was foisting it off on me because it hadn't been blocked properly.

I wanted to call her on it, but more than that, I wanted to hear the conversation at the other end of the counter. I gritted my teeth and said, "We should be able to correct the problem. No charge."

She smiled as if she'd put one over on me and left. By then, Julia had taken some bags of cleaning to the mark-in counter just inside the door to the plant. I dawdled as I slipped the knit dress into a bag with a note to clean and block it at no charge. That way, I could eavesdrop on what Brett was saying to Ann Marie.

"—and we could go to the Last Roundup on Saturday. It's a blast."

Damn it, say no, Ann Marie, especially to a place called the Last Roundup. It sounds so final.

I knew it was actually a country-and-western bar, famous as a place where you could get back to your western roots.

Mom had once told me more than I ever wanted to know about country-and-western dancing. I think the conversation was inspired by her idea that I needed to "get a life" so I wouldn't be such a workaholic.

Mom said line dancing was the in thing to do in her Phoenix social circle. She and Herb had taken lessons, and she'd mentioned that there'd even been line dancing at several wedding receptions they'd attended. She would probably want the deejay to have the guests do it at Nat and Laura's wedding.

Ann Marie cast a quick glance in my direction before she whispered something to Brett. Unfortunately, I'm not good at lip-reading, so her response was lost on me.

I fumed as she went in back to retrieve Brett's tuxedo from our conveyor. By the time she returned, Julia was back, as well.

Ann Marie completed the money transaction, and Brett gave her a businesslike nod as he left. It didn't fool me for a minute. He was up to no good, and I needed to take her aside and give her another warning about him.

I'm sure she guessed as much. She glanced at her watch. "Whoops," she said, "It's time for my break."

With that, she was off to our lunchroom. I would have followed her, except that I didn't want to leave Julia to handle the remaining customers by herself.

Finally, there was a lull in the traffic. I asked Julia if she knew anything about the Last Roundup.

"All I know about it is from my niece," she said. "On Wednesday's, they have ladies night, where women get in and drink for free.

My niece tells me that all the guys go there looking for a one-night stand. She says it's a real 'meat market.'"

A meat market. What about a slaughterhouse? The thought sent an icicle up my spine. I couldn't help wondering if that's where the killer had taken his dates, but I couldn't imagine straitlaced Ardith Brewster going there. However, there was the matter of that pair of jeans in her last cleaning order.

"Do you think you can handle the counter alone for a few minutes?" I asked Julia.

Julia said she could, and I headed to the lunchroom for a serious "big sister" talk with Ann Marie. When I got there, the room was crowded with the cleaning crew.

"Psssst." The noise came from behind my back.

I tried to ignore the sound as I looked around for Ann Marie. She wasn't there.

"Psssst." The noise was louder as I started over to Mack to ask if he'd seen Ann Marie. I turned around.

It was Betty the Bag Lady, and she was standing just outside the door. She looked wild-eyed, and her short gray hair was sticking up all over her head, as if she'd just had a bad scare. She used a sweeping motion with her hand to indicate that she wanted me to go with her. I knew she wouldn't take no for an answer.

I returned to the door. "Okay, Betty, what do you want?"

She grabbed me by the arm. "You gotta come with me!"

"Have you seen Ann Marie?" I asked.

She nodded. "You need to come right now or he'll get away."

Oh dear God, had she seen Brett in the act of abducting Ann Marie?

By then, we were at the back door. She tugged on it and pushed me outside.

"Over there," she said, pointing to our left.

I was looking in the other direction. Ann Marie was sitting in a fancy sports car with Brett. Where did a waiter get the money for a car like that?

"No, over this way," Betty said in disgust.

I glanced where she was pointing. Someone was scrunched down inside another car. The car had rusted paint, a crushed fender, and a cracked windshield.

"That's him—the creepy guy I was telling you about."

I could see the driver through an open window. "But you said the guy at the open house had a scraggly beard."

Betty looked up at the sky as if studying the cloud formations. "Don't let him know you're looking at him." Sure, like the way she'd been pointing at him hadn't already tipped him off.

"So where's the beard?" I asked. The man was in need of a shave, but there definitely was no beard.

Betty brought her gaze down from the heavens. "He must have shaved it off. Who cares? It's the same guy. Don't you think it's suspicious that he's still hanging around here?"

Ann Marie and Brett must have spotted me about the same time the man with the five o'clock shadow did. Brett revved up his sports car, and he and Ann Marie took off around the side of the building. Right then, Betty's scraggly mystery man shot forward, too, pulling onto the side street just north of First Avenue.

"Come on," Betty said. "We gotta follow him and see what he's up to."

I knew it was dumb to listen to Betty, but frankly, I was more concerned about following Brett and Ann Marie, in case she might be in danger.

I ran over to my Hyundai. My keys were back in my office, but I kept a spare set in a little magnetic container under the front fender. I don't know why I even bothered. No one would want to steal the car. It wasn't in much better shape than the one driven by the creepy guy.

I retrieved the key and unlocked the doors. By the time I started the engine, Betty was in the passenger seat. I drove around the side of the plant, still in the parking lot. To my relief, I saw that Brett had pulled up in front of the cleaners. Ann Marie bailed out of his car as soon as she saw us and ran into the call office. I came to a stop.

"What are you doing?" Betty screamed. "The guy's gettin' away."

Oh, yeah, Betty's creepy guy. His car had been idling on the street, but suddenly it took off. Without too much thought and without my driver's license, I headed out after him, making a right turn onto First Avenue in the direction the man had gone.

Call it rationalization, but in my own defense, I was desperate to find a suspect in Ardith's death—someone who wasn't connected to the cleaners in any way.

This guy might be the answer. Maybe he'd been staking out the cleaners just now, looking for another victim. If he'd also been hanging around at the open house, perhaps Ardith's death didn't have anything to do with the man in the well-pressed clothes, but was the act of the grungy pervert up ahead.

"You're losing the guy," Betty yelled. "Step on it."

We zoomed past the huge Cherry Creek Mall, a covered shopping center with a lot of other stores spreading west from it. Unfortunately, *zooming* was a relative term in the always-congested street in front of the mall.

The light changed to red up ahead. I could barely see the guy's car in the heavy traffic. He had pulled over in the left-turn lane, ready to shoot south on University as soon as the light changed. I would have to squeeze into one of the two turn lanes, or else I was going to lose him.

"Did you get the guy's license plate?" I asked, glancing over at Betty.

She glared at me. "Look, I was just standing outside, taking my break and minding my own business, when I saw the guy. Why would I have a piece of paper, for cripes sakes?"

"Okay, okay. Open the glove compartment and grab a pencil and something to write on. If we get close enough, try to get the number of his license plate."

She wasn't about to let it go. "Besides, you thought I was nuts when I told you about him. I didn't have time to get no license plate. I had to show you I wasn't crazy."

"All right. I'm sorry. Just get the paper."

Reluctantly, she reached into the glove compartment and re-trieved an old sales receipt and the stub of a pencil.

The light changed up ahead and the left-turn arrow came on. Since my own turn signal wasn't working—getting it fixed being something I needed to put on my to-do list—I signaled with my arm out the window that I wanted to move over a lane. The driver in back of me must not have known the rules for hand signals. He wasn't about to let me in. As soon as he went past, I edged the front fender into the lane in front of the next car.

The driver honked. I hoped he wasn't one of those road-rage people. He couldn't move forward unless he let me in, so he finally stopped long enough for me to squeeze my car in front of his. I waved my hand in a thank-you gesture, but when we turned the corner, he blasted around me and gave me the finger. I guess that was better than it could have been, although when I looked over at Betty, she was giving him the finger back.

I switched lanes and followed the angry driver around a slow-moving car on the right. Up ahead, I could see Betty's guy going along at the posted speed limit, unlike most of the drivers on the road. I assumed he didn't know I was on his tail.

I closed the distance between us until I was behind his rattletrap of a car. I could see that it had a Colorado license plate with the fa-miliar white mountains against a green background.

"Okay, write down the numbers on the plate," I said.

Betty squinted her eyes into tiny slits. "I can't see them from this far away. You'll have to get closer."

"If I get any closer, I'll be attached to his back bumper."

"Okay, you read 'em off to me. I'll write 'em down."

Now it was my turn to squint, and I called out the three num-bers, followed by three letters, which made them a lot easier to re-member than a whole string of numbers. Just to be sure I had them right, I edged closer and repeated them a second time.

All at once, the guy accelerated, and frankly, his car had a lot more oomph than mine, even though it looked worse. He must have noticed us and suspected that we were following him.

I was ready to call it quits, but Betty kept yelling at me to follow him. He continued south on University to Arkansas, where he took a left. I did the same, but I had to wait for an oncoming car. He ran a stop sign a few blocks later and made another left turn. I started to slow at the intersection.

"For Christ sakes, keep going," Betty yelled. "We're going to lose him if you don't quit being such a wimp."

A wimp without a driver's license is a wimp who's justified in being cautious. And besides, what else did I hope to achieve? We had the license number, and that's about all I could ask for. Nevertheless, I kept going without coming to a full stop.

Once I made the turn, I sped up. That was just before I heard the short blast of a police siren. I looked in the rearview mirror. A cop car had appeared out of nowhere. The driver had his sights set on me. I could tell.

"I told you to keep going," Betty said. "The only reason he spotted us was that you slowed down."

I came to a stop at the curb. The officer pulled in behind me. I thought fleetingly of laying out the whole story about Ardith and Lorraine Lovell, but the moment I saw the cop head toward my car, I knew that would be a mistake.

I recognized the man, and with the possible exception of Stan Foster, a homicide detective I'd once dated, this was the last cop I wanted to see right then.

Mel Sutton, who always brought us his uniforms to be cleaned, was a likable, slightly overweight guy with sandy hair and a cuddly teddy bear quality about him. However, he was also on my suspect list because he'd been in the call office the day of the open house. I wasn't about to tell him what was going on.

Mandy?" Mel sounded surprised when he reached the car.

"Mel," I said, trying for the wide-eyed, innocent look. "I hope I didn't do something wrong."

"I'm afraid you did." He motioned back to the intersection we'd just driven through. "You didn't come to a complete stop, and you failed to put on your turn signal."

Betty, who'd never voluntarily offered any information to the police while I'd known her, suddenly opened her mouth. "We were chasing a creepy guy who's been hanging around the cleaners since our open house back in March."

Oh swell. If Mel had anything to do with Ardith's death, he would be on high alert now.

Betty reached in her pocket and pulled out the scrap of paper with the license number written on it. "This is the guy's plate number." She reached across me and handed it to him before I had a chance to react.

There went the only evidence I had that might clear Mel or my other customers of involvement in Ardith's death.

"I'll go see if I can get a make on the car," Mel said.

I felt a moment of optimism. Maybe he would actually find out the name of Betty's creep.

He was gone a long time. "Sorry," he said when he returned, "there's no such license plate. You must have copied the numbers down wrong."

Betty took offense at that. "No way. I copied them down just the way the boss lady read 'em off to me." She looked at me accusatorily. "You must not have seen them right. Maybe you need glasses."

I seethed. "May I have the paper back?" I asked. "I need the receipt it's written on."

Mel shrugged and handed it to me. I took a quick look at what Betty had written. The numbers and letters were what I remembered calling out to her. I mentally moved Mel up a little closer to the top of my suspect list.

When I reached over and started to put the receipt in the glove compartment, Betty grabbed it out of my hands. "Yep, those are the numbers you gave me."

Either that, I thought, or Mel and the creepy guy are in cahoots. Was that getting paranoid or what?

"I'll need your registration and proof of insurance." Mel sounded almost apologetic for the inconvenience he was causing me.

I rummaged through the glove compartment until I found what he wanted.

Once he was through looking at the cards, he said, "Now I'll need your driver's license."

Here came the hard part. "Look, Mel, I'm afraid I rushed out of the cleaners without my purse. I don't have my license on me, but surely you can vouch for me." I stopped just short of offering to clean his uniforms free for a month.

"Sorry, Mandy. I can't do that." He busied himself with writing the ticket, and when he was through, he handed it to me. "I'm afraid you're going to have to find someone else to drive your car back to the cleaners."

"I can do it," Betty said. "I got a driver's license."

I'm sure my mouth dropped open. To my knowledge, Betty had

never had a driver's license, but quick as a flash, she reached in her pocket and pulled out a coin purse and an honest-to-God license.

"When did you get that?" I asked.

"Artie's been helping me with my driving skills," she said, referring to her live-in boyfriend, a courtly doll doctor who was the total opposite of Betty. "Next time your mom wants me to drive her someplace in a blizzard, I'm ready."

Obviously, she was referring to the time back in January when I'd had to rescue the middle-aged meddlers from a mountain restaurant.

Mel took a look at Betty's license and handed it back to her. "Okay, that should be fine."

She stuck it, along with the information on the license plate that didn't exist, in her coin purse, and we traded places under Mel's watchful eye.

As soon as he handed me the ticket and went back to his patrol car, Betty let out a shrill whistle. "I bet that's going to cost you a bundle, boss lady," she said.

"I don't want to talk about it," I said. "In fact, I don't want to talk about anything. Period. End of conversation."

Surprisingly, Betty obliged, but probably not because she respected the fact that I was mad. More likely, it was because it took all her concentration to get us back to the cleaners. If Arthur had been giving her driving lessons, it obviously wasn't in a stick-shift car.

I became more irritated every mile we went, and the only words I uttered during the whole trip were, "Damn it, put in the clutch." Otherwise, I gnashed my teeth each time she ground the gears. I was sure she'd probably stripped them clean, and I'd worn all the enamel off my teeth by the time she pulled into the parking lot in back of the plant.

Unfortunately, her silence ended soon thereafter. The moment she saw Mack at the spotting board, she became a veritable font of information.

"Wooee," she said. "The boss lady's in a world of hurt. She got a ticket for failing to stop, not using a turn signal, and driving with-out a driver's license."

I thought the least Mack could have done was been curious about what had gotten me in that predicament in the first place. In-stead, he looked pained at the thought of yet another irresponsible act on my part. It was all because he'd taken on the role of a substi-tute father years ago. He was always giving me advice or worrying about some impulsive thing I'd done or was about to do.

I wanted to point to Betty and scream that it was all her fault. I didn't. After all, I'm an adult, with the ability to make my own deci-sions. The person I was really mad at was me for getting swept up in her craziness in the first place.

"Can I see you in my office, Mack, when you have a minute?" I asked, my voice tight with suppressed anger.

He nodded.

I turned to Betty. "I'd like that license plate number back, if you don't mind." My voice actually quivered this time.

"The cop said it wasn't no good." Nevertheless, she went into the pocket in her pants, pulled out the coin purse, and produced the piece of paper on which she'd written down the number of the license plate.

"And just out of curiosity, why the devil do you carry your dri-ver's license around with you in that little purse?" I asked.

She snorted. "You think I'm going to leave my valuables in a locker in the lunchroom, where anyone can break in and steal me blind?" She gave me a gloating smile. "Besides, you never can tell when you're going to need your driver's license."

I was sure I would sputter something pathetic if I tried to re-spond. I turned abruptly and left. As soon as I got to my desk, I took another look at the license plate's series of numbers and letters. They were definitely what I remembered calling out to her. If they were wrong, maybe I did need glasses. Sixes and eights were begin-ning to look alike to me sometimes on the computer.

I put my head down on the desk and closed my eyes. I was still sitting that way, the traffic ticket and the scrap of paper clasped tightly in my hand, when Mack arrived.

"So, do you want to tell me what this is all about?" he asked.

I spilled out the whole sordid story, from the moment Betty whisked me out of the lunch room to the moment when Officer Mel Sutton, who'd signed the guest book at our open house, became the arresting officer.

Mack just sat across from me shaking his head.

I was tempted to rationalize aloud that if Mack hadn't corroborated her story of seeing the creepy guy at the open house, I would never have taken off on Betty's wild-goose chase. I decided that would be a cop-out and let the opportunity pass.

Finally, Mack voiced an opinion. "Don't you think that's awfully coincidental that a guy who was at the open house is the one who stopped you? Have you ever run into him before when you've had to call the police?"

I guess I hadn't had time to analyze the situation. But no, until now, Mel had never been one of the police officers I'd met during my many unfortunate contacts with the law.

"I suppose he works out of a district station in this area, though," Mack said. "That's probably why he brings us his uniforms to be cleaned."

I nodded.

"And didn't you say that he mentioned how you should have hired an off-duty policeman to handle crowd control that day? That doesn't sound like someone who had ulterior motives when he came in the cleaners."

Mack was raising doubts about Mel and then casting them aside. Still, there was the matter of the license plate that Mel had said didn't exist. Even if he were guilty of something, what possible motive could he have for lying about the plate?

"Well," Mack said, "I think it's high time you called the police and told them about Ardith Brewster and the other woman, as well as the incident today."

I protested. "Yes, but maybe I should wait. Travis is going to check out the names on the list for me."

Mack frowned. "And you neglected telling me that?"

"There's been a lot going on."

"Yes, but I thought you were going to keep from getting any more involved in this."

I didn't point out that this was our livelihood that was at risk. Instead, I said, "I'm just trying to narrow down the list, like we agreed I should."

"No." Mack was adamant. "You need to call as soon as possible."

"I suppose."

Mack started to get up. "Good. Let me know what happens."

I couldn't let him leave. I wasn't through venting yet. "Before you go back to work, I wanted to tell you that Nat and Laura are engaged. They're planning to get married next month."

Mack knew Nat from when I was in junior high and would bring my classmate into the cleaners with me. He knew Laura because of her connection to Mom and me, and I could tell he was surprised.

"Give them my best wishes," he said.

"I will, but that's not all. I'm afraid Mom is going to talk Herb into coming up here from Phoenix to oversee the arrangements."

"Well, give them my condolences, too," he said. He certainly knew my mother and Herb, thanks to his long association with Dyer's Cleaners.

He offered one final word of advice. "You have enough to worry about without getting involved in their wedding plans. You know, it's not really your problem."

"I know," I said just as my phone rang. I picked up the extension as Mack slipped out of his chair and headed back to the dry-cleaning machines. He waved at me and mouthed, "Good luck."

So the wedding wasn't my problem, huh? It became painfully obvious within seconds that Mack and I were both wrong.

Laura was on the phone, although it took me awhile to recognize her voice. "I don't know what to do, Mandy," she sobbed. "Your mother and Herb want to come up here to help plan the wedding. Your mother is talking about some crazy 'theme' wedding."

"What the devil is a theme wedding?" I asked.

"I don't know." Laura let out a tears-induced hiccup before she continued. "She mentioned something about a medieval or a Hawaiian motif."

"That's crazy." Mom had obviously been working overtime on wedding ideas since I talked to her the previous night.

"I know," Laura said. "All Nat and I want is something simple." She drew out the word *simple* like a wail. "Will you try to talk to her, Mandy?"

Suddenly, all the pent-up blame I'd wanted to place on Betty and Mack for my incursion into South Denver spilled out. "Didn't I tell you to wait awhile to tell them? Either that or say all the wedding plans were already made and set in stone?"

Now Laura was crying big-time.

"Please, Laura, you need to quit crying and be firm." It had never worked when I tried it on Mom, but I wasn't about to tell Laura that.

"I couldn't say the plans were all made," Laura said finally. "That would have been a lie. Besides, I had to tell them in time for them to make arrangements to come up here for the wedding."

Why? I wondered. Mom, at least, always seemed ready at a moment's notice to come up to Denver and complicate our lives.

"Would you just try to talk to your mother for me?" Laura's voice had turned husky from all the crying. "You seem to be able to stand up to her better than I can."

Stand up to her, maybe. Have any effect, no.

"Pleeeease," Laura said.

"Okay, I'll try, but it probably won't do any good."

"Bless you, Mandy." Laura hung up, a lot more confident of me than I was of myself.

I tried a few deep-breathing exercises before I tackled the phone again. I needed to get myself under control whether I planned to call Mom first or the cops. I finally decided the police would be easier.

My dilemma was whom to ask for when I reached the Crimes Against Persons Division. I could ask for Stan Foster, whom I'd once dated, but he'd always thought I was insufferably nosy, and this would confirm it in his mind. Despite all that, he'd seemed interested in our getting back together the last time we'd talked, and I didn't want to go there, either.

Another alternative was to ask to speak to Detective Jack Reilly. I'd met him during a couple of murder investigations that I was drawn into through no fault of my own. The bottom line was that he hated me.

I settled for calling the main number for the department. I knew it by heart from all the times I'd had to use it. When someone answered, I asked if I could speak to the detective in charge of the Ardith Brewster murder investigation.

I was immediately transferred to an extension. I prayed that neither Stan nor Reilly was the lead detective on the case.

After a few short rings, a man answered. "Ivinson here." He was surprisingly soft-spoken, which gave me hope that he might be easier to talk to than the detectives I'd had to deal with in the past.

Once we established that he was one of the detectives on the Brewster case, I identified myself and told him about Ardith's last visit to the cleaners and how she'd told us about the new man in her life. I even explained about his neat appearance—"the sharp creases in his pants and the brightness of his freshly pressed shirt," and how she'd complimented us for keeping his wardrobe in such good shape.

Ivinson was so attentive and polite that I almost felt as if I were talking to an old friend. "What's the man's name?" he asked.

"That's the problem. She wouldn't tell us his name, but she said they were planning to spend a quiet few days together at home this past weekend. Then I read she was murdered. I was afraid he was somehow involved in her death, but I'm thinking now that it might have been a suspicious character who's been hanging around the cleaners and maybe stalking women." I explained about Betty's creepy character.

"Do you have an ID on this second man?"

"No," I said, but I launched into a description of the man and his junker car. I even speculated that he lived someplace off of South Broadway, thanks to Betty's information that she'd seen him in her neighborhood. As the coup de grâce, I said, "I have the license plate from his car."

I didn't mention that a police officer had already run the plate and said it didn't exist. The more I'd thought about it, the more convinced I'd become that the sequence of numbers and letters on the license plate was correct. If Mel had been trying to pull some sort of fast one on me by saying the plate didn't exist, then his little game was over. I wasn't going to take his word for it. If the plate came back a second time as being nonexistent, then I'd have to accept that verdict.

I reeled off the three-number, three-letter plate to Detective Ivinson.

"Just a minute," he said. "I'll check it out."

He put me on hold, and while I waited, I thought about what Mack had said. Mel's appearance at the intersection had been just a bit too coincidental. Maybe he actually was in collusion with the shady character in the junker car, or what if he were somehow involved in Ardith's murder and simply wanted to muddy the waters? None of it made a lot of sense, but I didn't have any other explanation—unless maybe Mel was the one who needed glasses.

Ivinson came back on the phone. "I'd like to get a statement from you this afternoon. What if I stop by your store at four o'clock?"

"Sure," I said, eager to get the meeting behind me and pleased that he was being so accommodating.

"And thanks for coming forward with the information," he continued.

I was fixated on the shady character in the car. Maybe the man even had a record for molesting women. "So the license plate was helpful?" I asked. I even visualized that Ivinson would take care of all my traffic tickets for being such a good citizen.

"We'll discuss it this afternoon," he said.

I didn't want to wait, but in an effort to keep on his good side, I didn't say anything. His next words made me realize that cooperation probably wasn't possible.

"What I'm going to need," he said, "is a list of all your customers."

I'd been afraid of this, but I hadn't expected it to come so soon, especially not once I'd zeroed in on the creepy guy as the prime suspect.

I mumbled something about seeing Ivinson at four and hung up. I couldn't bring myself to tell him right then that I wasn't about to give up my list of customers without a fight.

I didn't feel up to calling Mom once I got through with Detective Ivinson. The thought of giving up the names of our customers had left me numb and unable to communicate on any serious level.

Instead, I went out to the dry-cleaning machines to talk to Mack. "A detective's coming here at four. He wants me to provide him with a list of all our customers."

I could tell Mack was as disappointed as I was. "But what about the guy in the beat-up car?"

"I gave him the license plate, and he was gone for a while checking it out. He said we'd discuss it later."

Mack frowned. "Why not right then?"

"I don't know. Maybe he's checking to see if the man has a rap sheet, and if he does, the police will forget about me giving them the database for my customers."

"And if they don't?"

"I'm going to tell him I won't provide a list."

Mack shook his head, but he didn't disagree. "Want me to stick around until after you talk to the guy?"

"No, you're off at four. Just go on home and I'll call you later."

"What if I come back at seven and we go over to Tico Taco's for dinner?"

I was glad to accept the offer. I'd probably need the company after taking a stand against Ivinson.

"Too bad we can't cull a few more names from your list," Mack said.

"That's why I asked Travis to run a background check on the names."

Mack didn't have a response to that.

"I asked everyone up front to write down the names of people they remember being at the open house," I said. "I'll check to see if they came up with anyone." If I got lucky, maybe I would find a match to a customer who'd been in the cleaners one of the days Lorraine Lovell had come in.

I headed to the counter to talk to Julia and Ann Marie. Especially Ann Marie. She needed to cool it with Brett until the police found Ardith's killer.

Lucille, who works behind the scenes marking in the clothes to be cleaned, stopped me before I got to the call office. "Where've you been?" she asked. "I had to work the counter during lunch, and you know how I hate that. Now I'm way behind." She seemed to think her gray hair and long years of service gave her the right to complain whenever she had to do something she didn't want to do— namely, deal with the public.

"I'm sorry," I said, glancing at my watch. Actually, I was glad to hear that Julia and Ann Marie had been able to get away for lunch.

"I hope it doesn't happen again tomorrow," she said.

If I left her alone to do the mark-in and help bag and hang the finished garments, she was a hard worker, albeit a little grouchy. That didn't excuse her from doing other things in a pinch.

I couldn't help myself. I stopped just before I entered the call office. "By the way, have you made out that list of people you remember being at the open house?" I asked. "I'd like you to give it to me before you go home tonight."

Lucille scowled. She hadn't liked being called into service at the open house, either, and apparently this was the final indignity. "If I *ever* get caught up with my work," she said, giving an exaggerated sigh.

This wasn't my day. As soon as I reached the counter, I headed for Ann Marie. She looked at me as if I was the last person in the world she wanted to see.

"I know you're probably mad at me," she said, beginning to talk even before I got there, "but I was wrong about Brett being in the cleaners the day of the open house, because, you know, he told me he wasn't here, and I believe him, so you shouldn't worry about me going out with him, because he's really a nice guy."

She always tended to run her sentences together when she was nervous, but she finally stopped to get my reaction. She obviously didn't know that I could check the computer to see if Brett was lying. At least I could if Brett had actually done any business with us that day.

I guess she decided my silence was approval. "So everything's great," Ann Marie said. "Okay?"

"I still think you should wait about dating him until this whole thing is cleared up." Having to offer such cautious advice made me feel old, fearful, and as grumpy as Lucille.

"Okeydoke," she said.

I knew her well enough to realize that she was agreeing with me just to bring this conversation to an end as quickly as possible and in a way that would satisfy me.

Frankly, I wanted to end it, too, so I asked if she or Julia had made a list of men they remembered being here during the open house. Ann Marie shrugged, but Julia produced a sheet of paper with a short list of names, including several rather decrepit elderly gentlemen who'd probably been here strictly for the food and drink. None of the names coincided with the ones I'd written down as possible suspects from the days Lorraine had been here.

I said I'd be in my office for a while and headed to the back of the plant.

When I reached my desk, I logged on to the computer and checked to see if Brett had dropped off or picked up an order during the open house. Okay, so maybe Ann Marie was right. There was no transaction for him that day. It didn't mean he hadn't been here, just that the place had been such a zoo that he couldn't get any service.

I checked for other customers who'd actually managed to pick up or drop off clothes during the festivities. Most of them were women, which apparently shows that the female of the species is more patient and persistent about getting clothes cleaned.

I couldn't help wondering for a few seconds if Ardith had been referring to another woman when she talked about the "sharply creased pants" and the "freshly pressed shirt." After all, I thought we are kind of a unisex society when it comes to clothes. I shook my head in disgust. I was getting crazy about the whole thing. Ardith had definitely said "he" and "so different from most of the men I know."

By the time I finished going through the list of customers that we'd served the day of the open house, including names in the guest book that I didn't recognize, it was after 3:30. I'd found only one other possible prospect to add to my list—an actor who tended to wear capes over his pressed pants and neatly starched shirts. He always reminded me of a vampire without the fangs.

I needed to get up front to intercept Detective Ivinson when he arrived. No need to let everyone know that yet another homicide detective was paying me a visit. Unfortunately, I had developed somewhat of a reputation for hosting members of the Crimes Against Persons Division of the Denver Police Department.

When I arrived at the counter, Julia and Ann Marie had already left for the day. Theresa, who was the afternoon counter manager, handed me a list of open house attendees she remembered.

My list was getting longer instead of shrinking, and I couldn't help remembering what Mack had said about culling names from the list. It seemed particularly important now to eliminate as many names as possible before Detective Ivinson was able to secure a subpoena or whatever the police used in these situations.

Narrow the list. Narrow the list. You need to narrow the list. I was repeating the words to myself like a mantra when Theresa's coworker Elaine provided me with a few more names.

The last name on the list gave me a start. I had a match. "Are you sure he was here?"

Elaine nodded. "I remember him distinctly. He always seems to be striking a pose. He stood around for a few minutes, but when he couldn't get waited on, he left."

I stared at the name she'd written down. It was Jason Arnell, the male model who'd also been here one of the days Lorraine Lovell had come in. Maybe I could give his name to Detective Ivinson when he got here and that would satisfy the police. But was being a frequent customer enough reason to be marked as a murder suspect, and could I give up the name without feeling guilty about it?

I didn't know, and I couldn't bear to think about it right now. I went over and logged on to one of the computers to help with the late-afternoon rush, and when I looked up, I couldn't believe my eyes.

Jason, who'd previously been famous around here mainly for his underwear ads in a mail-order catalog, was standing in front of me. It had to be serendipity, not mere coincidence. He must have come directly from a game of tennis or a modeling session. He was wearing white shorts and a white V-necked sweater, and he was striking one of the poses that Elaine had described. It seemed to say, Aren't I gorgeous?

"Hi, Jason," I said as I formulated the beginnings of an idea. What if I asked him about the open house? If he denied being here or seemed nervous about it, maybe that would be a tip-off as to his guilt.

"I'm doing a spot check of customers to see how many came to our open house back in March," I said. "Did you attend it, by any chance?"

Jason swiped a lock of sun-bleached blond hair off his forehead, blinked his big blue eyes at me, and looked as if I'd asked him to solve a problem in advanced calculus.

"We had champagne and cake and gave tours of the plant," I ex-

plained. "I was interested to see if customers thought I should do it
again."

I began to feel a familiar itch coming on. After all, I was lying
through my teeth. I had no intention of ever holding another open
house.

However, maybe I'd touched a nerve. Jason seemed to be turning the question over in his mind. Should he admit to being here—
in case someone had seen him—or should he play dumb about the
whole thing? Of course, there was always the possibility that he
didn't know what the devil I was talking about.

Finally, he answered. "I was here that day, come to think of it,
but the place was so crowded, I left without picking up my order."

Bull's-eye. I'd scored a direct hit. Not only had he been here the
same day as Lorraine but he was admitting that he'd been here the
day Ardith met her mystery man. I didn't know if it proved innocence
or guilt, however. What I'd wanted was for him to stutter out a denial.

"I would say that you probably shouldn't have another open
house," he continued, still mulling over my question. "I think a lot
of your regular customers got turned off that day because they
couldn't get any service."

Actually, I couldn't have agreed more, and I wanted to move on
now that I had his reaction to the question. "Well, let's make sure you
get fast service today." I grabbed the ticket he'd deposited on the
counter when he first came in and checked to see where his order
was located on our conveyor. "I'll get your clothes and be right back."

With that, I hurried to the conveyor and punched in the slot
number on a keypad. The conveyor began to whir around the
cleaners, giving me a chance to consider what I'd just done. Damn.
I probably shouldn't have acted so impulsively. If he'd been the one
who'd met Ardith that day, why tip him off to the fact that I was interested in whether he'd been at the open house? Why did I always
blurt out something without thinking about the consequences?

I returned to the counter, hung his order over a hook, and told
him how much he owed.

"I've been thinking," he continued as he handed over his money. "Maybe if you have another open house, you should hold it on a Sunday, when you're usually closed. That way, it won't interfere with your regular business."

I felt like saying, Give it up already. I wasn't really serious. All I wanted to do was see your reaction to the question. What I actually said was, "You're probably right. Thanks for the input."

Either he was sharper than I'd given him credit for or he was totally innocent of any wrongdoing and was serious about helping me with future promotions.

He gave me a big smile, suitable for an eight-by-ten glossy for his portfolio, and departed with his clothes.

Cal Ingalls took his place at the counter. What were the chances of that? Another name on my too-long list of suspects. The Marlboro Man, as Julia called him, had also been here one of the days Lorraine Lovell had come in.

Cal was tall but not as muscular or as handsome as I'd always visualized the Marlboro Man to be, but I wasn't going to quibble with Julia's fantasy. Still, with a head of curly brown hair and an unruly cowlick, he did have a certain disheveled appeal.

He was dressed the way he always was—in jeans, a dress shirt unbuttoned at the neck, and a sports jacket. He handed me several shirts and a corduroy jacket, but he held on to a pair of jeans, almost as if he'd forgotten about them.

"What was that about an open house?" he asked.

Now that I'd decided my questioning of Jason was probably a bad idea, I wanted to drop the whole thing.

Cal wouldn't let me. "Did I miss something?" he asked.

"I was just trying to see what people thought about the open house we had." Mistake or not, I decided I might as well continue. "Did you come to it, by any chance?"

"Nope. I'm afraid I never even heard about it. When was it, anyway?"

"Back in March."

"That probably explains it. I had to go out of town a lot in March to our oil-drilling site up in Wyoming."

"What about those jeans?" I asked.

He looked confused at the change of subject, and I pointed to the jeans with a Wrangler logo on them.

He pulled the jeans back and tucked them under his arm. "I don't know why I brought them in here. I'm going to the Laundromat later, and I had them in my car."

He'd seemed rattled by the question, but maybe it was because he was going to the coin-op for one of those singles' nights that Ann Marie had told me about. That sent a chill up my spine. Perhaps he was lying about not being at the open house, too, and he was going to the coin laundry looking for another victim.

God, I wished I'd never brought up the whole thing. I wondered if maybe I should turn over all the names of my customers and let the police handle the questioning of suspects, but the idea appalled me.

Cal gave me a crooked grin that seemed a lot more natural than Jason's perfect smile. "I've had a lot on my mind lately," he said, apparently as an explanation for why he'd brought the jeans into the cleaners. "We're down at seven thousand feet and still waiting for the well to come in."

I put his jacket and the shirts in a bag for mark-in. Lucille could separate them later, one bag for dry cleaning and the other for laundry.

"I'll be back in a couple of days to pick up the clothes," he said, turning to leave.

I nodded. "We'll have them ready."

I glanced at my watch. It was a few minutes after four. I looked out the door to see if I could spy someone who looked like a homicide detective.

I didn't. The person I did see was Brett Harrison, Ann Marie's waiter. He nodded at Cal, and they exchanged a few words. Now that was interesting. I'd seen them talking to each other on a few previous occasions, but now I wondered about it. Were they acquainted, other than through chance encounters at the cleaners? Could they have some other connection to each other, the way I'd thought Mel Sutton and the grungy man might have? I shook my head in disgust. I had to quit coming up with these conspiracy theories. It was highly doubtful that a serial killer would have an accomplice.

Suddenly, Brett broke away and disappeared from my line of sight. Why didn't he come inside? I wondered. I had to assume that he was waiting around for Ann Marie. Maybe he'd asked Cal if she was here, and when Cal said no, he decided to leave. Even though the only evidence I had against him was what Ann Marie had told me about him being here the day of the open house—later recanted—I was still on edge about the relationship.

Or maybe my nervousness was because I was dreading the prospect of telling Detective Ivinson I couldn't bring myself to give up the names of my customers. My only hope was that the license number I'd given the detective would lead to Betty's creepy suspect, who, as it would turn out, had a record for stalking women. Case closed.

Another customer came up to me. At first glance, I thought the man was the priest with the turned collar whom I'd reluctantly put on my list of suspects—people who'd been here during one of Lorraine Lovell's visits. After all, the priest's garb was different from that of the other men Ardith knew, which was the only clue I had to go on.

"Father—" I began, then stopped. He had the same short gray hair, thin face, and kindly eyes as the priest, but something was a little off. Maybe it was just the fact that he wasn't wearing his normal black shirt and white collar, but I wasn't about to try the question about the open house on him. After all, this might be God's way of telling me I should never suspect a man of the cloth.

"Ms. Dyer?" the man asked.

I nodded.

"I'm Detective Ivinson. We had an appointment at four o'clock. Sorry I'm late."

Panic set in, and for a moment I toyed with the idea of telling him that I'd misunderstood the question and Ms. Dyer wasn't here. I wondered if he'd heard me call him "Father." At least I could take some comfort in the fact that he had a kindly face to go with the soft-spoken voice on the phone. Maybe he would turn out to have an understanding heart, as well.

I fought down my impulse to flee. "Oh, yes, why don't you come back to my office with me?"

He nodded and followed me through the plant. When he was seated across from me at my desk, he pulled out a notebook and a ballpoint pen. "Now if we could review what you told me over the phone. Start at the beginning."

"First," I said, "I'm wondering what you found out from that license plate I gave you. Does the man have a record?" After all, I'd hoped the reason he hadn't wanted to tell me anything over the phone was that the guy was a real scumbag and Ivinson had wanted to see how many prior arrests he had.

"I'm afraid I can't give you that information," he said.

"But I'm the one—"

He shook his head. "Sorry, I can't say any more."

My mind was reeling. It wasn't so much from the fact that Ivinson wouldn't tell me what he'd found out as it was from the realization that Mel Sutton must have lied to me.

If Mel had been right that there was no such license plate, wouldn't Ivinson have told me I'd copied the plate number down wrong?

No, there was definitely something about the plate that had made Mel feel he had to lie about it. I had no idea what it was, but some frightening possibilities came to mind.

SEVEN

As soon as Ivinson told me he couldn't give me any information about the license plate, he moved on. "As I said before, why don't you—"

I had already tuned out. I was still hung up on Mel. What if he and the grungy stranger in the beat-up car really were in some sort of collusion? Okay, the thought had flitted through my mind at the time, but I'd decided it was one of those off-the-wall ideas of an overworked mind. Now it seemed like a real possibility. Or what if the grungy guy had seen Mel leave the cleaners with Ardith and was blackmailing him? Mel would want to see that the guy got away.

"Ms. Dyer?"

Ivinson's voice startled me. I had to get a grip. "Yes," I said, as if I'd been hanging on his every word. I didn't fool him for a minute.

"I said, 'Just start at the beginning.'"

I repeated the whole conversation with Ardith about the open house and what she'd said about her mystery man. Now I had a dilemma. When I'd talked to the detective on the phone, I hadn't mentioned Lorraine Lovell and the fact that she'd also been in the cleaners shortly before she was killed. Nat had told me that was off the record. I didn't want to get him in trouble, but no matter what, I had to tell Ivinson about her.

"About a year ago," I said, "another customer was murdered in her home. She'd been in the cleaners only a couple of times, but I remember reading about her. The circumstances sounded similar to Ardith's death because the article said she appeared to be entertaining someone and there was no sign of forced entry."

I didn't know whether there'd been an article at the time or not. I was hoping he wouldn't remember, either.

My hands were clammy with sweat. Perspiration beaded my forehead. My nose began to itch the way it always does when I stray from the truth, but at least I hadn't betrayed Nat's confidence.

I mentioned Lorraine's name, and I saw Ivinson perk up. "I don't know if there's a connection, but I thought I should let you know."

"Hmmm," he said, seeming to write more in his notebook than what I'd told him. "You said she'd only been here a few times. Do you have the dates for her visits?"

"Yes, I looked them up." I gave him the days she'd dropped off and picked up her clothes. "Those were the only times she was here, but I remembered her name when I read about her in the paper—Lorraine Lovell. It was so alliterative."

Stop it, will you? I warned myself. You always have a tendency to overexplain.

I rubbed the side of my nose while Ivinson wasn't looking. It was going to grow as long as Pinocchio's if I didn't quit fibbing. I'd read once that a study by a group of scientists in Chicago showed that a person's nose actually does grow when the person lies. Nasal tissues become engorged with blood, causing them to swell, during a deception. While the effect might not be noticeable to the naked eye, the liar is drawn to touch his/her itching nose, betraying guilt.

Someone pounded on the door as Ivinson continued to write in his notebook. We both jumped. Damn, it was probably Betty. She had a habit of interrupting me at the most awkward times.

I started to yell that I was busy. No, I decided, it was better to go to the door and shoo her away.

But it wasn't Betty. Before I could even get out of my chair, the door swung open. Lucille came stomping into the room.

She tossed a folded sheet of paper on my desk. "Here. That's the only thing I remember. You know I don't like to work out front, and I don't know any of the customers by name." She did a quick 180-degree turn and marched out of the room, slamming the door behind her.

"What was that about?" Ivinson asked.

"Just an employee completing her garment count for the day." I cringed. If I was going to lie, why didn't I make up something consistent with what Lucille had just said? What did a garment count have to do with customers' names? Fortunately, Ivinson didn't seem to care. He was more interested in getting on with the interview.

"So when did you find out about Ms. Brewster's murder?" he asked.

I was suddenly obsessed with the idea that I needed to put Lucille's list away in my desk. I didn't want Ivinson to see it, in case it said "People at open house."

I opened a drawer and slid the paper inside. "Well," I said, "I didn't know about it until—" I should never have decided to sneak a look at Lucille's list once it was safely tucked away in the drawer. Considering her remark, though, I guess I was curious to see if it would be a blank page.

I flipped the paper open, and there *was* something inside. Lucille had written a single sentence, not a list. It said, "The only person I saw around the cleaners that afternoon was that Travis fellow you've been going out with."

I slammed the drawer shut, but I was in free fall after that. Travis couldn't have been here during the open house. He'd had trouble even remembering it, for God sakes, and he would have had a hard time forgetting the confusion if he'd come inside. Besides, I was sure I hadn't seen him.

I finally flashed back to what Ivinson had asked. "The newspaper—I read it in the newspaper."

Ivinson nodded. "As we discussed earlier, what I need from you is a list of customers who were here the days in question. If you can't provide that, I'll need your whole database."

Now came the part I'd been dreading—well, one of the many things I was beginning to dread these days.

"No," I said. "I can't do that. I'm sorry. It would violate customer confidentiality, and I certainly can't have you going around questioning everyone just because they bring us their dry cleaning."

"This is a murder investigation, Ms. Dyer."

Suddenly, Ivinson seemed to transform in front of me from the kindly, thin-faced man of the cloth to an evil wolflike carnivore with beady eyes, a too-long nose, a pointed chin, and sharp little teeth. Talk about a metamorphic change.

"Is that your final decision?" He was no longer the soft-spoken man I'd talked to on the phone, either.

I stood up. "Look, Detective Ivinson, there's no way I'll voluntarily provide you with the names of my customers."

"Then I believe this conversation is over." Ivinson got out of his chair.

"I can't have all my customers become suspects in a murder investigation. Surely you can understand my position."

Apparently, he didn't. He put his pen and notebook in his pocket. "Good day, Ms. Dyer. We have other ways of dealing with people like you."

I started to get up. "I'll try to find out who the man was that Ardith met here, and I'll let you know."

My words were lost on him, which was probably just as well. I'd been told more than once not to stick my nose in a police investigation. But this was personal. It could affect my whole livelihood. Not to mention the principle of the thing.

Ivinson had already shut the door, not quite as hard as Lucille, but close. I gathered he'd decided to show himself out of the plant.

Normally, I would have insisted on accompanying him to the front door, but right then I was just glad he was gone.

I wondered if he would return with a warrant to search the place. The police had threatened to do that once before, but I'd willingly granted them access to the building after a competitor was killed on the premises. I really didn't know what the police could or would do in this case, but at the moment, I was more concerned about the note.

Dropping back into my chair, I opened the drawer and took another look at the piece of paper. Yes, I'd read it correctly. Lucille had definitely said that Travis had been here the day of the open house. Had she been trying to get back at me for ordering her to deliver a list or was she telling the truth? She had no real reason to make it up, however. She could simply have said she didn't remember anyone.

More to the point, if Travis had been here, why had he denied remembering the open house when I'd mentioned it last night? We hadn't seen each other over the past weekend, when Ardith had been entertaining her lover. That much I knew. He'd been tied up on this undercover job, or so he said.

I couldn't help thinking how Ardith had described her mystery man as different from the other men she knew. Travis usually wore slacks and sports jackets and open-necked shirts. Was that different enough from the people Ardith worked with? Maybe. What was really different was the scar, which gave Travis a somewhat cynical, hard-edged, albeit sexy, appearance. He didn't look like someone who would work at a bank.

I shook my head, slammed the drawer shut again, and locked the note inside. I refused to put Travis on my list of suspects. No way. It was ridiculous. He wasn't even a customer. Ardith had said her lover was a customer, so it couldn't be Travis—unless, of course, he'd told her he was a customer rather than say he was here to see me.

Damn it, stop thinking this way, I scolded myself. When I told him about Ardith, hadn't he offered to do whatever he could to help me? Sure, my inner voice said, but what if he did that just to find out what I knew and steer me off in the wrong direction?

I would talk the situation over with Mack at dinner, and hopefully he would be able to reassure me that Travis didn't have anything to do with this. Hadn't Travis come to my rescue on a couple of occasions? Surely no serial killer would do that. But hadn't Ted Bundy once warned Ann Rule, the true-crime writer, about the dangers of being outside alone at night? It was when he'd escorted her to her car after both had spent a late shift volunteering at a crisis center in Seattle.

Quit it, Mandy. Get to work. Stop wallowing in fear.

I'd promised Laura I would call Mom and talk her out of coming to Denver right now. I reached for the phone, but just then it rang. I picked it up.

"It's me." I recognized Travis's voice.

"Hi." As long as I stuck to short answers, I decided my voice wouldn't reveal the terrible thoughts I'd been having about him.

"I'm glad I caught you," he said. "I wanted to let you know what I found out so far." I assumed he was referring to the list of names I'd given him. "But first, how're you doing?"

"Okay." But of course I wasn't.

"Good," he said. "Are you ready?"

My hands were shaking as I grabbed a pen and paper. "All right." My voice shook, too.

"Here goes. The cop, Mel Sutton, the air force lieutenant, and the state representative, Barry Sampson, are all married."

I already knew about Sampson's weird *War of the Roses* living arrangement, but I wrote down his name anyway.

"The others are single, although Cal Ingalls had a messy divorce a few years ago."

I wondered how he'd found that out, but I wasn't sure if my voice would hold up if I tried to ask him about it.

"Brett Harrison, the waiter you mentioned, had a couple of arrests for drug possession a few years ago." He referred to the dates.

"None of the other men you mentioned appear to have criminal records, either for sex offenses or anything else.

"But Jason Arnell has a credit rating that's the pits. Seems he doesn't work all that much as a model, and between jobs, he's a parking attendant."

I was having a hard time absorbing all this, and I was getting writer's cramp from trying to write it down.

Travis didn't even pause to take a breath, and I decided he must be in a hurry. "You've probably read some of the articles about State Representative Sampson. There've been rumors that he's been taking payoffs from lobbyists, but as of now, that's all they are—rumors. I haven't been able to find anything on Bill Merrick, the owner of that men's store down by you, Reverend Woodley, or any of the other people you mentioned, but I'll keep digging."

"Th-thanks." The word came out as if it had two syllables because I was stuttering now. I couldn't help wondering what secrets would turn up if I had someone investigate Travis.

"Look," he said. "I'm already late for work, but this job should be over soon, and we'll get together and talk this out as soon as I'm through. Okay?"

I willed myself not to stumble over my words as we said good-bye. "Sure thing. Take care."

"You, too."

With that, he hung up, but I knew I'd have to resolve my suspicions about him before I saw him again. I turned on the computer and checked to see if Travis, unbeknownst to me, had ever been a customer here at the cleaners. I couldn't find any evidence that he had. So why didn't I feel better about him?

I'd been ready to call Mom when Travis called. I might as well get it over with, since I'd promised Laura that I would. I punched in her number in Phoenix, and her answering machine came on. "Mom, I need to talk to you. Call me as soon as possible. It's urgent."

It wouldn't have been quite so urgent earlier in the day, when

Laura had asked me to call. As it was, I feared Mom and Herb could be on their way to Denver at this very moment. "Call me on my cell phone. You know the number, don't you?" I gave it to her just in case she'd lost it. After all, I'd told her it was only for emergencies. As far as I could tell, this qualified as one. "Uh . . ." I continued, "we really think it would be better if you waited to come to Denver until it's closer to the wedding. Call so we can discuss it."

Having accomplished nothing with the phone call except to tip Mom off as to why I was calling, I went up front. At least I could help at the counter until it was time to meet Mack. Work, I've found, is the best antidote for hysteria, and I was feeling a little better by closing time. I'd stood up to Ivinson even though I knew I might regret it later, and at least Mom hadn't called from here in Denver. I still had doubts about Travis, but I was hoping Mack could dispel them at dinner.

When I finally got to Tico Taco's in the strip shopping center behind the cleaners, he was waiting for me in our usual booth. Manuel, the plump and genial owner, who'd recently grown what I thought of as a Pancho Villa mustache, was hovering nearby, ready to take our order as soon as I sat down.

Well, that wasn't quite true. He'd just returned from a vacation in Mexico, and what he wanted to do was tell us all about the trip—a day-by-day account.

"Can you imagine my Maria actually surprising me with the trip for my birthday?" He was referring to his wife, a plump, pleasant woman he'd married several years before. "What a birthday present!" He hit his cheeks with the palms of his hands. "And to think she kept it a secret until my party."

We'd heard all about the gift at the time, and after we listened to the story again, Manuel finally got around to taking our orders, chicken fajitas and a margarita for me and the same for Mack, only his were beef fajitas.

"What'd you find out?" Mack asked as soon as Manuel left.

I told him what Ivinson had said about the license plate and how I'd turned down his request to give up my customer database.

"Do you think he'll be back with a court order?" Mack asked when I finished.

"I don't know," I said, "but—"

I didn't finish because Manuel returned with our drinks just then. He insisted on hanging around until we tasted them and gave him the thumbs-up.

Once he left, I continued. "I'm still trying to narrow down the list of suspects in case he does." I told Mack about my impulsive and possibly ill-conceived discussion with Jason Arnell and later with Cal Ingalls about the open house. "Elaine thinks Jason was at the open house, and he and Cal were both at the cleaners when Lorraine Lovell was there."

I could see Mack begin to shake his head before I finished. "I'm not sure you should have done that. You have to be more careful, Mandy."

I came very close to telling him that he was the one who'd mentioned my need to go over the list, but I didn't. "I suppose," I said. "It didn't do much good anyway. Cal said he hadn't even heard about the open house. Jason admitted being at it and insisted on giving me advice on how to run the next one so it wouldn't inconvenience my regular customers. I don't think he would have done that if he'd been guilty of something."

We'd hardly had time to take a few sips of our drinks before Manuel was back with the sizzling pans of fajitas and all the fixings.

"Where's Señor Kincaid?" he asked. "I haven't seen him for a while."

"He's been working on an assignment at night," I said.

Manuel nodded his head. "Ah, *bueno*. I was afraid you'd broken up." Ever the romantic, he was always happy when people paired off, and he hired musicians to serenade them on Saturday nights. Needless to say, I avoided Tico Taco's like the plague on those nights.

Eventually, he left again, and I tried to figure out how to tell Mack what I'd learned about Travis. Manuel had given me an opening, but I didn't want to spoil Mack's dinner. Instead, I had to listen to him fret about my getting "too involved" as we worked our way through the meal. His litany of my indiscretions covered my wild-goose chase with Betty that morning and my questioning of customers in the afternoon. He even invoked past offenses and how he'd had to come to my aid, or, at the very least, worry about me.

By then, we'd finished the meal, and I couldn't help smiling. "If someone has to worry about me, I'm glad it's you. You remind me of Lucy in 'Peanuts.' You're such a fussbudget."

He seemed irritated and pleased at the same time.

I really hated to break the spell, and I dreaded bringing up Travis, but I needed a less emotional opinion than my own.

"I value your opinion, Mack, and I want to run something by you." I launched into the tale of Lucille's note and my reaction to it. "I didn't see Travis that day, and he never mentioned one word about stopping by during the open house. At first, he said he couldn't even remember it. Do you think it means anything?"

"Are you asking if I think he's a suspect?"

"I didn't quite want to put it that way."

"For God sakes, no. You're letting this whole thing get to you. He's never been a customer, has he?"

"Well, no."

"So he wasn't even around back when this other woman was killed, and we're going on the assumption that she met someone at the cleaners, too. It wouldn't have been him."

"I suppose." As an afterthought, I told Mack what Travis had found out about our suspects.

"Now let's get out of here. You need to get home and get a good night's sleep." He grabbed the check and started to get up.

"It's my turn to pay," I protested.

"No, this is my treat."

There was no sense arguing with him when he'd made up his

mind. "Okay, I'll get the tip." I dug in my purse and left a five-dollar bill on the table.

It was already dark as we left the restaurant.

"I'll walk you to your car," he said, now in full protective-father mode.

"No, you don't have to do that." It was one thing for him to lecture me, but this was going too far. The Hyundai was across the parking lot from where he'd left his truck, and I decided I never should have told him about my conversations with Jason and Cal earlier in the day. "Really, I can get to my car by myself."

My protest didn't do any good.

He opened the door for me and waited until I was safely locked inside the car before he headed back to his truck. I put my head down on the steering wheel and wondered if maybe I should quit using him as a sounding board. He worried about me too much.

When I started the car and drove out onto First Avenue, I noticed he was right behind me. That wasn't surprising, because we both had to go up Speer Boulevard toward downtown Denver to get home.

I didn't become suspicious about his motives until he failed to turn off on the one-way street that would have taken him to his house. Good grief, don't tell me he's going to follow me to my front door.

Not only that, but he was following so close, there didn't seem to be more than an arm's length between our two vehicles. In fact, it looked as if I was towing the truck on a very short chain. Where was a policeman now, when I needed him to tell Mack to back off?

I even toyed with the idea of detouring from my normal route home to see how long Mack would keep after me. I decided that was an immature thing to do; it would only prove to Mack that I was too irresponsible to take care of myself.

We continued the two-car parade to my apartment, and when I found a parking space, I jumped out of my car and headed back to where he'd pulled to the curb by a fire hydrant.

"What do you think you're doing?" I yelled as I went over to his truck and stuck my head in the rolled-down passenger window.

"I was making sure you got home safely."

I put out my hands in a gesture of frustration. "Well, I'm here now, so your responsibility is over."

Apparently, Mack felt he had to explain. "A car pulled out of the parking lot just behind us, and I'm worried that the driver was trying to follow you. I wasn't about to let his car get in between us."

I guess Mack was thinking of the time last winter when he was behind a pickup that ran me off a mountain road and into a snowbank.

"Didn't you see the guy?" he asked.

No, all I'd seen was Mack's truck, with its lights blinding me whenever I tried to look in my rearview mirror.

"So where is he?" I looked up and down the deserted street.

"He turned off at the last corner." Mack sounded a little embarrassed, and I couldn't help feeling sorry for him.

"Well, thanks for the concern, Mack." I echoed what he'd said to me in the restaurant. "Now go home and get a good night's sleep."

He was the most stubborn person I'd ever known. "I'll just wait here until you get inside."

I gave up and left him in the no-parking zone.

When I looked out the window from my apartment ten minutes later, he was still there. I guess he was waiting to make sure he didn't spot the car again.

EIGHT

Once I converted my sofa into a bed and climbed under the covers, I had trouble getting to sleep. Could Mack have been right about someone following me, and was it only because of him inserting his truck between our two cars that the driver finally backed off? Even worse, could it have been one of the men Betty the blabbermouth or I tipped off today about my interest in the open house? I wondered.

I got up and looked out the window again. Mack's truck was no longer at the corner. In a strange way, I found that comforting. He must have decided he'd been wrong about the car and gone home to get some rest.

I tossed and turned when I went back to bed, but I finally dropped off into a restless sleep, now that I had convinced myself that Mack had been his normally overcautious self when he thought someone was following me. After all, the driver had turned off before we reached my place.

When the alarm went off the next morning, I bolted up from bed. I'd been having a dream of some kind, but whatever it was faded from my mind before I had a chance to grab hold of it.

I was just as happy that it had. It was probably some ghoulish nightmare about Travis trying to run Mack and me down in his car, and it would have resurrected all the doubts about him that I'd tried to purge from my mind the previous night.

No, the dream had to have been something else, because I suddenly had a flash of inspiration. I knew what the next thing was that I needed to do to narrow down the list, as Mack had suggested.

My subconscious must have been working overtime while I slept. I seldom have sleep-induced and brilliant ideas the way other people claim to do all the time. Okay, there was the time I remembered where I'd put a set of keys after I "slept on it" overnight, but usually my nighttime flashes of genius don't hold up in the light of day. The time I thought of adding a taco stand inside the call office came to mind. It had seemed like such a good idea when I scribbled it down on a piece of paper during the night.

No matter. I now had a motivation for going to work. Why hadn't I thought of it before? I needed to talk to some of the people who'd known the victims and figured it shouldn't be that hard to do. I was on a first-name basis with one of the tellers at the bank. I could ask her about Ardith. And as I recalled from looking up Lorraine Lovell's name on the computer, she had listed a work number. I bet it was somewhere in the Cherry Creek area, either in the mall or in the string of stores on Second and Third Avenues, in what's called Cherry Creek North.

Maybe I would find out that they both had a preference for a certain type of man. I was hoping for "grungy," but I would settle for "snazzy." I guess I was thinking of Jason Arnell, the male model who wasn't quite as slick as the glossies in his portfolio. Or maybe I would find out that the two women had shared a mutual interest in politics or had a thing for military men. That might lead to the state representative who had a *War of the Roses* relationship with his wife or to the air force lieutenant in the "spit-and-polish" uniform.

After I fed Spot to keep him from being underfoot, I took a quick look out the front window. The street was quiet—just a few people heading off to work and a solitary jogger who looked as if his feet hurt.

I even had the nerve to check my phone messages, both on my home phone and on my cell. There was only one call, which was from a telemarketer. Nothing from my mother. I was surprised Mom hadn't called. She must be pouting about the message I'd left on her machine to stay away from Denver until the wedding.

I zapped a cup of water in the microwave and had a quick coffee and a piece of toast while I put on a freshly pressed uniform—a tan skirt and blouse with a gold Dyer's Cleaners logo on the pocket, which was standard garb for any of us who worked the counter.

It was nearly eight when I reached the plant, thanks to Mack being the one to open up this week. I had a lot to do before ten o'clock, when the bank and most of the stores in the Cherry Creek area opened for business: Find out where Lorraine Lovell had worked before she was murdered, plan questions to ask her and Ardith's coworkers, and, of course, work at the front counter until the morning rush was over.

My carefully laid plans for how to proceed were dashed the moment I pulled into the parking lot. There was a big black Lexus in the spot where I usually parked at the back of the plant. Why did I suddenly have a bad feeling about this? Maybe it was because that is exactly the type of car my mother and Herb liked to rent when they came to Denver.

I tried to steel myself for what I might find inside the cleaners. I did a few deep-breathing exercises. They didn't work. I was still too chicken to enter. I opened the back door just enough to give a hissing sound, the way Betty had when she'd summoned me outside the day before to see the grungy guy.

When I had Mack's attention, I motioned him with a crook of my finger to come outside. "Is that who I think it is?" I asked the moment he crossed the threshold. Despite my panic, I couldn't help noticing that Mack looked tired.

"And you better get in there," he said. "Betty has your mother and Herb trapped in your office, and the fur could be flying by now."

God, I hoped that didn't mean that Mom was still wearing the mink coat from her January trip to Denver. Actually, the image of Mom and Betty as two scraggly alley cats perched on a back fence wasn't much better.

Unfortunately, Betty thought that she and my mother were bosom buddies after their unfortunate road trips together. Mom had a less favorable opinion of Betty. Still, she had a somewhat mystifying belief that Betty's street smarts and dubious driving skills would help her out in a jam whenever she ventured into the mountains. Knowing that Mom had been jailed in Aspen on one of their junkets and had been left stranded with Betty in a blinding snowstorm on another, I hoped she'd come to her senses.

I had to admit, however, that despite Mom's tendency to overdress and Betty's preference for the same bilious green outfits day after day, they were sisters under the skin—or in this case, the fabric they chose to wear. What I mean is that both have a tendency to stick their noses into things that are none of their business. If that sounds like me, I most emphatically disagree. I always have a good reason for nosing around. In this case, it was because my business was in imminent danger of going down the drain.

I took one final gulp of fresh air and followed Mack into the plant.

"I was in your office with the three of them, but I had to come back out here to tend to the machines," Mack said, sounding relieved that I was there to handle the people problems.

I left him in the dry-cleaning department, pasted on a smile, and feigned surprise as I rounded a corner to my office. "Mom, Herb. What are you doing here?"

Conversation came to an abrupt stop.

Mom rose from her chair and gave me a kiss on the cheek. I couldn't help noticing that she looked like a piece of modern art in a full-skirted dress of orange and green swirls and curlicues.

"Don't you remember? I told you we needed to come up here so Herbert could get acquainted with Nat"—I could tell she still didn't approve of him—"and I could help Laura with the wedding plans."

Apparently, she'd never picked up my rather cryptic message

from her answering machine, telling her to stay away until the wedding. Otherwise, I was pretty sure she wouldn't have kissed me.

My stepfather got up and gave me a big bear hug. He was in plaid walking shorts, knee-high socks, white shoes, and a white golfing shirt. The plaid clashed rather dramatically with Mom's bright swirls and curlicues. "Good to see you, Mandy-Pie," he said. "How about that niece of mine finally deciding to get hitched?"

"That was a surprise, wasn't it?" When you're at a loss for words, always answer with another question.

Betty interrupted from her perch on top of my desk. "Here I thought they were coming to Denver to help you find the creepy guy who mighta killed that woman."

I glared at her, wondering how the devil she'd found out the real reason for my interest in the men who'd attended the open house. I needed to have a serious conversation with her as soon as I could clear everyone out of my office.

"Yes, Betty was just telling us all about it," Mom said, quickly sitting back down, as if she might faint otherwise. "I hope you aren't getting yourself in another situation that we'll have to help straighten out."

I turned my glare in her direction, but she was oblivious to the look. She was busy fanning herself, as if she couldn't take any more bad news.

"No sir," Herb said, still on his feet. "We don't want anything to happen to our little girl. So, do you want to talk about it?"

"I really don't have time right now. I have a lot of work to do." Besides, it was obvious that Betty the blabbermouth had already filled them in. "What are you doing here so early in the morning, anyway?"

"Our plane had mechanical problems on the way to Denver," Herb said. "We were so late coming in to DIA that we decided to check into a hotel and wait until this morning to surprise you."

I was still hung up on the hour of their arrival. "But why so early?"

"We didn't want to bother Laura yet, and we knew you're always here at the crack of dawn," Herb said. "We figured you might like to go out for breakfast with us."

I was already shaking my head before he finished. "I'm sorry. I have too much to do."

Betty jumped down from the desk. "Well, I could use a break, and pancakes sound pretty good about now."

"No, Betty," I said. "You need to get back to work. *Right now.*"

It was Betty's turn to glare, and for once, Mom looked downright relieved.

Betty stopped moving as soon as I mentioned work instead of breakfast. "*Now,* Betty."

She stomped out of the room, and I turned to Mom and Herb. "I really have a lot of work piled up. Maybe we can all get together tonight for dinner." The moment the words were out of my mouth, I wished I hadn't suggested an alternate meal, but I knew I was going to have to face everyone sooner or later. Later was better.

I edged them toward the door, a skill I'd developed by handling some of the more difficult employees.

I escorted them outside, with only a quick stopover for them to say good-bye to Mack. "And please," I said, "we can't discuss what Betty was telling you with Nat and Laura."

Mom shook her head. "No, we don't want that nosy Nat to get wind of whatever it is. He's as bad as the paparazzi."

They both gave me a good-bye hug, which, I knew, might be the last one I'd get from Mom once she checked her answering machine. As soon as Herb started the car and drove away, I went back into the cleaners and started across to the laundry department, but Mack stopped me to offer a few fatherly words of concern and advice.

"Nobody suspicious drove by last night, and I hung around until two in the morning," he said.

"But I looked out the window before I went to bed and you were gone."

"I didn't want to stay by a fire hydrant all night, so I pulled into a parking space up the block."

I didn't know what to say. I finally said thank you. "Please, take the rest of the day off and go home and get some sleep."

"I might just do that." He yawned. "I guess maybe it was all in my imagination after all."

That was a relief, but Mack wasn't about to let me off the hook that easily. He changed the subject.

"Now don't go getting messed up in that wedding stuff between your folks and Laura. You have enough problems already."

I nodded and pointed in Betty's direction. "And one of them is right over there. Somehow, she found out why we were trying to track down people who'd been at the open house."

When I got to the washing machines, Betty was intent on watching the spin cycle on one of our industrial-size washers. She ignored the angry look on my face and gave me a conspiratorial grin. "That Herbie is really something, ain't he? I always wondered what type of fella Cece was married to. He takes the cake, don't he? He looks like one of them Scottish guys that wears skirts and plays the bagpipe."

I guess she was referring to his knee-length plaid pants, which might have looked like a kilt from certain angles. She'd once referred to my mother as looking like an overgrown garden in a floral-patterned dress, but I wasn't amused by her colorful description this time.

"Who gave you the idea that the creepy guy might have something to do with a murder?"

Betty shrugged. "I just figured it out."

"No, you didn't."

She thought about it for a while. "Then maybe I overheard it in the lunchroom."

"From whom?"

" 'From whom?' " she mimicked me, as if I was using too fancy a language for her. "Well, I was just sitting in there minding my own business, if you know what I mean, and I happened to hear Ann Marie talking about it with that new girl who bags the clothes. I didn't know it was some big secret."

Now I wanted to throttle Ann Marie as well as Betty.

"Well, don't say any more about it to anyone. Do you understand?"

"Gotcha, boss lady. Nobody's gettin' nothin' more out of me." With that, she made a gesture as if to zip her lips.

Before I went up front to have a word with Ann Marie, I returned to my office and booted up my computer. I typed in Lorraine Lovell's name, and the information we had on her appeared on the screen. It was just what I'd been hoping for. She'd given both a home and a work phone number. The place where she'd worked had a prefix that sounded as if it was in this general area of town.

Without waiting, I picked up the phone and punched in the numbers. I got a recorded message: "You have reached the Party Hearty Party Shop. Our store hours are ten A.M. to nine P.M. Monday through Friday and—"

That's all I needed to know. In fact, it was better than I'd hoped for. I knew the owner, Pam Kelsey. We used each other's services from time to time.

I glanced at my watch. It was only 8:30, but by the time I finished helping at the counter, the party shop should be open.

With that, I headed to the call office. Lucille ignored me as I started by the mark-in station. I stopped anyway. I couldn't stand it any longer. I had to find out why she'd said Travis was at the open house.

"About that list you gave me yesterday—why did you say Travis was here?"

She gave me a disapproving look, apparently still feeling put upon for having to make a list, short though it was. "You know I don't know any of the customers by name, so he's the only one I know for sure I saw around here."

"But I would have remembered if he were here." I stopped short of saying that he wouldn't have stopped by without talking to me. I didn't want to let her know how upset I was and give her a chance to gloat.

"Well, he was here all right—sneaking around out back," she said.

"What do you mean, 'out back'?"

"I had to get away from all the confusion around here, so I went out back to get some fresh air. When he saw me come out the back door, he acted kind of guilty and ducked into his car out in the parking lot. He just sat there until I came back inside."

"Are you sure it was him?"

"Of course I'm sure. There isn't nothing wrong with my eyesight. Besides, he was limping when he got to his car."

Okay, that sounded like Travis. He was still limping back in March from a gunshot wound he'd taken in his leg a few months earlier. But there must have been a lot of people limping around Denver at that time of year, considering the accidents that happen on the ski slopes every day.

I wasn't going to challenge her about it, though. "Well, thanks," I said. "I'll have to ask him about it."

Like that was going to happen. I didn't think I could bring myself to ask him right then. If he'd been here that day, I knew there was no way he could have missed our big OPEN HOUSE signs and the balloons out in front of the plant, courtesy, strangely enough, of the Party Hearty Party Shop. After all, he'd already said he could hardly remember the open house.

Lucille shrugged and went back to marking in the clothes. I continued through the door to the call office and my next task. I waited until Ann Marie finished with a customer. Then I pulled her aside and chewed her out.

"What's the idea of telling people about the connection between Ardith and the open house?"

"I didn't tell anyone."

"Betty said you were discussing it in the lunchroom."

Ann Marie shook her ponytail back and forth as if she were swatting flies. "I didn't bring it up. That new girl, Dottie, who bags the clothes asked me about it, honest. That's why I was talking about it."

I sighed, but I wasn't through yet. "Did you happen to go out with Brett yesterday afternoon?"

This time, she shook her head so hard, I thought she might throw her neck out of joint.

"No, why?" She actually looked puzzled, and I decided she was telling the truth, so I let it go.

Either he'd been looking for her and hadn't found her or he'd been hanging around for some other reason. I wondered why.

We returned to the counter, where I tried for a more cheerful attitude. "How're you doing, Julia?" I asked of my more mature and sensible counter manager.

She looked as tired as Mack had seemed. "I didn't get any sleep last night," she said. "Charlie took the kids on a camping trip, and I thought it would be fun to have some time to myself, but it wasn't. Our dog got spooked by something, and he kept running to the back door and barking all night. I had this picture of someone outside just waiting to break in when I went to sleep. I got so scared that I was even afraid to let Rambo out to do his business, so he did it inside instead."

I was sorry I'd asked and relieved when a customer came in the door. "I'll take this one," I said, in hopes of ending the conversation.

"Don't you ever get scared at night, living alone the way you do?" Julia whispered as a woman with a load of clothes came up to my station.

I wasn't about to tell her about the nerve-racking night I'd had myself. "Never," I said, "but I have a cat, and fortunately he doesn't bark and get me all shook up."

*　*　*

When I reached the back door an hour later, Mack wasn't around. Kim, his Korean assistant, was busy sorting clothes for the next load of cleaning to be put in one of the machines.

"Hi, boss lady," he said, a term he'd picked up from Betty in his quest to improve his English.

"Hi, Kim. Where's Mack?"

"He went home." He looked pleased at his use of the proper verb form. "He be back later." He corrected himself. "He *will* be back later."

"Good, Kim, and thanks."

I was relieved that Mack had taken my advice for once. Besides, now I didn't have to go through an interrogation about where I was going.

Outside, it was a perfect spring day. I wished my mood fit the weather. There wasn't a cloud in the sky, only a few jet trails left by planes high above.

I decided to walk, hoping it would cheer me up to be out of the plant for a while. The party shop was only four blocks away. I got there with time to spare and had to wait until five after the hour for someone to let me in.

"We don't generally have people waiting at ten o'clock," a woman about my age said as she held the door for me. "What can I do for you?"

The party shop always seemed like a happy place, full of helium-filled balloons, costumes for every occasion, and all sorts of paper tablecloths and party favors.

I didn't see the owner, only a couple of other clerks in the back stocking shelves. "Is Pamela here?"

"Sorry," the woman said. "She won't be in until noon, but I'm Joan. Maybe I can help you."

I wondered if I should come back later and talk to Pam or see what I could find out from her employee. Finally, I cleared my throat and introduced myself. "Do you remember an employee named Lorraine Lovell?"

Her eyes widened, and I could tell she did. "I had only been working here for a few weeks when she—" Joan's words trailed off, and she looked at me suspiciously.

"I'm aware of what happened to her, and this is a little awkward," I said, grappling for some words that would reassure her. "We're going through a lot of unclaimed clothes at Dyer's Cleaners, and someone said she thought one of the dresses had belonged to Lorraine. It's an expensive black evening gown with a slit up the side, and I thought her family might want it if it was actually hers. Do you know if she had any designer gowns?"

Joan thought for a minute and shook her head. "No, I don't think she could have afforded something like that. She was always complaining about money problems."

My nose had begun to itch, but since she didn't know about the problem I had with lying, I rubbed the sides with my forefinger and thumb. It helped.

"What kind of clothes did she wear?"

"I know she bought one skirt and blouse at Wal-Mart. She showed it to me, and even though she didn't like the color, she said her boyfriend would like it because it was purple."

I immediately came to attention. It sounded just like Ardith, whose wardrobe had changed to please her lover. I needed to find out if Lorraine's wardrobe had changed drastically, too.

"Uh . . . so you don't think she might have worn a slinky dress like I described. It's probably a size two—for someone with a model's figure."

Joan shook her head. "No, she was definitely not a size two. More like a twelve." She thought about it for a minute. "I think there's a picture of her over here from a birthday party we had for Pam just before—you know."

She went behind the counter and pulled a framed photograph off the wall. I hadn't noticed it before, but if I had, I would have assumed it was some sort of promotion for the store. There were balloons and party hats and favors galore in the picture.

"Here she is." Joan pointed to a woman next to Pam, but I would have been able to pick her out anyway.

Lorraine Lovell looked so much like Ardith that they could have been twins.

NĬNE

y mind went blank. I couldn't think of anything else to ask. I mumbled that the gown at the cleaners must not have belonged to Lorraine, then fled the party shop.

I couldn't get over the fact that the killer seemed to have turned Ardith into a clone of Lorraine. Had he picked Ardith because she bore a resemblance to Lorraine, or had he gone around searching for look-alikes for the other women he was said to have killed? How could I find out about those other victims, even though they had no connection to the cleaners, and what would it matter if I did? It wouldn't help me narrow down my list of possible suspects.

I was so puzzled by the similar appearance of the two women that I was almost back at the cleaners before I realized I'd been planning to stop at the bank. I'd even taken along some twenty-dollar bills, with the idea that I could request change for our cash registers. I did a quick about-face and headed for the bank, where I had to stand in a long line of customers waiting to be helped.

When I finally worked my way to the front of the line, one of the tellers motioned me to her counter. "I'm waiting for *her*," I said, pointing to Nadine Woodruff, a blonde with teased hair, long, brightly painted fingernails, and a propensity to gossip.

I stepped aside so the next person in line could go to the other teller. Unfortunately, I had to keep doing it until Nadine finally completed some complicated transaction and was free.

"Hi, Nadine," I said, stepping up to her cage. "I want to get some small bills—ones and fives—and ten dollars' worth of change." I placed five twenty-dollar bills on the counter, even though I really didn't need any petty cash.

"It was a terrible thing about Ardith Brewster, wasn't it?" I said, leaning over close to her.

Nadine stopped counting my money with those nails so long that I wondered how she could even hit the keys on her computer. "We're still in a state of shock around here," she said. "Ardith was so businesslike that most of us didn't think she had a life outside of work."

I was afraid that answered my main question. "You mean none of you knew anything about a boyfriend? The newspaper said the police thought she'd been entertaining someone."

Nadine nodded. "Yeah, that was a big surprise to us. The police were asking us if she was dating someone, but no one here knew anything about her personal life."

"Maybe she had a hobby or some outside activity where she met someone," I said.

"If she did, it was news to everyone at the bank. I always figured she went home and studied loan applications all night, although she had loosened up a little lately. At least she'd quit carrying her briefcase back and forth to work."

This line of questioning wasn't leading me anywhere, so I tried a different tack. "I wonder if her family knew anything about her love life."

Nadine started through my short stack of bills. "You know, that was really kind of sad. Her next of kin was listed as a brother in Texas, but apparently he hadn't seen her in years."

I seemed to be striking out no matter what approach I used, and if Nadine didn't know the answers, I figured no one at the bank did.

"Well, I was really sorry to hear about her death," I said finally.

"Yeah, it was spooky, besides," Nadine said, and began to give me change in small bills and coins.

When I was loaded up with the money that we didn't really need, I stuffed it into my purse and headed back for work. Somehow Ardith's death seemed even sadder, since she apparently hadn't had any close family to mourn her loss. When I reached the cleaners, I went directly to the front counter.

"You've had several calls from your cousin Laura," Julia said as soon as I arrived.

That figured. Mom and Herb had apparently made contact with her.

I called Laura at her photo studio. "Mandy, your Mom and Uncle Herb were here," she said with a slightly hysterical tone to her voice. "They want to take us to dinner tonight so Herb can get to know Nat, and they said you'd agreed to come, too. I just wanted to make sure."

"Yes, I'll be there." It was what I deserved for copping out of breakfast.

"And your mother has a million ideas for our wedding."

I wanted to say, I told you so, but I held my tongue. I had the feeling that Mom's plan A was to break up Nat and Laura, and if that didn't work out, plan B was to give them a wedding that was sure to lead to a divorce.

"The dinner reservation is at the Briarwood at seven-thirty."

Of course my mother would pick some place on the far end of town, way out west in Golden. I was sure I would be late, since we didn't close until seven, and I pointed that out. Maybe I'd get caught in traffic and be unable to make it at all.

"You have to promise you'll be there to give me moral support," Laura said.

"I promise." I knew it was the only way I could get Laura off the phone. I also deduced that Mom still hadn't heard the message to stay away that I'd left on her answering machine in Phoenix. It gave me an additional reason to dread the evening that lay ahead.

Once I was through relieving Julia and Ann Marie while they went to lunch, I decided to hit the party shop again. Maybe Pamela could shed some more light on Lorraine, since I hadn't learned anything about Ardith at the bank.

Unfortunately, I felt as if I were in a race against the clock. I expected Ivinson to come back at any moment with a search warrant and demand my database of customers. Every time the door to the call office opened, I had a jolt of fear that it would be the kindly cop turned carnivore, come to the cleaners to arrest me. It was another reason to leave the premises. If I wasn't there, they couldn't issue me with papers to turn my business upside down.

I didn't realize how fast I'd been walking in my effort to escape the cleaners until I got to the party shop. I'd worked up a sweat in the early-afternoon sun that was baking down on the sidewalks. I should have had the good sense to cross to the shady side of the street, but I guess I wasn't thinking clearly. I was too wrapped up in contemplating everything that lay ahead.

I saw Pam as soon as I went inside the party shop. She was a plump middle-aged redhead whose happy-go-lucky personality fit the business she'd chosen for herself. For a fee, she would deliver the balloons in person to a child's birthday party. She would even dress up as a clown, something I knew about because she had us clean her clown suit on a regular basis, and she had mastered the art of making balloon animals just so she could entertain the kids at the parties.

She was busy blowing up balloons with a tank of helium in the back of the store. I'd always thought it was a novel idea she'd had to thumbtack the balloons to blocks of wood, which she covered with wrapping paper, to keep them from floating away when she made her deliveries. Otherwise, customers would have to buy special mounts if they wanted to anchor the balloons.

I didn't see Joan, the employee I'd talked to earlier, so I headed back toward the owner.

"Hi, Pam," I said, waving at her.

"Oh, hi, Mandy. Joan said you were here earlier, asking about Lorraine. It was such a tragedy what happened to her."

I waited while she blew up a final balloon for what she called her "balloon bouquets." It was obviously for a child's party. In addition to "Happy Birthday," the balloons were imprinted with characters from the TV cartoon series *Clifford the Big Red Dog*.

"Why were you asking about her?" Pam glanced up at me as soon as she affixed the balloons to one of the blocks and set the arrangement aside. "Joan said it had to do with a dress that you thought might have belonged to Lorraine."

I decided to come clean this time, although maybe not squeaky-clean. I admitted that had been an excuse because I didn't want to scare her employee. "You read about Ardith Brewster, the officer from the bank, didn't you?" I asked when I was through confessing the ruse.

"Yes, it was another terrible crime, wasn't it?"

"I remembered that Lorraine Lovell had worked for you," I said, although I didn't mention how I'd come to learn that. "Anyway, I was wondering if the killer might be stalking women in this neighborhood."

"Dear God. Do you really think that could be true?" She began to twist a loose scrap of wrapping paper around her finger.

"I don't know, but that's why I didn't mention it to Joan. Do you happen to remember if Lorraine met someone here in the party shop or in the neighborhood and started dating him?"

Pam shook her head, but it was half a shiver at the thought. "I remember that she had a boyfriend, but she was really secretive about him, said they didn't want to go public with it for a while."

Now it was my turn to shiver, although I didn't do it overtly. I did it inside. My stomach churned, and my heart pounded in my ears. The man had to be the same one who'd swept Ardith off her feet.

"Did Lorraine ever say where she met him?"

"No. To tell you the truth, I thought she'd probably met him in one of those chat rooms on the Internet and was embarrassed about it."

I nodded, but, unfortunately, I knew that Ardith hadn't met her lover that way.

"Maybe she went to singles bars or political rallies or someplace else where she could have met him," I suggested.

"Not that I know of. She was pretty quiet and didn't seem to have many interests except surfing the Internet."

"I have to tell you, Pam, that Joan showed me a picture of her at your birthday party. It really jolted me, because she looked so much like Ardith that they could have been sisters."

Pam finally tossed the scrap of wrapping paper in the wastebasket. "Really, what do you mean?"

"Oh, the shape of her face and her brownish red shoulder-length hair."

Pam began to shake her head. "Oh, that wasn't the real color of her hair. She'd just dyed it a lighter shade because her boyfriend liked it that way. Before that, it was a dark brown." Pam motioned to my short, dark hair. "In fact, it was about the same color as yours."

We talked a little more, even though I was reeling from the information. Pam wondered if there should be an alert put out to women who worked or lived in the neighborhood.

"Maybe I could talk to the police about it," I said as I started to leave.

"That's right. You have an in with the police, don't you?"

Apparently, she'd heard of my involvement with the cops on more than one occasion. But oh, if only she knew that the police were on the outs with me now.

As I walked back to the cleaners, I couldn't help but dwell on what Pam had just told me. It seemed apparent that the killer, whoever he was, was creating women in the image of someone he'd once known. But who? A mother, an ex-wife, an old girlfriend, or even his first victim?

I suddenly felt cold, despite the fact that the sun was still baking down on me. I hadn't learned a damned thing except that the murderer was some weird Svengali, turning women into what he wanted them to be, and once he achieved the desired look, he killed them.

I was late when I reached the Briarwood. I knew I would be, but I decided if Mom had wanted me to be there on time, she would have made the dinner reservation for later in the evening or chosen a closer location.

The restaurant was well known for its Christmas decorations and a huge tree that stood beneath a beamed ceiling during the holidays. At this time of year, it still had a warm atmosphere, with its dark woodwork, antique furniture, and the glass etchings that served as dividers for the smaller dining areas.

When the hostess led me to the table where the other four diners were waiting, Mom and Herb stood out like neon signs. Mismatched neon signs, besides.

Herb had changed from his plaid golfing shorts to western wear. I didn't know if it was in recognition of being in Colorado or in honor of coming from Arizona. I opted in favor of the Southwest because he was loaded down with turquoise jewelry.

Herb's outfit was accessorized with a turquoise nugget to hold his string tie in place, a huge belt buckle festooned with dozens of turquoise chips, and several rings with turquoise stones. When he stood up to give me a hug, I couldn't help noticing his cowboy boots. They had white toes, like wing-tip shoes.

Mom hadn't carried out the western theme. She was wearing a gold-colored cocktail dress with a full skirt and a low neckline. It practically glowed. However, she was wearing a squash-blossom necklace with an enormous chunk of turquoise in the center. She didn't budge from her chair, and I decided it was because the necklace probably weighed a ton. Okay, maybe it was because there seemed to be a definite chill in the air where I was concerned.

"You're late," Mom said, managing to pout and talk at the same time.

"I told Laura I might be."

Laura remained strangely quiet.

"I'm afraid we ate all the goodies before you got here," Herb said, taking the last shrimp in a bowl that was served along with crackers, pâté, and cheese as appetizers leading up to every meal.

Nat gave me a devilish grin. "I was just telling Herb here about some of our exploits."

"You mean when we were kids?" I asked. "Don't believe anything he says."

"No, about how you went along with me on some of my interviews and pretended to be a photographer."

"And how you didn't know a damned thing about cameras." Herb chuckled. "Well, now you have Laura, a real photographer, to go along with you on stories." He gave Nat a playful punch on the shoulder, as if putting his seal of approval on Nat's upcoming marriage to Laura.

No wonder Mom was pouting. It wasn't the only reason, however, which became abundantly clear when she spoke. "Laura and I don't understand why you left that message on my machine not to come up here until the wedding."

Laura looked as if she might slink to the floor at any moment. She obviously hadn't had the nerve to tell Mom that she'd begged me to intervene on her behalf. She was a wimp, and she was going to rue her wimpiness as soon as Mom took over control of the wedding preparations.

That time seemed to be right now. "As soon as I heard that Laura and Nat want to be married up in the mountains, I knew they should have a western theme for their wedding."

I wondered if that was the reason she'd made Herb dress up like Kenny Rogers.

"I can just see them now—riding off on horseback after the ceremony," she continued. "Laura could ride sidesaddle in her beautiful old-fashioned wedding gown."

Laura looked as if she might cry.

"Now, wait a damned—" That was Nat.

I knew for a fact that he wasn't much of an equestrian. We'd gone horseback riding once as kids, and his horse had bucked him off. Nat had developed a phobia about horses after that.

A waitress came up to the table before Nat could finish. "Are you ready to order now that the rest of your party has joined you?"

I nodded, even though I hadn't looked at the menu. I ordered the first thing I spotted on it. I think it was chicken, although I never had a chance to find out.

My cell phone started ringing right then. It was like one of those fake calls you arrange for when you're on a blind date and are afraid the guy will turn out to be a real loser. Only thing was, I hadn't had the foresight to make plans for someone to call me.

I grabbed the phone as if it were a lifeline and a possible means of escape from what had already started out to be a more unpleasant experience than even I had anticipated.

"Hello, this is Mandy."

"This is Paulette Thompson, a nurse at Denver Health Medical Center."

My stomach tightened into a knot. I hadn't wanted a real emergency, just an imaginary one.

"Your sister, Julia Bartlett, has been in an accident, and—"

My sister? Julia wasn't my sister, but who cared?

I didn't let the nurse finish. "What kind of accident?"

"She was apparently attacked by a mugger while she was out walking her dog."

My conversation with Julia that morning came back to me.

"That doesn't sound like an accident," I said, practically shouting into the phone.

It didn't sound like a mugger, either. It sounded exactly like what Julia had related to me earlier in the day—that someone had deliberately been staking out her house the previous night with the intention of doing her bodily harm.

TEN

I needed to get away from the din of diners and the clatter of dishes. I rose to my feet and headed for the entrance to the restaurant.

"How badly is she hurt?" I asked, afraid of the answer. I had reached the relative quiet of the reception area by then.

"What's going on?" Nat had followed me from the dining room, and either his nose for news had overwhelmed his desire to make a good impression on Herb or else he wanted to get away.

"Shhh." I put a finger to my lips as I tried to hear the nurse.

"She has some bruises, but otherwise she seems to be okay," the woman said.

I felt a surge of relief.

"But the doctor wants to keep her overnight for observation," she continued. "She's really agitated, and unfortunately, we're unable to reach her husband."

I was sure it was because he couldn't pick up a signal on his cell phone from wherever he and the children were camping in the mountains.

"Anyway, she asked me to call you. She wants to see you."

Luckily, I'd given my cell number to my counter people. Obviously, Julia had kept it, although I was sure Ann Marie had lost it long ago.

"Okay, where is she in the hospital?" I asked.

"We're going to be taking her upstairs to a room, but you can come to the ER when you get here. Do you know how to find it?"

I said I did. I'd been to the hospital on more occasions than I cared to remember. "I'll be right there." I thanked the nurse and hung up.

Nat was still standing close to me, obviously trying to overhear my conversation.

"So what was that about?" he asked. "Does it have something to do with those murders you were so worried about?"

"God, I hope not." I wasn't lying when I said that, but I had a funny feeling that it did. "Look, I have to go."

Nat grabbed my arm. "Not before you tell me what's going on."

"It's Julia, my morning counter manager. She was attacked by a mugger."

I could tell Nat was skeptical about the mugging, even though he didn't know the whole story. "I've been thinking about it," he said, "and your reason for wanting to know about the murder of that Brewster woman doesn't hold water."

I pushed his hand away. "I'm sorry, Nat. I'm not going to stand here and talk to you about this. Tell everybody I'm sorry I can't stay, and if it isn't too late, cancel my dinner order, will you?" Fortunately, I'd had the foresight to bring my shoulder bag with me, or I'd have had to go back to the table and face Laura and my folks again.

Nat looked as if he were having second thoughts about facing them himself. Maybe it had finally occurred to him that he was no longer the freewheeling reporter who could drop everything at a moment's notice to go off in pursuit of a story.

He nodded his head in defeat. "I'll talk to you later," he said as he started back to the dining room.

I almost felt sorry for him, but I didn't have time right then to think about the changes that were going to take place in Nat's life. I rushed out to my car and headed back to Denver. There was no left turn allowed on the road in front of the restaurant, the route that would have taken me directly back to the main highway.

Considering my recent traffic ticket, I decided not to tempt fate by making a left turn anyway. Instead, I headed east, then swung south through downtown Golden before getting back on the extension of Sixth Avenue that would take me right by the hospital complex.

On the way, I kept thinking about the "mugger." Had the police caught him? If not, did Julia remember anything about him? And if it wasn't a random act, could it have been a deliberate attack because someone feared she might remember something about the open house that could lead to Ardith's killer?

I pulled into the parking lot twenty-five minutes after I'd taken the call. I was anxious to ask Julia all the questions that were swirling around in my head. When I reached the emergency room, I had to go through a metal detector to gain entry to the hospital.

"I'm here to see Julia Bartlett," I said to a receptionist, who gave me a long, complicated set of instructions on how to get to the upper floors. After working my way through the maze of hallways and asking the help of half a dozen people along the way, I finally reached Julia's room.

"Oh, thank goodness. I'm so glad you came," Julia said as soon as she spotted me at the door. "I told the nurse you were my sister so she'd call you."

I winced when I saw the bruises on her neck and heard the hoarseness of her voice. Someone must have tried to strangle her— the way they had Ardith. Well, not exactly that way, because, according to Nat, Ardith had been trussed up from head to foot.

Julia grabbed my hand the moment I reached her bed. "Somebody tried to kill me, Mandy." Every word seemed like an effort for her. "If it hadn't been for a neighbor, I'd be dead." A tear rolled down her cheek, and she wiped it away.

"Don't try to talk right now. I'm here, and I'll stay with you all night if you want me to."

She started shaking her head as she pulled herself up from the already-elevated bed. "No, no, no."

"Okay," I said, surprised at her reaction. "Whatever you want, I'm here for you."

"You have to find Rambo. He got away, and the kids will never forgive me if something happens to him." Now her voice sounded as if she were gargling gravel.

"Oh, right. Rambo, your dog."

Julia fell back on the pillow.

A tall, heavyset nurse came in the room right then. She reminded me of the way I'd always pictured Nurse Ratched in *One Flew Over the Cuckoo's Nest*. "Mrs. Bartlett really shouldn't be talking right now." The woman glared at me as she pointed at Julia.

"You 'member where I live, don' you?" Julia's voice was getting weaker now and her eyelids were beginning to droop.

"Yes." I'd been to her house once several years before, when her husband threw her a party for her fortieth birthday. I'd even taken balloons from Pam's party shop, which seemed like another odd quirk of fate just then.

"Tha's where it happened," Julia whispered, her words slurring even more. "Jus' call for Rambo, and if he barks, say 'Sit.' He'll calm—"

"Please, Mrs. Bartlett," the nurse scolded, "you shouldn't be straining your voice like that." She turned to me, her scowl still in place. "She needs her rest, so don't pester her with any more questions tonight."

"I just need to know a couple of things."

The nurse rose up to her full six feet, as if daring me to say anything else.

"Okay, just one question." I turned to Julia. "What kind of dog is Rambo?"

She was sound asleep.

"Good, the sedative is finally working," the nurse said. "You won't be able to find out any more tonight." She had a satisfied Nurse Ratched look on her face.

Okay, so I wasn't going to learn any more about Rambo. With a name like that, I was beginning to fear that he would turn out to be a rottweiler or a pit bull.

"I'll be back first thing in the morning." I knew Julia couldn't hear me, even if I went over and shook her, and I was afraid Nurse Ratched might tackle me if I tried. I left the room in defeat, much as Nat had slunk back to Laura and my folks at the restaurant.

I had the foresight to check a phone book and copy down Julia's exact address before I left the hospital and headed for South Denver, where she lived. I even pulled over to the curb en route, with the idea of calling Mack to see if he could help me corral a possible attack dog. He'd returned to work midafternoon, after taking a few hours off to get some rest, but I hadn't told him what I'd found out from Pam earlier in the day. I hadn't wanted to upset him again, which would surely happen if I called him about the dog.

Too bad Nat is otherwise involved, I thought. I even thought of calling Travis, although as much as I tried to purge the thought from my mind, I was upset about what Lucille had told me. Besides, he was probably still involved with that undercover warehouse job, and I couldn't think of anyone else to call.

If it seemed chicken of me to have thought about seeking help in catching a dog, it was because I'd never had a very good relationship with members of the canine family.

When I was five, there was an unfortunate incident when a beagle mistook my favorite stuffed animal for a chew toy. Needless to say, I waged a losing battle in a tug-of-war with the pooch.

I could cite other examples of various breeds and their aversion to me through the years, but the most recent altercation was with a Saint Bernard that I'd promised to feed while his owner was away.

Yukon, as he was called, took an instant dislike to me and didn't want to let me in the kitchen, apparently under the misguided impression that I was there to steal his dog food. After he kept me pinned to the wall for an interminable length of time, I finally called Mack to come over and feed the dog so he wouldn't starve. Mack got along with Yukon just fine, so to save my pride, I decided the dog simply didn't like women.

Now I was faced with trying to catch a dog that might or might not want to be caught—and a dog named Rambo, besides. It sounded like another disaster waiting to happen. That's the only explanation I have for why I didn't even bother to think about the wisdom of wandering around a darkened neighborhood where my friend had just been attacked.

As a matter of fact, it didn't occur to me to consider how really dark the area would be until I pulled up in front of what I thought was Julia's house. A thick overhang of elm trees, only recently leafed out, shut out the moon and a streetlight at the end of the block. I couldn't begin to see the address on the front of the house. Fortunately, Julia's last name was affixed to her mailbox in iridescent letters that caught the glint of my headlights as I pulled up to the curb.

The homes on either side of Julia's house were dark; apparently, the neighbor who'd saved Julia's life had gone to bed or left the premises. That's when it hit me that I might have been focusing on the wrong thing up to then. I must have been out of my mind to agree to go searching for Julia's dog in a dark and deserted neighborhood where a strangler was on the loose.

So what was the best way to handle the situation? I decided to keep the car doors locked but roll down the window and yell out "Rambo" as I drove around the neighborhood.

Frankly, my actions reminded me a little of *A Streetcar Named Desire,* which I'd recently watched on late-night TV. I couldn't help thinking that calling for Rambo was not unlike Marlon Brando yelling, "Stella. Stella."

I wished Mack were there so I could have shared that bit of

movie trivia with him. After all, he had a movie quote for nearly every life experience. Okay, the real reasons I wanted him there were for moral support and to be my backup in case I got into trouble.

"Rambo," I yelled as I sat in front of Julia's house. "Rambo," I kept yelling as I drove down the street, rounded the corner, and circled the block. Occasionally, I interspersed the name with whistling. It didn't work a damn with my cat, but I thought it might lure Rambo out of hiding.

By my second pass in front of Julia's house, I was beginning to get discouraged. Apparently, I was also irritating the neighbors. I saw a light go on at a house across the street as I reached the end of the block. A bare-chested, muscular man came out on his front porch and stared at my passing car as I yelled "Rambo" again. For a minute, I could almost imagine that he was Sylvester Stallone, responding to his movie name.

Get a grip, I told myself. You're getting giddy with all these thoughts about movies. That's Mack's thing, not yours.

I pulled to the curb and got out of the car with the intention of asking for the man's help. A guy with the biceps of Stallone would be a nice ally to have in my current predicament. Before I could yell at him, he went back in the house and slammed the door.

I returned to the driver's seat and resumed my search. On my third pass in front of Julia's house, a huge black dog bounded across the path of my car. I slammed on the brakes. This had to be Rambo, and it was just as I'd feared. He was as big as a horse.

There was nothing for it but to try to capture him. I pulled to the curb, grabbed a flashlight—the better to follow him if he took off into the bushes—and got out of the car.

He stood at attention a few feet away from me, cocking his head to the side as he watched me with the interest of a hungry wolf.

"Come on, Rambo," I coaxed.

When he ignored me, I ordered him to sit. He didn't respond to that, either. So much for Julia's comforting suggestion.

I sneaked up on him and grabbed him by the collar. He growled and tried to back away, but at least he didn't bite. After we tussled for a few minutes, I managed to drag him to the car. I tried to push his rump so he would jump into the passenger's seat, but he was resistant to taking a ride with a stranger.

I don't know what made me decide to use the flashlight at that point. I pointed it at the tag attached to his collar and checked it. The tag said his name was Willie.

Willie? It also said his owner lived over on the next block. Damn, damn, damn. I'd almost rescued the wrong dog. I released him, and he bounded away between Julia's house and the one next door, presumably heading toward home.

After coming out of the incident unscathed, I was ready to call off the hunt. I watched Willie disappear, and that's when I noticed a hint of movement on Julia's front porch. I was around the car and back in the driver's seat before I dared to take another look.

I half-expected to see the hulking shape of Julia's attacker coming toward me. Instead, I heard a yapping sound and saw a streak of something small and white in hot pursuit of Willie.

Good grief. That couldn't be Rambo. I wasn't about to take off into the black hole of Julia's backyard, but I waited until the yapping died down and the tiny white apparition reappeared in the front yard and climbed the steps to the front door.

Okay, I'd give it one more try, but I couldn't believe that this puff of white was actually Rambo. I headed for the house, flashlight still in hand. As soon as I reached the porch, the yapping resumed.

The dog looked like a toy poodle. It had a leash dangling from its neck. I should have thought of that when I snatched Willie, I realized. Julia had been taking her dog for a walk, and Willie didn't have a leash. Still, I had trouble convincing myself that this bit of fluff could have a name like Rambo. I tried it anyway.

"Sit, Rambo." The poodle quivered, apparently almost as unnerved as I was, and sat back on his haunches.

I scooped him up before he knew what was happening and beamed the flashlight down on his tag. Sure enough, it said Rambo.

Who would be dumb enough to name a toy poodle Rambo? Maybe Snowball or Fluffy, but not Rambo. Okay, Fluffy might be a more appropriate name for a cat, but after all, my late uncle Chet had chosen the name Spot for the big yellow tabby I'd inherited from him. Who ever heard of a cat named Spot? Never mind that my uncle had named him for the spots we were famous for removing from clothes, not in memory of a dog he'd had as a child.

Once I was sure I wasn't absconding with the wrong pet, I put Rambo in the car and drove out of the neighborhood as fast as I could. But now I had another problem. What about Spot? The cat wouldn't take kindly to my bringing home another pet, especially one of the canine variety.

I would cross that threshold when I got home. For now, I decided just to be thankful I hadn't gotten mugged, killed—or even bitten during my first and, I hoped, only attempt as an amateur dogcatcher.

Rambo seemed to like riding in the car. He put his paws up on the window so that he could look outside as we made our way to Capitol Hill.

I got lucky and found a parking space only a few yards from the old Victorian house where I lived. It was about time my luck changed, but I was still on guard. I looked up and down the street to make sure Mack's mystery car wasn't around before I climbed out from behind the steering wheel and grabbed Rambo.

"Nice doggy," I said in an effort to calm Rambo and myself. "We'll be home soon."

I made a run for the front door. When we reached the entryway, Rambo licked my face, as if he realized I'd rescued him from a long and lonely night on the mean streets of Denver. I couldn't believe that a dog actually liked me. I have to admit it was kind of flattering.

I climbed the stairs to my third-floor apartment, Rambo in my arms. When we reached the landing that led to the final set of steps, I came to an abrupt stop. Someone was waiting up above, hunched over on the steps in front of my door.

"Don't worry. It's just me." I recognized the voice before I had a chance to panic.

"What are you doing here, Betty?" Actually, I was too tired and relieved to care, and besides, I thought this might be a good thing. I needed someone to capture Spot and put him in my walk-in closet so there wouldn't be a confrontation between the two animals.

"I was tailin' that grungy guy from yesterday," Betty said as I continued up the steps.

"I told you not to do that."

"Don't matter. He gave me the slip, so I figured I better let you know."

I'd reached the third-floor landing by then. "Why would you feel the need to tell me that tonight?"

" 'Cause I lost him here in your neighborhood, and I thought he might be comin' to kill you, seein' as how he prob'ly killed all those other ladies."

eLeven

After the evening I'd had, it took me a few seconds to grasp what Betty was saying. "Why would the grungy guy be coming after me? He doesn't even know me, much less know where I live."

I stopped. If Mack was right and someone had followed us home, maybe he did know where I lived, even if he didn't know my name.

"You never can tell," Betty said. "What if he's been stalking you the whole time, and now he's got you picked out as his next victim?"

"Thanks a lot, Betty." I knew I sounded ungrateful for the information, but I didn't want to hear any more bad news that night. Still, if he was the one who'd tried to strangle Julia, maybe Betty was actually right and he was now on my trail.

As quickly as that thought rattled through my head, I rejected it. After all, Ardith had indicated that her mysterious boyfriend was a customer, and "grungy" didn't quite cut it as a description for the people who patronized the cleaners.

I still couldn't see Betty well, due to the thirty-watt bulb above the landing, but apparently Betty had noticed Rambo.

"What in bloody blue blazes you got there?" she asked.

Rambo had ducked his head into my shoulder. "It's a dog, and since you're here, maybe you can give me a hand." I fumbled in my shoulder bag for my keys.

"It looks more like a big old fur ball that Spot spit up," Betty said.

I unlocked my door. "Are you going to help me or not?"

"Depends what you want me to do."

I had my hand on the doorknob. "I want you to go inside and put Spot in the closet so we don't have a fight on our hands."

"Okay, I can do that. Like I always say, me and Spot get along because we're both old alley cats. I don't like dogs so much." With that, she entered the apartment, turned on the light, and shut the door.

I waited outside until she gave me the all-clear. "Okay, I got Spot in the closet, but he ain't too happy about it."

I entered the room and put Rambo on the floor. He streaked toward Spot's food dish, although how he spied it so quickly, I didn't know.

He was gulping down some dry food Spot had left in his dish by the time I tried to grab him. He growled. I drew back my hand.

"Okay, if you want to eat cat food, that's your business." Besides, I didn't have any dog food around the place, and I wasn't about to go out and get some at that time of night, especially after what Betty had said.

Spot began to meow and scratch the door of my walk-in closet. Ordinarily, he liked the closet, where he had a basket that he slept in sometimes. Not tonight.

He kept on meowing and scratching, but I ignored the sounds and took a look at Betty. It was the first good view I'd had of her. She was dressed in a baggy pair of black corduroy pants, a black sweatshirt, and a black Oakland Raiders cap with the bill turned down to hide her eyes. No wonder I hadn't been able to recognize her on the landing. A pair of combat boots completed her ensemble.

"Why the outfit?" I asked. She looked like a gang member, all dressed in black.

"I figure if you're going to tail somebody, you oughta dress so they can't see you."

"What do you mean? Surely you weren't walking."

"Nope, Artie let me use the car."

Artie, or Arthur, as I preferred to call him, was her "significant other," and a more mismatched pair I'd never seen. He was a chubby doll doctor who looked like a Kewpie doll himself, and she was a loose canon about to go off at any moment. For reasons I couldn't fathom, he seemed to find her antics amusing.

"But I thought I might have to follow Grungy on foot," she continued as an explanation of her attire, "and I sure didn't want him to put the finger on me."

I was glad she'd lost him, if that had been her plan.

"So where'd you get the mutt?" she asked.

"He belongs to a friend." I was in no mood to tell her about Julia's alleged mugging. If I did, the information would soon be zipping around the cleaners as fast as the news about Ardith's murder had.

She gave Rambo a disapproving look, and I wanted to get her off the subject of Julia's dog. "So, would you like a cup of coffee?" I asked.

I would have liked a stiff drink myself, but I wasn't going to tempt Betty, who'd been on the wagon since she gave up being a street person and went to work for me.

"Sure," Betty said just as a knock sounded on my door. She and Rambo instantly went on alert. Rambo began to bark. Betty hissed, "Shhh. It could be the grungy guy."

The knocking came again.

Rambo kept barking.

"Don't let him in," Betty said, her voice loud enough to shake the rafters.

Oh, that was smart. Maybe the visitor would have accepted the fact that the dog was home alone, but not once he heard a human voice.

I picked up Rambo in hopes he'd quit barking and started for the door.

"If you think that pipsqueak's going to protect you, I got news for you," Betty said. "He ain't no guard dog."

"Who is it?" I asked.

A male voice answered. "What's going on in there?"

"Who is it?" I repeated.

"It's your mom and Herb," Herb said.

I held on to Rambo and opened the door. "What are you two doing here?"

Mom entered the apartment first. She ignored Rambo and glanced from Betty to me as if we were in some kind of conspiracy. "We wanted to find out what happened to poor Julia," Mom said. "Nat said she was mugged."

Julia was one of the few people, besides Mack, that Mom liked at the cleaners. In order to get information about her, I gathered that Mom was now willing to forget that she was mad at me for the message I'd left on her answering machine.

"She's going to be okay," I said.

Betty perked up the moment she heard the name of a coworker. "What about Julia? I bet it was the grungy guy, not no mugger."

My stepfather followed Mom into the room. "What's with the dog?" he asked.

"He belongs to Julia, and I'm keeping him while she's in the hospital."

Herb nodded, then shut the door. As soon as he did, I put Rambo on the floor.

"We brought your dinner, too," Herb said. "Here's the doggie bag."

Rambo took one look at Herb as he held out the bag and hurled himself forward as if he were a bull attacking a toreador in a red cape. By the time I could get to the dog, he had bitten into the white tip of one of Herb's boots. He was gnawing on it as if it were a chicken breast, and I was afraid he would go for a leg next.

I grabbed the tiny ball of fury. Rambo tried to nip at me as I pulled him away and hauled him into the bathroom, the only other enclosed room in my studio apartment besides the one currently occupied by a cat.

"Bad dog," I said just so he'd know he couldn't get away with such behavior. I shut the door.

Now two animals were meowing and barking in what sounded like an off-key duet from behind their respective doors. That was the least of my problems. I came back to Herb. "Are you okay? Rambo didn't actually bite you, did he?"

"No, but he put a gash in my best pair of boots," Herb said, bending down to inspect them.

"Whoee," Betty said. "That little mutt sure don't like men too much, does he?"

"Maybe he doesn't like the ostrich skin on your boots," Mom said with a little shudder. "I know I don't. Those little dots on the skin remind me of pimples."

Herb looked irritated. "How many times do I have to tell you those dots are where the feathers were removed? They're called 'full quill.'"

If we were going to offer far-out theories, I chose to think the half-starved pooch had gone berserk at the mention of a doggie bag. I didn't share the thought with the other people, for fear they wouldn't think it was as amusing as I did in my overwrought condition.

"I'm sorry about Rambo, Herb," I said.

At the sound of his name, the dog barked even louder, and Spot, not to be outdone, continued his indignant meows. I went over and took the doggie bag from Herb as I gently tried to push them to the door. "And thanks for bringing my dinner."

"Hey, what about that coffee you promised me?" Betty asked. "Maybe Cece and Herbie would like some, too." Ah, yes, Betty— always the gracious hostess even when it wasn't her house.

"Sure," Herb said. "That'd be great."

"I might take a cup of tea," Mom said.

"You know I don't have any tea," I told her.

"Well then, three coffees coming up," Betty said.

She'd shared my apartment on several occasions that I'd just as soon have forgotten, and she knew how to make herself at home in my kitchen. She started over behind the counter that separated the kitchen from the rest of the apartment, and I handed her my doggie-bag dinner to put in the refrigerator. I figured she might as well make herself useful while she was playing hostess.

I had a hunch she was being so hospitable because she wanted to hear more about Julia's mugging and she thought she could get more information out of me if Mom and Herb were around.

I tried my best to steer the conversation away from Julia. I gave my guests a blow-by-blow account of my attempt to capture Julia's dog. None of them seemed to think it was funny. I was glad I hadn't shared my theory about Rambo and the doggie bag, but at least my story seemed to have lulled the animals into an uneasy calm.

Betty finished zapping water in the microwave, and when the beeper went off, it caused another round of barking and meowing. Betty, oblivious to the noise, came out of the kitchen with two cups of instant coffee for Herb and me. "So what happened to Julia?" she asked.

I couldn't stand it. I went over to the bathroom door and scolded Rambo. He quit barking.

"Do you think it had anything to do with the murders that Betty was telling us about?" Mom asked.

I decided it wouldn't do any good to stonewall it at this point, and besides, the sooner I told them what had happened, the sooner they would leave. At least I hoped so.

"I don't know," I said. "A man came up behind her and attacked her while she was out walking her dog. Fortunately, a neighbor scared him away and called the police. Julia's spending the night in the hospital, but it doesn't look as if she has any serious injuries."

"Poor Julia," Mom said.

"Don't sound like no mugging to me," Betty said as she glanced over at Mom and Herb. "Like I already told you, the boss lady here figures the guy who killed the banker lady met her in the cleaners the day of the open house." The microwave beeped that her own cup of water was hot. Rambo and Spot began barking and meowing again; Betty ignored the noise and the beep. "I still think the killer is this bum who's been hanging around in the parking lot. I followed him up to this neighborhood tonight, but then I lost him."

"Oh, dear," Mom said. "Maybe he's coming after you, Mandy." Her eyes got as big as silver dollars, a phenomena that was enhanced by her heavy eyeliner and Tammy Faye–style eyelashes.

Since the grungy guy looked a lot like Betty's other friends from her days as a homeless person, I suggested that she might be better served by asking them about him. At least that would keep her from trailing him around Denver all the time. She shrugged at the suggestion. Apparently, that wasn't exciting enough for her.

"Did Julia see who grabbed her?" Herb asked, getting us back on track.

"A nurse gave her a sedative, and she was out before I could ask her." Thankfully, Rambo and Spot had quieted down again, as well.

"Maybe she seen something the day of the open house that she don't remember, and the killer is scared it'll come back to her," Betty said.

My thoughts exactly. I hated it when Betty and I were on the same wavelength.

"If Julia can't remember, maybe you should ask some of your other women customers who were there at the same time as the murder victim," Mom said.

I hated it even more when my mother came up with an idea I hadn't even thought of. Of course.

We hadn't uncovered any real clues from the men who'd signed the guest book, but what about the women? They'd outnumbered the men five to one that day, and they'd be far more apt to recall bits of conversation than the employees, who had been busy with crowd control.

When Mack and I had reviewed the guest book, I remembered seeing that Ardith had signed it. I could start by checking with women who'd signed it right before or after she was there.

Just then, there was another knock on the door. I recognized the Morse code bangs; it was Nat's signature knock, and not a sound I wanted to hear at this particular moment.

Almost simultaneously, the phone rang. It set off another round of noises from the closet and the bathroom. Meow. Scratch. Meow. Yip, yip, yip, and a bang against the bathroom door. Thump. Whimper. Poor Rambo sounded as if he'd fallen from a considerable height.

"Just a minute," I yelled at the door.

I grabbed the phone and told the party on the other end to hold for a minute. I went to check on Rambo. He appeared to be okay after his assault on the door. I shut him inside the bathroom again.

"Okay, I'm here," I said into the phone as the banging on the door got louder.

"This is Mrs. Humphrey."

Whoops. It was the manager, who lived on the first floor.

"Your neighbors have been calling about the noise coming from your apartment, Mandy," she said.

"I'm sorry."

"I've never had a complaint about you before, so I thought I better call you. The Simpsons on two said it sounded like you were running a kennel."

I told her in as few words as possible that I was keeping a dog for a hospitalized friend but that it was only for the night.

She said something else, but I couldn't hear her because of Nat and the animals. Bang. Bang, bang, bang. Bang. He wasn't about to give up.

Rambo's yapping resumed, along with Spot's plaintive meows.

"What did you say?" I asked, covering the ear that wasn't pressed against the phone.

"I said that you need to keep the barking down, dear. It's getting late." She hung up.

Actually, this wasn't a bad thing. It gave me an excuse to throw everyone out of the apartment.

"I'm afraid you'll all have to leave, because the neighbors are complaining about the noise," I said. "I need to let Rambo out of the bathroom, and I don't want him to attack Herb again."

Apparently, Herb didn't, either. He rose to his feet and motioned for Mom to follow.

"But someone's at the door," Mom protested.

"It's Nat," I said, "and whatever you do, don't say anything to him about the murders on your way out. That goes for you, too, Betty."

She gave her standard zip across her lips. I wasn't so sure what Mom would do.

At the door, Nat tried to push his way inside. "You can't come in, Nat," I said. "I'm sorry. I have Julia's dog for the night, and I'm about to get evicted if I can't get him to quit barking."

Nat stood his ground. "So what'd you find out from Julia?"

"Nothing. They gave her a sedative, and I didn't find out anything."

"But—" he said.

"I'll talk to you later."

The rest of the party trooped out of the apartment and down the stairs. Nat turned and followed them, but I'm sure his intention was to grill them when they got outside.

I knew I would have to put my faith in Mom and Betty not to blab. It was probably a foolish hope, but at the moment, it was the only thing I could think to do.

I shut the door, but before I let Rambo out of the bathroom, I turned my attention to the cat in the closet. Spot wasn't too happy to see me, but once I provided him with his favorite canned cat food and an ample supply of water, I think he forgave me, although it was hard to tell. While he was busy eating, I dragged his litter box from the hallway to the closet and shut the door again.

Finally, I released Rambo from the bathroom and plopped down on the sofa. That's when the enormity of what had happened to Julia finally hit me. What if she'd been killed? I couldn't have her life and the lives of all the other potential victims of an unknown killer on my hands.

What I needed to do was turn over the names of my customers to the police, no matter what the consequences to my business.

I'd just read about a minister who'd given the police the names of worshipers who had access to the church's computer. It had led to the apprehension of the infamous BTK killer. If a church would do that, maybe it was time for me to do so, too.

I began to shake at the thought of Julia's close call. Rambo jumped up on my lap and licked my cheek, as if he sensed my agitation and was trying to comfort me.

TWELVE

Rambo and I had a restless night, mainly because I kept having nightmares. This time, I knew they were nightmares. Each time I nodded off, I could see a faceless killer on the loose somewhere in Denver. Sometimes he would be chasing Julia, and I would be watching him but was unable to do anything to stop him.

I would jerk awake, and Rambo would crawl up closer to me and nuzzle my cheek. I couldn't help wondering if maybe I should get a dog. Spot was never much comfort.

When morning came, I dragged myself out of bed, glad at least to be rid of the bad dreams. Rambo jumped down on the floor beside me, his stub of a tail shaking, apparently in anticipation of being fed.

After a complicated game to keep Spot and Rambo away from each other, I got dressed and gave Rambo some chicken from the doggie-bag meal I hadn't felt like eating the night before. I knew enough not to give chicken bones to a dog, but I hoped pieces of the chicken breast were okay.

My final act before I left the apartment was to leash Rambo to the doorknob in the hall while I let Spot out of his overnight confinement. As I left, the cat was going around the place and sniffing to see if he could smell the intruder. I hoped to God he didn't spray the walls in an effort to take back his territory.

Rambo and I set off for Denver Health Medical Center after a brief pit stop outside so the dog could relieve himself. My first priority when I reached the hospital was to get a key from Julia so I could stash Rambo in his house for the day. Once I pulled into the parking lot, I locked him in the car, careful to leave the window cracked so he wouldn't suffocate. Actually, it was still cool, with early-morning dew on the grass, but I knew it would warm up quickly, since it was another cloudless day.

Julia was sitting up in bed and finishing her breakfast when I got to her room. It made me realize I should have taken time to have a cup of coffee and a piece of toast, or maybe even a piece of chicken, before I left home.

"Did you find Rambo?" she asked the moment she spotted me. "I've been so worried about him."

Her voice still sounded gravelly, and the bruises on her neck had changed from a fierce red to a bluish black. I felt another wave of guilt. Could I have prevented this if I'd cooperated with the police earlier?

I assured her that I had found her dog, but I decided not to tell her about the harrowing time I'd had capturing him. Instead, I asked her if she could give me a key to her house so I could lock Rambo inside until I got off work.

"I'll go feed him and walk him later," I said. "And if the doctor releases you today, I'll come back and get you and stay with you until your family gets home." It was the least I could do.

It turned out she had a better solution. She said her husband had finally retrieved the hospital's message from his cell phone, called in, and had driven most of the night to get back to Denver. He'd arrived an hour ago.

"He and the kids are down in the cafeteria right now having breakfast," she said.

I was relieved. Not only could I transfer Rambo to his family but also her husband was back to take care of her. I moved on to my second and most important priority.

"Do you know if the police arrested the man who attacked you?" I asked.

Julia shook her head. "I don't think so."

I held my breath for a moment, praying she'd be able to answer the next question. "Were you able to tell them anything about the man that might help identify him?"

She shook her head again. "No, he came up from behind me, and then he ran when Joe, the guy next door, heard Rambo barking." Her eyes filled with tears. "I'm sorry."

"Don't be sorry. None of this is your fault."

She grabbed my hand. "Remember how I told you that I thought someone had been in the backyard the night before?"

I nodded.

"I can't help wondering if this had something to do with the open house and Ardith's mur—" She stopped, unable to finish.

"I don't know," I said. "But if it did, there has to be something that the killer thinks you saw or heard at the open house that would tie him to Ardith."

"I've racked my brain, but I can't think of anything."

"Well, maybe something will come to you later." God, I hoped it would, but at the same time I wanted to put her mind at ease. "Please don't worry about it, and take as long as you need away from work." I patted her hand and tried to get her mind off the subject by telling her about the adventures of Rambo and Spot in my apartment.

She laughed but said it hurt her throat. I decided not to share the tale of Rambo's attack on Herb, but I was running out of material. Luckily, her husband, Charlie, and their three children came back to the room about then, and the kids insisted on going with their father and me to make the Rambo exchange from my car to their father's pickup.

"That's crazy about someone attacking Julia in our neighborhood," Charlie said as I led him to the parking lot.

Apparently, Julia hadn't told him about the person in the back-yard the night before. I decided to leave it up to her if she wanted to tell him or not.

Rambo jumped into Charlie's arms when I opened the door, and I have to admit I was a little jealous to see how glad he was to see his family. When I got home from work, Spot begrudgingly acknowledged me as the person who fed him, but that was about all. Rambo, on the other hand, almost shook himself off his feet at the sight of the children when Charlie put him down on the ground.

I left the family in the parking lot and headed for work, but I stopped en route to call Mack and tell him I was on my way. When I got to the plant, I spent a few minutes bringing him up-to-date about what had happened to Julia and my decision, painful though it was, to give the police the names of the customers who'd been at the open house and at the cleaners the days of Lorraine Lovell's visits.

Mack, who was always on my side even though he sometimes disagreed with my methods, nodded his head in agreement. "Yeah, I think it's time."

"We'll talk some more later," I said. "Right now, I need to call the detective and tell him my decision. Then I need to get up front. Ann Marie and Lucille are probably going crazy at the counter without Julia's calming influence."

I took a deep breath and called Ivinson's extension at police headquarters. I reached his voice mail. Good. I left a message. That ought to buy me some time to compile a list, I thought.

First, I checked the front counter. I'd been right about what was going on there. The place was in a state of chaos.

Ann Marie seemed to be flirting with a young preppy-looking guy, and I wondered if she was checking him out to see if he'd been in the cleaners the day of the open house. Lucille, never happy to work the counter, was having an argument with a woman about a stain that was still on a blouse. Meanwhile, customers were stacking up behind them.

I frowned at Ann Marie, a signal for her to quit flirting. I took over with the aggrieved owner of the blouse, thus freeing my two employees to get to the other people waiting in line. All it took with the angry customer was an offer to redo the blouse at no charge or else pay her for it if the stain wouldn't come out. She left happy.

Eventually, order was restored to the call office, and I was about ready to head back to my office as soon as I explained about Julia's attack.

I didn't have a chance to bring up the subject. "We heard some-one tried to strangle Julia," Ann Marie said. "Do you think it had something to do with you know what?"

Obviously, Betty had been busy spreading the word. She might have zipped her lip with Nat, but the zipper hadn't stayed shut for long.

"I don't know, but she's going to be all right." I turned to Lucille. "You'll have to work up here for a while, and I'll see if Theresa can come in early." Theresa was my afternoon counter manager, who normally didn't arrive until two o'clock.

Lucille gave me a surly look. "Doesn't seem to me like it's safe to work the counter anymore."

"I'm sorry," I said, "but we're shorthanded, and I have to do something in my office."

I was about to make my escape, when Harvey Campbell came in the door. He was the owner of a western-wear store, and a collector of all sorts of western memorabilia—everything from cowboy hats to saddles. He always called them his "ranch dressing," a play on words that my late uncle would have enjoyed.

I would have expected Harvey to be wearing a western outfit himself—like my stepfather had the previous night. Instead, he was wearing a short-sleeved plaid shirt and brown slacks, but he was carrying a cowboy shirt.

It was two-tone—black and tan—and had bright orange flowers and green leaves embroidered on the front, the collar, upper arms, and cuffs, along with fabric-covered cord used as decorative edging along the seams and around the pockets.

I could see this even before he reached the counter because he was holding the shirt out in front of him on a hanger. That wasn't the way garments usually arrived at the cleaners.

"Howdy, Miss Mandy," he said, sounding for all the world like a throwback to the Wild West.

He quickly zeroed in on me as if he had me in the sight on a rifle. "Hey, I struck gold this morning," he said, pushing the shirt toward me for a better look.

It was a formfitting shirt that was probably from the 1940s or 1950s. I knew this from the many facts about cowboy clothes that Harvey had shared with me through the years. I also knew that he couldn't possibly wear the slim-fit shirt himself.

He was the very antithesis of the lean, laconic cowboy depicted in film. Not only was he pudgy and balding but he was also a real talker. I was faced with the need to try politely to keep this conversation short.

"Ain't it a sight for sore eyes," he said, still sounding like a wrangler right off the range. "I got it at an estate sale, of all places, and it still has the original hang tags on it. It also has most of the design features that make it a classic."

I was afraid he was about to launch into the fact that western wear was America's only truly original fashion, and although it was an interesting fact, he'd already mentioned it to me many times.

"So what can we possibly do for you, since it seems to be in pristine condition?" I asked.

He ignored the question. "Look at this."

Before I could say any more, he began to point out the many elements that made it a collectible, starting with the snaps on the front of the shirt. "That's one of the main differences between a western shirt and every other shirt in the world," he said.

"But why do you want it dry-cleaned?" I asked again.

Not to be deterred, he said, "Did I ever tell you that Denver was one of the main centers for the development of western wear, and that Jack A. Weil, founder of Rockmount Ranch Wear, which is still down on Wazee Street, came up with the idea of putting snaps on shirts, instead of buttons, way back in the forties?"

"I think you did," I said, trying to think of a way to rephrase the question about what Dyer's Cleaners could do for him.

Before I could figure out what to say, the front door opened and Nat came in. Damn. Mom or Betty must have blabbed to him about Ardith's murder and the possibility that Julia's mugging might be connected to it. Suddenly, I was in no hurry to break off the conversation with Harvey.

I saw Nat waving at me in the background, but I tried to ignore him. I knew it was too much to hope for that he'd come to talk about the wedding. Of course, I didn't want to talk about that, either. I figured if I stalled long enough, he might go away.

Meanwhile, Harvey was warming to his subject. "Those snaps were an inspiration. Not only did they give way if the shirt got caught on a fence or a saddle horn but that meant cowboys didn't have to be handy with a needle and thread."

"So you say it has a lot of the design features that make it a classic," I said, now hoping he would stay long enough to outlast Nat.

"You bet," Harvey said. "It's got—"

Nat had come over to the counter by then. "I need to talk to you right away," he said.

I shooed him away with a wave of my hand, as if my conversation with Harvey was too important to interrupt. He backed off a few steps as Harvey gave him an annoyed look.

"Now what were you saying, Harvey?" I asked.

He began to point to different areas on the shirt. "As you can see, it's got a double yoke, smile pockets, and shotgun cuffs."

Nat started to pace as he glanced at his watch. Good, maybe he had to get to an interview or was going to be late for work. If I could keep Harvey talking—which was not a problem, Nat might go away.

"Didn't you say that the word *yoke* actually came from the wooden harness worn by oxen to pull wagons?" I asked.

Harvey beamed. "Good, you remembered. The yoke is sewn from the shoulder down over the top part of the shirt, usually in a heavier fabric, but what makes this shirt unusual is that it has a double yoke in front."

I tried to remember some of the other things he'd told me about cowboy shirts. "And I remember you talking about shotgun cuffs before," I said. "That's because the cuffs extend up the arm like the barrel of a gun," I said.

"Yes, ma'am. Shotgun cuffs make the sleeves tighter so they don't get caught on saddles or barbed-wire fences. They also provide reinforcement for the snaps." He pointed to one of the cuffs. "See, it has multiple snaps, which is another difference from regular shirts, which only have one or two buttons."

I took a quick look at Nat. He had walked back to the windows and was glancing outside as if he might be thinking of leaving. Just a few minutes more and maybe he would go.

"My favorite feature is the smile pockets," I said of the upturned openings for the pockets. "They must have been the inspiration for the mouths on smiley faces." Harvey gave me a puzzled look. Apparently, he didn't draw smiley faces on greeting cards the way some people did.

I took another quick peek at Nat. Oh my God. I saw what he'd been looking at. Actually, not *what* but *whom*. Detective Ivinson was heading for the door. He must have used his siren to get here so fast.

At the sight of Ivinson, I could see that Nat's eyes had lighted up with the hungry look of the die-hard crime reporter. I had to bring my conversation with Harvey to a quick end.

I sure didn't want Nat to start badgering Ivinson about why the detective had stopped by, or, God forbid, have Ivinson think that Nat was waiting for me so I could act like some kind of small-time Deep Throat.

Unfortunately, trying to separate these two carnivores, both hungry for information, might be even more of a challenge than it had been to keep Spot and Rambo apart.

THIRTEEN

Harvey remained oblivious to the turmoil I was experiencing. "You got to admit," he said, admiring the shirt as he held it out at arm's length, "no one's going to take this for a city slicker's shirt. That's one of the things cowboys liked—that western wear was a departure from conventional fashion, the clothes that everyone else wore."

I leaned across the counter toward him. "Excuse me, Harvey . . ."

But Harvey was still on a roll. "Of course, John Travolta changed all that when he made *Urban Cowboy*. Suddenly, western wear went from a niche market to a mass market, but the trend didn't last too long."

Near the front door, Nat was all over Ivinson like . . . well, like ranch dressing on a tossed salad. I hoped Ivinson would have the sense to say he had come by to pick up some cleaning, but Nat would never swallow that.

I tried again with Harvey, and this time I raised my voice. "I'm really sorry, Harvey. I'd love to continue this conversation some other time, but right now I have to keep an urgent appointment."

"Why didn't you just say so?" He looked hurt, and I had to admit I had been giving him mixed signals.

"I'm sorry," I said. "So what do you want me to do with the shirt—clean it for you because it's been hanging in the closet all these years?"

"Good grief, no." He pulled the shirt back toward him, as if I suddenly might snatch it out of his hands. "Like I said, I got it from the estate of a guy who used to have a big cattle spread. He lived in one of those mansions over west of here by the Denver Country Club, and since I happened to be in the neighborhood, I thought I'd bring it in and show it to you."

Okay, it takes all kinds, I decided, even customers who just come in to chat and show off their latest purchase. However, my current predicament wasn't Harvey's fault.

"Well, thanks for showing me the shirt," I said as he turned to leave.

I was right behind him, wishing I could join arms and walk out the door with him, but it wasn't an option. I had to stop when I reached Nat and Ivinson. I told Nat in as few words as possible that we hadn't been able to find the missing item from the suit he'd brought in to be cleaned.

"I'll be in touch as soon as we locate it, Mr. Wilcox," I said.

I could almost see the cogs turning in his brain. The suit? What suit?

"Oh, yeah, the suit," he said finally. "What exactly did you say was missing?"

Now I was the one caught off guard. "Uh . . . the vest. We can't find the vest."

"Well, be sure and let me know the minute you find it." He winked at me with the eye that faced away from the detective.

All I could do was twitch my itching nose nervously, like a bad actress trying out for a role on the latter-day version of *Bewitched*.

Nat turned and headed for the door, but I knew he wouldn't wait for my call. He'd be outside in the parking lot and on the phone the moment the detective left.

"I got your message," Ivinson said. "It's a good thing. I was about to get a search warrant."

I don't know why I felt the need to explain. "One of my employees was attacked when she was out walking her dog last night. I decided it might have something to do with the case. That's why—"

He didn't give me time to finish the story. "I'll take the information right now, Ms. Dyer."

"Right."

I escorted him to my office, but I couldn't help feeling guilty for betraying my customers somehow. At the same time, I felt guilty for waiting so long, and maybe, putting Julia's life in jeopardy. A real "damned if you do, damned if you don't" dilemma.

"This is going to take awhile," I said. "I didn't expect you to get here so soon."

Ivinson didn't look happy about waiting. I'd been hoping my cooperation would bring out his "smiley face" like the ones on Harvey's shirt, but it didn't.

Finally, I was able to assemble the information on who'd come in the days of Lorraine Lovell's visit and the day of the open house.

When I handed the computer list to him, I said, "As you know, I was trying to figure out any customers who might fit the profile and were here the days of Ardith's and Lorraine's visits—I mean men who were well dressed, but different from the bank employees Ardith worked with."

"And did you come up with any names?" Sarcasm tinged his voice.

"Some." I gave him the handwritten list that Mack and I had made. "That doesn't mean they're guilty of anything, you understand, just that they dressed a little differently from the men at the bank."

I also gave him the lists my employees had made, but I have to admit the one name I withheld was Travis Kincaid's. I rationalized that he wasn't a customer and that he'd only been outside the cleaners, not in the call office. It didn't make me feel any better that I was still suspicious of him, and frankly, I needed to confront him about it and be done with it.

Ivinson broke into my thoughts. "Is that all?"

"There's a guest book I had people sign at the open house. I'd like it back when you're through with it."

"I'll give you a receipt."

As I pulled it out of a desk drawer, I realized I'd never gotten around to checking for the names of women who'd come in at the same time as Ardith. I glanced at the people who'd signed just before she did and then looked at the signatures right after hers. Much to my surprise, a few lines later was a name I'd overlooked, probably because Mack and I had only been checking out the names of men. Nadine Woodruff, the gossipy teller from Ardith's bank, had been at the cleaners about the same time as Ardith.

"I'm waiting, Ms. Dyer," Ivinson said.

I slammed the book shut and handed it to him. In return, he handed me the promised receipt.

"Before you go, I need to talk to you about my employee who was attacked last night." I gave him her name and address and what little information I had about it, including the fact that she'd thought someone had been in her backyard the night before.

Ivinson looked unimpressed, but at least he wrote something down in his notebook. "And what makes you think she might be a target for the killer?"

"I don't know. She can't remember seeing or hearing anything suspicious on the day of the open house, but maybe the killer thinks she did."

I thought of Julia's light brown hair. "Or maybe he thought she looked like the other women he'd killed." I launched into the eerie resemblance between Ardith and Lorraine Lovell. "I was told that Lorraine actually dyed her hair the lighter color just after she met some mysterious stranger."

"And just how did you happen to discover that, Ms. Dyer?"

Whoops. I probably should have notified the police earlier about the look-alike appearance of the two victims. "I talked to the owner of the party shop where Lorraine had worked, but I didn't find out about it until yesterday. I was going to let you know when I called about handing over the information."

I stopped just short of raising my right hand and saying, Honest, I swear that's the truth and the whole truth.

He looked at me as if to say, Right, like I'm going to believe that.

I needed to stop having conversations in my head. "I hope you'll use discretion when you talk to my customers," I said aloud.

He gave me a blank look. I couldn't even imagine what he was thinking, but it probably didn't have anything to do with the gentle treatment of the people on my list.

"That should do it," he said after he reviewed the material I'd given him.

I wanted to ask him about the status of the investigation, but I knew he wouldn't answer me. Yet I couldn't resist the temptation to get in the last word.

"I still think the most likely suspect is that man I was telling you about," I said. "You know, the one in the beat-up car. I hope you've tracked him down from the license plate I gave you."

That was the last word all right. Ivinson didn't bother to dignify the statement with a response. He turned abruptly and left, and since he'd found his way out on his previous visit, I didn't bother to accompany him.

Exhausted and shaken by what I'd just done, I dropped into my chair and stared into space. Before I could compose myself, Nat was in my office and in my face.

Julia would never have allowed him to get by the front desk without alerting me, but Lucille and Ann Marie were probably only too happy to let him pass. At least they wouldn't have to wait on him.

"A suit?" he said. "A suit with a *vest,* for God's sakes. At first, I didn't even know what the devil you were talking about. You know damned well I wouldn't be caught dead in one of those monkey suits."

But how about for a wedding? I resisted the temptation to tell him that he might have to wear something even worse—a tuxedo and ruffled shirt—for his upcoming nuptials. Of course, if Mom had her way, he might even wind up wearing one of Harvey's embroidered cowboy shirts.

"Look, I didn't want Ivinson to know we were friends," I said.

"Yeah, and it might have worked, too, if I hadn't just got through telling him I was here to take you to lunch."

I was appalled. Now, if Nat developed any stories about the murders, Ivinson would be sure I was his unidentified source.

"No way am I going to lunch with you, Nat." I got out of my chair and was halfway to the door. "I have to get back to work. I'll talk to you later."

He blocked my way. "Not so fast. I know something's going on, and I'm going to camp here until I find out what it is."

I knew he meant it.

"Besides, I was kidding about telling Ivinson I was taking you to lunch," he added. "There's no way I'm going to foot the bill for another meal for you."

"That's fine with me."

"I'm still not leaving until you tell me what's going on."

"Okay, Nat, but this has to be off the record, and by that, I mean it has to be buried six feet under."

"When have I gone back on my word about something like that? I'd even go to jail to protect my sources, Mandy."

Yes, and he'd probably relish the opportunity to become part of the story. That thought only made me feel a second wave of guilt about having given up even a part of my customer list without a fight.

"Okay, so I want to hear you promise that this is off the record."

"Scout's honor." Nat held up his hands in front of him, apparently so I'd know he wasn't crossing his fingers behind his back. After all, he's the one who taught me back in junior high that a promise didn't count if you did that.

I went back behind my desk, sat down, and poured out the whole story and the connections I'd found between Ardith Brewster and Lorraine Lovell.

Nat could hardly contain himself. "I knew you weren't worried simply because you thought a serial killer might be attacking women in your neighborhood. I should have followed my instincts right then and demanded the truth."

I also filled him in on the grungy man and the beat-up car and what had happened to Julia.

"So you think the attack might have something to do with the murders?" I could tell by the way he kept twisting a pencil around in his hand that Nat was itching to start taking notes.

"I don't know, but I keep thinking the killer may think she overheard something the day of the open house that might be a tip-off to his identity. However, Julia swears she can't think of anything unusual."

After that, I filled him in on my contact with the police and the painful decision to turn over the names of my customers.

Nat finally stuck the pencil behind his ear. "Well, I did find out something sort of interesting this morning. The cops think the guy is a smoker."

"Really. You mean maybe they can get his DNA off a cigarette butt or something?"

"Nope, they didn't find any butts, but they did find evidence of ashes in a saucer on the table by Ardith's bed. They also found ashtrays or dishes with ashes in them in similar locations in the other victims' houses—almost like the killer was leaving them as a clue."

I don't know why I felt as if I had to play devil's advocate. "Maybe all the women smoked, and he picked them because they did."

"Nope. People swear that Ardith, at least, never smoked—so it's more like this guy had a cigarette after a tryst in the boudoir."

"Maybe Ardith was a closet smoker."

"Ugh," Nat said. "It would be pretty gross to light up in a closet. Talk about a smoke-filled room."

I couldn't help wondering why I stayed friends with a guy who could be so irritating sometimes.

Nat always knew when he'd gone too far with me. "Besides," he said, "even a closet smoker would probably have an ashtray, not have to pull out a saucer from her cupboard."

He had me there.

"So do you know if any of your customer suspects were smokers?" he asked.

"Not offhand."

I'd given up the habit myself after the cleaners became a smoke-free facility, but at the moment I had a yearning to light up—a sure sign of stress.

I glanced at my watch. "Look, I have to get to work."

Ann Marie and Lucille were probably at each other's throats up in the call office, and I might need to intervene.

"Okay, okay." Nat got up to leave, but he had one final request, guaranteed to raise my stress level even higher. "Look, you've got to do something about your mother. No one else seems to be able to get through to her, and now she's decided it might be nice to have a destination wedding on the beach in Hawaii instead of here. For all I know, she'd want everyone to wear grass skirts."

"I'll talk to her, but that's all I can do. You've been around my mother long enough that you ought to know what she's like."

Nat nodded his head. "Why do you think I never proposed to you?"

"I thought it was because I wasn't tall and blond, not to mention there was no chemistry between us."

"Well, yeah, there's that, but I didn't know she'd want to run Laura's life, too."

I was on my feet now, anxious to end this conversation. "Frankly, you and Laura need to be the ones to tell her in no uncertain terms that you're going to plan your own wedding."

"Laura doesn't seem to want to confront her."

"Then I guess it's up to you."

I walked out of the office and accompanied Nat to the back door. As soon as he left, Mack turned to me.

"It sure didn't take the police long to get here," he said.

"Yeah, I guess it's over—for better or worse." Jeeze, on top of everything else, Nat and Laura's upcoming nuptials must be getting to me. I was quoting wedding vows.

Mack nodded. "At least now I won't have to worry about you getting into any more trouble." He sounded relieved.

"Nope, no trouble at all—except that our business is probably going to wind up in the sewer."

"Look, if you hadn't called them, the police would probably have served you with papers and taken all your records, and I doubt that a dry cleaner would have any protection under the law, even if your attorney tried to fight it."

Mack usually made me feel better, but right then, I didn't think anyone could. After all, what person would ever think he'd become a suspect in a murder investigation simply for bringing us his clothes to be cleaned?

He must have sensed my unhappiness, as he changed the subject. "So what did Nat want?"

"To find out what was going on with me and the police."

"You didn't tell him, did you?"

"Yes, but strictly off the record."

Mack didn't look as if he approved.

"But he did tell me something interesting. The police think the killer is a smoker." I relayed the rest of what Nat had told me about the saucer that had been used as an ashtray by the bed.

"Just because he smokes, I don't want you checking out the computer to see who might have cigarette burns in his clothes," Mack said.

Why hadn't I thought of that before? Maybe it was one last avenue to explore.

Mack must have regretted the comment as soon as the words were out of his mouth. "Don't forget. You're out of it. No more investigating. You have to promise me that."

"All right, Mack. I promise." I crossed my fingers behind my back.

I had this niggling feeling that I should talk to Nadine again. I'd tried to ignore the thought. It was probably a stupid idea. If it had been worth anything, I should have mentioned it to Ivinson.

But I did have some checks I needed to deposit at the bank. I really did.

FOURTEEN

I had an argument with myself about what I should do: Stay out of any further detecting, the way Mack wanted me to do, or try to find out something more to give to the police.

Back and forth, back and forth. I finally rationalized that if I could uncover even a small clue, it might keep the cops away from my customers' doors.

I called Theresa, explained what had happened to Julia, and asked her to come in early for her afternoon shift. As soon as I finished, I headed up front and told Ann Marie and Lucille I'd be back as soon as I could. Then I sneaked out the front door and headed for the bank so Mack wouldn't question where I was going.

Clouds were boiling toward Denver from the mountains, and it looked as if we might have a spring storm. I picked up my pace, anxious to get back to the cleaners before it rained.

When I reached the bank, it was crowded, the way it always was on Fridays. I had to wait for my favorite teller to get free.

If anyone would remember seeing Ardith at the cleaners during the open house, I was convinced it would be her coworker. Maybe she and Nadine had even walked over there together.

Had I subconsciously noticed Nadine's name in the guest book when Mack and I first looked at it? Maybe that's why I'd thought to go to the bank to talk to her earlier. It's strange how the mind works sometimes, and it wouldn't have been the first time that something hidden away in the recesses of my brain had triggered an action that I wasn't even aware of.

I just wished it had worked up to the surface when I came to see her the first time. I'd have to be careful not to make her wonder why I was asking.

"Next," Nadine said.

I stepped up to her counter. "Hi, Nadine, I'm here with my regular Friday deposits." I regretted the remark immediately. It sounded as if I was trying to justify why I was there.

The teller started going through the checks I'd brought and tallying them up on her computer with her extra-long fingernails. This time, her nails had tiny stars painted on them.

"Nadine," I said, leaning over toward her. "Do you remember being at the cleaners the day of the open house back in March?"

She nodded but didn't stop adding up my checks.

"I noticed where you'd signed the guest book, and it was just after Ardith wrote in it. Did you happen to go over there together, by any chance?"

This time, she shook her head. Suddenly, she was being uncommunicative, but I wasn't giving her much to communicate about.

"There was so much confusion that day, and someone else's order got mixed up with Ardith's. I wondered if you happened to see who was with her at the counter that day. We'd like to return the man's clothes, but we don't know who he is."

Nadine paused at her keyboard and gazed off into space, and for a moment, I wondered if she was questioning why I hadn't brought up the clothes mix-up with Ardith long before she was killed. "No, I don't remember seeing her at the counter," she said finally.

I was disappointed but not really surprised.

She was silent for a few more seconds. "I do remember seeing her there that day, though. She was talking to another customer."

I held my breath, waiting for her to continue. She didn't.

"Do you know who it was—someone else from the bank maybe?"

"Nooooo." She strung out the word like it needed a question mark at the end. "I saw her talking to this guy when I was over getting some champagne."

Already, this was more than I had any right to expect. "Do you remember what he looked like? It could have been the customer whose order got mixed in with hers."

This time, Nadine closed her eyes as if she were trying to re-create the scene in her head. Finally, she opened them. "I'm sorry. I didn't see his face because he was turned away from me. That's the only reason I remember Ardith. She was facing me."

"Do you happen to recall anything distinctive about what he was wearing? That might help me decide if the order belonged to him."

I was freewheeling now, and since there'd never really been an order, I continued to ad-lib. "It included a blue blazer with an emblem on the pocket and gray slacks." I realized I was describing the way Jason Arnell had looked on his way to one of his recent modeling assignments. I stopped. I didn't want to plant any images in her mind. Fortunately, I hadn't.

"No," she said. "That doesn't sound like him. He was wearing blue jeans."

Damn, damn, damn. Blue jeans? That could have been anyone, given the fact that almost any American male between birth and old age wore blue jeans at one time or another. I had to admit it sounded different from the people at the bank, but how could it have been the well-dressed man Ardith described?

"What about a shirt or jacket?" I asked.

She shook her head. "I'm sorry. I don't remember." She grinned at me. "I was looking at his cute butt, and I guess I wondered why Ardith was talking to him. I figured she'd prefer the stuffed-shirt type."

A cute butt, huh? Maybe that could be a clue.

Was there any other question I should ask? I tried to think of one. "You didn't happen to walk back to the bank with her, did you? Maybe she said something then or later."

"No. Frankly, she seemed so involved in the conversation that I didn't want to interrupt. In fact—" Nadine had given up going through the checks, her fingers frozen on the keys. I hoped she wasn't thinking that this might be Ardith's mystery man/killer, but I was afraid maybe she was. "In fact, it was almost as if she was flirting with him, and I didn't want to say anything about it to her afterward. She always acted so snooty when anyone tried to talk to her."

God, it sure sounded like the right guy, but in blue jeans? So different from the other men she knew, but Ardith really had said he was well dressed, hadn't she?

I decided that was all I was going to get out of Nadine, at least without raising her suspicions more than they probably were already. "Okay, I appreciate your trying to help, but I guess we'll have to keep digging to find the owner of the clothes. I shouldn't have interrupted your work."

"No problem," she said as she finished up the transaction and gave me a deposit slip.

When I turned to leave, I noticed that the line of customers was even longer than when I'd come in.

The next person in line gave me an "It's about time" look as I passed. It was the same look some people gave us at the cleaners when we paused to chat with customers.

I would have liked to stop and browse in a bookstore or have a cup of cappuccino at one of the coffeehouses in the area. I didn't dare give into temptation, though. I wasn't sure Lucille would ever forgive me for keeping her on the counter for so long. Besides, I felt the first drops of rain as I crossed the street to the cleaners. I made a run for the front door.

As soon as I got inside, Ann Marie said, "I'm starving. I'm going to pass out if I don't get something to eat."

"Aren't there rules that say you have to give us a lunch break in a timely fashion?" Lucille asked. "And, pray tell, how am I ever going to get all my own work done back at mark-in?"

"Go to lunch, both of you," I said. "And if you don't get done, I'll do the rest of the mark-in for you after you leave, Lucille. Okay?"

"Hmmph," Lucille said as she followed Ann Marie into the back of the plant.

Fortunately, the rain meant that business was slow and I could handle it easily by myself. I did pick up a new customer, Mrs. Lawrence Martin, Jr., with the emphasis on the *Mrs.*

"We just got back from our honeymoon," the young woman said shyly. "My husband has this shirt, and some of the buttons got torn off. I was wondering if you can replace them."

"Sure." I pointed to one of our signs. "We replace buttons free of charge."

"And I have this pair of trousers." She seemed almost embarrassed now. "The zipper got stuck, and I thought maybe you could put in a new one after you clean them."

All I could think was that it must have been some kind of honeymoon, but I didn't blink an eye. "Done," I said.

Cal Ingalls showed up later and gave me a ticket for the shirts he'd left the day I tried to play detective with the handsome Jason. Cal was wearing gray slacks, a white shirt, and a windbreaker. No blue jeans today. It made me wonder. . . .

"What are you doing here all by yourself?" he asked. "Where's the woman who normally works here with you?"

I wondered if he was referring to Julia. "She had an—"

I stopped short of saying the word *accident.* "She took the day off."

"She picked a good day for it. You're usually so busy, and I was afraid I wouldn't be able to pick up my shirts before I left town."

"I'll get them right now."

I hurried back to the area where we stored the boxed shirts and grabbed his order, then picked his sports jacket off the conveyor.

"Thanks," he said when I returned to the counter and gave him the shirts and jacket. As soon as I added up his bill, he handed me the exact change.

"Where are you going this time?" I asked.

"Back to the oil field up near Casper."

I couldn't resist watching him as he started to leave. I decided he qualified in the "cute butt" category, but who else on the list Mack and I had made fit the description Nadine had just given me? Lots of men on the list, unfortunately.

Cal stopped abruptly and came back to the counter. "Say, what was that guy so nervous about the other day? You know, the one you were talking to just ahead of me in line."

Obviously, he meant Jason. "I don't remember him being nervous," I said. In fact, as I recalled, Jason had sounded bored and boring as he offered me advice about what to do if we ever held another open house.

"Well, he stopped me as soon as I got to my car," Cal said. "He asked if you'd grilled me about the open house, too. I told him no, but I thought the whole thing was a little strange."

So did I. In fact, it was red flag strange, but I didn't say so to Cal. Instead, I wondered if I should ask him some questions about Brett Harrison while we were exchanging information about other customers.

After all, I'd seen him talking to Brett on more than one occasion, so I decided maybe I should ask him what Brett had talked to him about before Jason waylaid him at his car. What did a petroleum engineer and a waiter have in common? Had Brett happened to ask if Ann Marie was working that day? Had Brett taken off when he found out she wasn't around, and what about his car? How could a waiter afford such an expensive car?

Before I could think of what to ask, Cal turned and was out the door. "I'll see you when I get back," he said as the door closed behind him.

Theresa arrived just before Ann Marie came back from lunch,

and I retreated to my office. Lucille was back, too, but she didn't even look at me, much less speak, as I passed her station.

I was having hunger pangs myself. After all, I hadn't had anything to eat since—well, I couldn't even remember when. I stopped en route to my desk and picked up a couple of candy bars. So much for lunch.

As soon as I sat down, the first thing I did was try to call Julia's phone number. No answer. Presumably, she hadn't yet been released from the hospital, and I couldn't help wondering about Rambo, now that I'd developed an attachment to him. I hoped he wasn't locked inside the truck.

I made another call, this time to a florist, and ordered a bouquet of spring flowers for Julia. "Just sign the card 'From the gang at work.'"

I'd just unwrapped a Baby Ruth when Mack appeared at the door. "Anything new?" he asked.

I shook my head. I thought it best not to tell him what I'd learned about the blue jeans and Jason Arnell.

"Ted just went home sick," he said.

Ted was one of our pants pressers, so I finished the candy bar and spent the rest of the afternoon at the press. At least it gave me time to ponder what Nadine had said.

Should I put Jason at the top of my suspect list because of what Cal said? Frankly, the moment I'd heard about the jeans, I'd tended to put him lower on the list. I had a hard time picturing him in jeans, but for all I knew, maybe he even modeled them sometimes.

Almost everyone on my list could fit Nadine's description at one time or another. Certainly Mel Sutton when he was off duty as a cop. In fact, I was almost certain that Mel had been wearing jeans at the open house.

Ditto for Brett Harrison, who wore tuxedos on the job and drove a car too expensive for his salary as a waiter. Although I hadn't seen him at the open house, I thought he'd been wearing Levi's the day Ann Marie had been flirting with him.

Maybe Ardith had simply been impressed with the neatly pressed garments the men were picking up—a tux for Brett, and uniforms for Mel and the air force lieutenant.

And what about Cal? He was the obvious choice, since he almost always wore jeans with a sports jacket and dress shirt—except today. I'd added his name to my list simply because he'd come in one of the days Lorraine Lovell had.

However, he'd said he'd never even heard about the open house after my only attempt at a one-on-one interview of Jason. Of course, he could have been lying, and if he'd been lying about that, he could just as easily be making up the story about a nervous Jason.

Finally, there was the grungy guy. I'd never seen him except through his car window, but he definitely was the jeans type, the more tattered the better. I could almost picture him with torn knees in his pants, and maybe even a rip in the posterior, so his boxer shorts showed through.

Ugh. It was not a pretty picture, but it might have drawn Nadine's attention to his derriere. It was certainly not a picture that went with Ardith's glowing description of her mystery man. Unless, of course, she was leading me astray, too, because she feared she'd said too much already about her lover. And Nadine had said the man didn't really seem the type Ardith would be having a conversation and even flirting with.

Before I let the whole thing go, I couldn't help thinking about Travis. He'd cut off a leg on several pairs of jeans and worn them when he was recovering from the gunshot wound to his leg and was still on crutches. That would have been a clue, except he wasn't wearing them by March.

Besides, no one had actually seen him in the call office, only outside the plant. But why hadn't he told me about being in the vicinity that day? I might have given him the benefit of the doubt—except for that long, poignant pause when I'd mentioned the open house to him.

About the time I finished at the pants press, I reached the conclusion that Nadine's clue was no clue at all. I was no closer to finding Ardith's killer than I had been before.

I moved on to the front counter to help Theresa and Elaine wait on customers. For the remainder of the day, I divided my time between waiting on customers and marking in the clothes from Lucille's backlog.

It was after seven before I finally had a chance to call Julia again. Her husband answered the phone this time.

I identified myself. "How's Julia doing?"

"We got her home this afternoon. The doctor thinks she's going to be all right now. I guess her blood pressure went sky-high after the attack, but now it's gone down."

"That's a relief."

"She's asleep right now, but I can wake her up."

"No, no. Just tell her I called, and that I'm thinking about her. I'll call back tomorrow."

I resisted the temptation to ask about Rambo and went home to my surly cat. As soon as I opened the door, Spot tried to escape. Obviously, he'd decided that anyplace that would take in a dog was not a place he wanted to be.

I was too fast for him, but he began to wail and scratch at the door as soon as I closed it. It had been an almost impossible task to turn this outdoor cat into an indoor cat, and now he seemed to be regressing.

I bent down to rub him behind his ears. "Come on, Spot, how about some milk?"

He stuck his nose in the air and walked away.

"Okay, I'll share my doggie bag with you." At least he didn't go berserk at the mention of a doggie bag the way Rambo had the previous night. Maybe there was some advantage to having a cat after all.

I went to the refrigerator, zapped the leftovers in the microwave, and sat down at the table to eat. I was glad Nat hadn't been able to cancel my order at the Briarwood the night before.

I wondered if Nat had actually paid for the dinner, even though he'd said he wasn't buying me any more meals. Or maybe he'd just been referring to the cheeseburger he'd bought me the night he and Laura told me they were engaged. Normally, we went Dutch, and it irritated Nat when he had to pay. Good.

Unfortunately, thinking of Nat reminded me that I'd promised him I would talk to my mother again. Boy, that ought to be payback to Nat for a lot of meals. But I'd do that later—when I'd had a chance to relax for a while.

I cut off a piece of chicken and put it on the floor. Spot sauntered over to it as if he really wasn't interested. When he thought I wasn't looking, he grabbed it and carried it into his closet hiding place.

The phone rang before I had a chance to take a bite myself. I didn't want to talk to anyone. Not my mother, Nat, Laura, or Travis, all of whom I'd have to confront at some point.

I let the answering machine pick up.

I couldn't recognize the voice on the other end at first. The person was whispering. "Mandy, pick up. Are you there? If you are, pick up."

No way. Not until you identify yourself.

The voice rose an octave. "Hey, pick up. I gotta talk to you. It's life-or-death."

Okay, now I knew. It was Betty, and that was always bad news.

"Look, it's really important. I wanta know what you think I should do next."

Oh great, I thought. Was this another of Betty's escapades that I could avert if I picked up the phone? I went over to the counter, but I couldn't make my hand grab the receiver. I really didn't want to talk to her.

"Oh boy, I gotta get out of here. I'll have to call you later."

Now I had to pick up. "It's me," I said. "What the devil's going on?"

"Never mind. It was a false alarm."

I tried to get the words out from between clenched teeth. "What was a false alarm?"

"I thought there for a minute the guy'd spotted me, but he didn't."

Oh dear God. "Where are you?"

"At a pay phone in a bar over on Colfax."

"Are we talking about the guy in the beat-up car?"

"Damn, he's lookin' back this way again." The line went dead, and with it, any hope I had of enjoying my meal. My heart had settled in the pit of my stomach.

FIFTEEN

I sat on a stool at the kitchen counter, waiting for Betty to call me back. Ten minutes went by.

I'd just about decided to go cruising Colfax Avenue, looking for her, when the phone finally rang. No waiting for the answering machine to pick up this time.

I grabbed the receiver.

"Hey, it's me again." Betty sounded as casual as if we'd simply been disconnected.

"What happened?"

"I hid out in the ladies' room until the guy left." My relief didn't last long. "But I'm sure he's outside the bar waiting for me."

"And who are we talking about?" I asked.

"You know, the grungy guy, just like you said."

Okay, I could call the police. But Mel Sutton had already told me the grungy guy didn't exist. Detective Ivinson had been unwilling to give me any information about him, as if he were someone in the Witness Protection Program the detective was trying to shield.

I decided my best bet would be to check things out myself before calling in the cops. Then maybe they'd believe me when I told them the man was up to no good. Also, I needed to rescue Betty, not just from being trapped in the bar but also from the temptation to have a drink while she was there. After all, she was a recovering alcoholic.

I picked up my purse. "Where are you?"

"At the Crow Bar and Grill."

I knew where it was. Who could forget a place with a name like that?

"I'll be right there. Don't leave, but don't have a drink while you're waiting." This time, I was the one who hung up.

Keys in hand, I hurried out the door and down the stairs. When I reached the Crow Bar, I drove around the block, trying to spot the beat-up car. I didn't see it. I gave up looking and pulled into a parking spot a few stores east of the bar.

Once I entered the place, the smell of stale beer and cigarette smoke assailed me, but I couldn't see for a few minutes because of the dimly lit interior. I waited until my eyes adjusted to the dark, but I still didn't see Betty. I glanced at the few people on stools and at a table as I walked to the rear. I found the pay phone and went in the ladies' room, which was next to it in a back hallway. No Betty anywhere.

I glanced at the rear exit, wondering if Betty had fled that way. I tried the door, but it was locked. A fire violation, I was sure.

What had possessed her to leave? Had the guy come back inside and forced her out of the place with him? Now my stomach was in my throat. I thought about going back in the restroom and throwing up. Instead, I swallowed hard and headed for the front door. The bartender gave me a dirty look, as if I was one of those people who came in to use the facilities and then left without buying anything.

I stopped and went over to him. "I was looking for a woman who made a call from here a few minutes ago. Did you see her leave, by any chance?"

"Can't say as I did."

I handed him ten dollars, the way I'd seen private eyes on TV do when they were trying to get information.

"Yeah, now that you mention it," he said, "she kept looking out the window and finally took off." He pointed to the left of the front door. "She went thataway."

"Was anyone with her?"

"Nope, she was all by her lonesome."

Well, that was something. Apparently, she'd left of her own volition, but where had she gone? Why hadn't she waited for me? The only reason I could think of was that something had scared her so much that she didn't want to hang around.

I thanked the bartender and went out to the sidewalk. It was probably stupid, but I looked up and down the street, walked to the corner, then turned north on a one-way residential street. I was hoping I'd find her lurking in some bushes, the way I had the time she and Mom had gotten in trouble in Aspen. As soon as I was partway up the block, I regretted my impulse. The street was as dark as the bar had been, especially after the bright lights along Colfax.

As I started to turn back, I heard a sound. I stopped, every muscle tense, and listened. All I could hear was the traffic out on Colfax. I began to retreat, when I heard the sound again. This time, it sounded like a *pssst*—the same sound Betty had made when she was hiding in the bushes.

I looked around, but I didn't see anyone.

"Pssst. Over here."

I glanced toward a parked car, and as I drew closer, I saw two eyes peering up at me from just above the rolled-down passenger's window. It was Betty, hunkered down as she stretched across from the driver's seat.

"What are you doing out here?" I asked, irritation making my voice louder than I intended. "You were supposed to wait inside."

"Shhh." She motioned with a hand. "Get in. Don't stand out there."

I took one step toward her and stopped. "Is this Arthur's car?" I asked, referring to her live-in boyfriend. Knowing Betty, I figured I couldn't be too careful. It would be just my luck if the car belonged to a complete stranger, and we got arrested for sitting in it. An arrest on top of all those traffic violations was more than I could stand right now.

"Of course it's Artie's car. Get in. I got a lot to tell you." Somehow, she managed to open the passenger door as she pushed herself up into the driver's seat. I should have gone back to my own car right then and driven home as fast as I could, but I needed to give her a strong talking-to. I climbed in the car.

"Betty, you have to quit going off on these wild-goose chases. The guy may do something to you if he figures out you're following him, but anyway, I don't think he's the killer."

She folded her arms across her chest. "Why not?"

"I just don't." I could be as irrational as she was, even though I'd considered him a suspect only a few hours ago. Still, he really didn't fit the profile.

"Phooey," she said.

"So why don't we call it a night?"

"Nope, I'm waiting until I see what he does next." She motioned to an apartment building across the street. "He's hanging around back there in a parking lot."

"How do you know he hasn't left by now?"

"I just do." She sounded as contrary as I had a few moments earlier.

"This is ridiculous. I'm going home." I started to get out of the car.

As I did, a man came out of the apartment building she'd been pointing at. I ducked back into the car and leaned over toward Betty to get a look at him through the driver's window. A porch light was on above the door, and I could see him plainly.

It wasn't the grungy guy, but even more of a shock, it was someone I recognized—Brett Harrison, Ann Marie's waiter, who always brought us his tuxedos to be cleaned. Only he wasn't wearing a tux tonight; it looked as if he had on a pair of jeans.

He went down the steps and climbed in his expensive sports car. As soon as he drove past us, another car zoomed out of the driveway behind the building and headed after him. Betty had been right. It was a rattletrap of a car, and I had to believe the grungy guy was inside.

Now this was really getting weird—first Mel and now Brett in such close proximity to the spooky guy in the beat-up car.

"Go. Follow them, Betty." I yanked my cell phone out of my purse.

Betty just sat there.

"Start the car, damn it. We don't want to lose him this time."

"What d'ya mean?" she asked. "The other day, you were bent all out of shape when I made you follow him."

"This time, I'm going to be the one to call the police." She ought to have realized that I'd been mad on the previous occasion because of the three traffic citations.

"Okay, boss lady, whatever you say."

Betty turned the key in the ignition and slammed down on the gas pedal. The engine made a grinding sound, as if it were in great pain. She switched the key off, then tried again.

The car gave a death rattle.

She kept pumping and the engine kept protesting. I could smell gas fumes in the car.

That's what I got for putting my trust in a former bag lady who'd just gotten her driver's license. "You might as well quit. You've flooded the car."

"So what do you want me to do now?" She turned off the ignition and stared at me.

"Wait until it'll start, and then go home and stay there."

"Aren't we going to try to look for the guy?"

"We won't find him now."

Despite my advice, she pumped on the gas pedal and tried again.

My irritation index was rising, but I made an effort to remain calm. "Frankly, it sounds like the battery's dead." My first clue should have been when the dome light didn't go on when I got in the car.

She jerked the key out of the ignition. "Then it's not going to start, no matter how long we wait."

"You got it. You'll have to get someone to jump-start it tomorrow." Fortunately, I didn't have any jumper cables, and I was happy about that. I wasn't in any mood to help her get the car started, but of course that meant I'd wind up having to take her home.

Why oh why was I always getting myself in these ridiculous predicaments with Betty?

"So, what am I going to tell Artie?" she asked after we went to my car and I pulled away from the curb.

I wasn't about to offer any advice on how to handle the doll doctor, although I could think of a few words of advice for him. "I'm afraid that's something you're going to have to figure out for yourself," I said.

"I guess I shouldn't have left the headlights on while I was in the bar," she said.

My fingers gripped the steering wheel as if it were her neck, and I didn't dare answer.

"What's the matter?" she asked. "You still shook up about getting that ticket the other day?"

"I don't want to talk about it. In fact, I'd prefer total silence until I get you home."

"Fine, if that's the way you want to be about it. Next time, I'll just handle things by myself."

I didn't answer.

She unbuckled her fanny pack from around her waist and, using it as a pillow behind her neck, leaned back in the seat and went to sleep. She snored, and I fumed all the way to her apartment just off South Broadway.

When I pulled into a loading zone in front of her building, I nudged her awake. She snorted and made a production of getting out of the car.

"Whoops, I forgot my fanny pack," she said from the sidewalk before I could make a clean getaway.

She came back to the car, and just then Arthur came running down the steps. He must have been watching for her from their window.

"I was worried about you, cupcake," he said, giving her a hug. "Are you all right?'

She nodded.

"What happened to the car?"

Most of the guys I knew would have asked about the car first and me later.

"The battery went dead on it," Betty said.

He rubbed the top of his head, making his whiff of white hair stand up in a Kewpie-doll curl. "I knew I should have had it in for a tune-up before I let you use it to go see Mandy."

She winked at me, and I was sorely tempted to tell him that she'd left the lights on while she was in a bar.

He came over to the car. "Thanks, Miss Dyer, for giving her a ride home. If there's anything I can do to return the favor, let me know."

"Maybe you shouldn't let her drive at night until you're sure the car is fixed."

She frowned at me from just behind his shoulder. "Grab my fanny pack out of the car, sweetie," she said, all sugar and spice to him.

I handed him the fanny pack, and he turned back to her. "Before I forget, Mandy's mother called a few minutes ago and left her number."

My mother? I was out of the car and around to the sidewalk in a flash. "What did she want?"

Arthur looked puzzled. "Oh, I'm sorry, I don't know. She asked for Betty, but you're probably right. She must have been looking for you."

I had my cell phone out of my purse, but of course I couldn't remember her number at the hotel. Meanwhile, Betty was already up the steps and going through the front door.

"Why don't you come up to our apartment and then you can

both talk to her?" Arthur, always the gentleman, said. "I've just made a pot of coffee and some apple strudel."

It was an invitation I couldn't refuse, mainly because I needed to find out what these two middle-aged meddlers, not Arthur, were cooking up. They'd wrought havoc on so many previous occasions, and I knew in my gut that this call wasn't because Mom had been looking for me.

When we reached the apartment, Betty was on the phone and looked surprised and irritated that Arthur had invited me up. The smell of the freshly baked strudel was inviting, even if Betty wasn't.

"Just a minute," she said into the phone. "I'll take this in the bedroom."

"Is that my mother?" I asked. "I want to talk to her."

Betty shrugged. "Okay, your daughter wants to talk to you first, and then I'll get back to you."

I grabbed the receiver. "What are you doing calling here? I know damned well you weren't looking for me."

Arthur looked shocked, but Mom and Betty together always brought out the worst in me.

"Well, dear," Mom said. "I was just trying to find out what was going on about the murders and poor Julia. I've been trying to call you, but you weren't answering your phone." I guess it had never occurred to her to call my cell phone, since she thought I had no social life.

"Besides, you're so tight-lipped about everything, and I figured Betty would tell me even if you didn't," Mom added.

I was fuming. "Swell, talk to Betty, then. Just don't go planning some harebrained scheme to help me out." I handed the phone back to Betty.

"Look, Cece," Betty said, "I'll call you back just as soon as we have some of Artie's strudel." She looked smug as she hung up the phone.

I was about to leave, when Arthur handed me a huge slice of the strudel. The aroma wafted up to my nose, and I couldn't resist. Besides, I didn't want to hurt his feelings. He couldn't help it if the object of his affection was a buttinsky.

He handed another piece of strudel to Betty and poured us both a cup of coffee.

"Hey, I can't help it if your ma called me," Betty said. "I promise to zip my lip when I talk to her." She ran her fingers from one side of her mouth to the other the way she always did—not that it ever did much good.

"Okay," I said, trying to be agreeable for Arthur's sake.

The strudel was delicious, but I gulped it and the coffee down as fast as I could. I needed to get out of there before I exploded again. Arthur handed me a paper bag, and for a minute, I thought he intended for me to blow into it in case I hyperventilated on the way home.

"That's another piece of strudel for you to take home," he said.

I wondered if Betty had any idea how lucky she was.

She walked me to the door, and out of hearing of her boyfriend, I couldn't resist a final warning. "The same goes for you—no more crazy schemes hatched up by my mother."

"Gottcha, boss lady. I'm not doin' no more favors for that crazy lady." With that, she shut the door.

I shook my head at the thought of how Mom had talked Betty into joining her on those two disastrous trips to the mountains. Both had sent me on nerve-racking missions to rescue them. The most baffling thing about their relationship was that they didn't even like each other.

Halfway down the hall, I realized that while I'd had Mom on the phone, I should have said something to her about butting out of Nat and Laura's wedding plans. It would have been a good opportunity, since I was already mad. Now I'd have to do it when I got home.

I got to my car and started to climb inside, when I noticed something on the windshield. I yanked the paper out from under the wiper and looked at it. I couldn't believe it. In fact, it was the crowning blow—a ticket for parking in a loading zone. Never mind that it was the middle of the night. Surely nothing more could happen to me until morning.

CHAPTER
SIXTEEN

When I got home, I found a parking spot a few houses south of where I lived. I parked the car and started to open the door. The dome light came on, unlike what had happened with Arthur's car. It lit up the interior as I started to get out.

Suddenly, I heard a sharp zinging noise, and my whole world seemed to explode. The driver's window shattered into a thousand pieces, spewing glass pellets all over me. Something whizzed by my left ear. I slammed the door shut and dived for the floor.

What had just happened? A bomb? A bullet? I curled my body around the gearshift, my head under the dashboard of the passenger seat and my feet still back on the driver's side of the car. I was afraid at any moment that the whole car would blow up or someone would stick a gun in the window and finish me off.

I heard the squeal of rubber as a car took off or else skidded to a stop. Someone yelled. Feet pounded toward me, and a dog barked. I fumbled for my purse on the passenger's seat and tried to locate my cell phone. By the time I found it and dialed 911, a man I'd never seen before opened the passenger door. I shrank down even farther under the dash.

"Help," I yelled into the phone. "Someone just tried to kill me."

I almost added that the person was standing by my car right now, but the man said, "My God, lady, are you all right?"

I gave my location to the person on the phone. She said to keep the line open and she would dispatch an officer at once.

A black Lab stuck his nose in the car. The man pulled back on a leash. "I was walking my dog," he said, sounding almost as scared as I was. "I saw someone stick the barrel of a rifle out a car window up the street, and, *bang,* your whole window disintegrated. You were lucky you weren't killed."

All I could do was nod. I tried to squeeze out from under the dash. The man saw me struggling and helped me up, but it still took a contortionist's skill I'd never known I possessed to get free. That didn't mean I was ready to leave the car.

"The shooter's gone," the man said. "He took off as soon as he fired at you, so it's safe for you to get out now."

At his urging, I finally crawled out of the car. By the time I reached the sidewalk, several people had spilled out of the houses and apartment buildings up and down the street. One of them was a neighbor, Patrick McCarthy, whom I knew only slightly.

He rushed over to where I was standing, and he made the sign of the cross. "Dear God, are you okay? What happened?"

I couldn't answer. I was afraid my voice would shake the way my legs were doing. I wasn't sure how long I could remain standing.

"Someone in a car over there tried to kill her," my rescuer said. He pointed to an empty parking space slightly to the north of us and across the street. "He took off as soon as he saw me."

"Did you get a license plate on the car?" another man asked as he came trotting up to us. Apparently, he was a late-night jogger, and he kept bouncing up and down in place.

The man who'd helped pry me out of the car shook his head. "I didn't notice. I just started running toward the car. I was sure someone had been shot."

"What about a description of the car?" the jogger asked.

My rescuer shook his head as he kept a tight grip on his dog's leash. "I'm sorry."

I wondered if it had been the beat-up car with the grungy guy inside. Surely the man with the dog would have noticed a car with dented fenders and rusted paint. I couldn't help thinking of what Mack had said about someone following us home the other night. Maybe he'd been right, and the guy had been waiting until the right moment to make his move.

My hands were shaking as I held the cell phone. I couldn't hear if the dispatcher was saying anything or not because of all the spectators' questions and comments.

"Why do you think someone would take a shot at you?" Patrick asked.

My shoulders began to heave involuntarily, but I tried to pass it off as a shrug. "I don't know." But of course I did know. It had to have something to do with Ardith's murder. There was no other explanation.

A siren began to shriek in the distance. Finally, a patrol car rounded the corner and double-parked beside us. I told the dispatcher I was hanging up, and I turned off the phone. The last thing I wanted was for my mother to call me right then.

An ambulance and a fire truck arrived as I stuffed the cell phone back in my purse. Three more police cruisers followed and blocked traffic on the street. The first officer on the scene told the onlookers they'd have to move back. Patrick wasn't about to leave. Neither was the stranger who'd come to my aid.

I heard him tell the officer that his name was Harold and that he'd seen the whole thing. I knew from what he'd already said that he was going to be a big disappointment as an eyewitness.

"A guy shoved a rifle out his car window, and he took a shot at this lady. Then, *ka-boom,* her whole car seemed to self-destruct," Harold said.

The lead officer told another cop to talk to Harold while he interviewed me.

He introduced himself as Officer Babcock. "Are you all right?" he asked.

I nodded.

"I can see you've got some cuts on your face, and you have some glass in your hair."

I patted my cheek, and it was only then that I realized a piece of glass was embedded in the palm of my hand. Blood had run up my arm as I held the phone. I dragged a Kleenex out of my purse, yanked out the piece of glass, and tried to stem the flow of blood.

"You'll probably need to let one of the medics check out your cuts," Babcock said, motioning to the ambulance. "But first, I'll need to get your name."

I gave it to him, along with my address, and told him that I was the owner of Dyer's Cleaners in the Cherry Creek area. Then I asked if we could talk privately. This time, he managed to get Patrick to move back from where we were standing.

"Any idea who shot at you?" he asked. "Did you have a fight with your husband or boyfriend?"

I shook my head.

"Anybody else you can think of who has a grudge against you?"

Another shake of my head.

I interrupted his questions and tried to explain about Ardith and all the information I'd given to Detective Ivinson. He took copious notes.

"But I don't know who the killer is." I said. "There is one strange guy who's been hanging around the cleaners. I have no idea what his name is, but I have his license number."

I might as well run it by one more policeman, I decided. Maybe I'd get a different answer this time. I dug the sheet of paper with the letters and numbers written on it from my purse. I read them off to him. I wasn't about to give up the scrap of paper with the license plate information written on it, since it was the only proof I had that the guy was real. So far, all I knew was that either the plate didn't exist or it did and Detective Ivinson wouldn't talk about it.

Babcock looked inside the car and said he'd have the vehicle towed to the police impound so the lab techs could take a look at it. He thought the bullet might be lodged in the upholstery in back, since it hadn't shattered the rear window. I hadn't even noticed.

"I'll get someone to look at your cuts." He started to walk away, then turned. "Do you live with someone?"

"No."

"Is there someone who can spend the night with you?"

I shook my head. I didn't want to call Mack, or, God forbid, my mother about this. "I'll be okay once I get upstairs in my apartment."

Most of the crowd began to disperse, but Patrick was still standing off at a distance. I looked over to where he was. I stiffened.

He was talking to Travis, but why was Travis here? He should have been at his undercover job on the loading dock at this time of night. Why would he be in my neighborhood just after the shooting had occurred? The only reason I could think of—and I definitely didn't want to believe it—was that he was the shooter, and he'd returned just now to see if he'd killed me or, at the very least, scared me to death. I began to tremble big-time, and I had to lean against the car for support.

"We need to get a coat for you," Babcock said.

It was a little chilly after the rain earlier in the day, but I was shaking as if I were stuck in a ground blizzard in January. "Th-th-there's a jacket in the back of the car," I stuttered.

Babcock retrieved it for me and put it around my shoulders. It didn't do much good to stem my tremors.

"Sign this statement," he said, and thrust a clipboard at me. I wrote my name and handed it back to him. "I'm going to have a medic take a look at you. Then you can go inside." He headed over to the ambulance.

Travis broke away from Patrick and started in my direction as soon as Babcock left. He was wearing jeans and a T-shirt, which further unnerved me. Were these the clothes he wore while working undercover, or were they what he'd been wearing when Nadine saw him talking to Ardith?

I knew I wasn't thinking clearly, and I couldn't stand watching him as he walked toward me. He still had a slight limp from the bullet he'd taken in his leg back in January. Did he blame me for it? I turned and began to walk away, but he caught up with me.

He grabbed my arm and turned me around. "Christ, what happened, Mandy? Are you all right?"

Before I could answer, he put his arms around me, but I stiffened at his touch. My hands dangled at my sides, and I couldn't make them move. He pulled back.

"What's the matter?" He had a hurt look on his face, and I knew he wasn't referring to the shooting. I couldn't bring myself to tell him that the real reason for my panic was his sudden appearance from out of nowhere.

"Someone took a shot at me. That's what." I dropped my head because I couldn't look in his eyes. "And I can't deal with any more questions right now. Okay?" "

He backed up a few more steps and put his hands out in front of him, apparently to show me he wouldn't press me for any more details. "Look, when you're through talking to the cops, let's go for a drink."

"No." The ferocity in my voice surprised me. "I just need to be alone for a while. I'm shook up right now, and I don't want to talk to anyone."

"Okay. No more questions. I promise." He seemed to be waiting for me to say something else.

"I'm sorry." My voice choked up, and I was afraid I was going to burst into tears.

Patrick had followed Travis over to where we were standing by my car. "Who would want to take a shot at you?" he asked.

"I don't know." My eyes flickered toward Travis for a split second. Talk about giving myself away with my body language, but I couldn't help wondering what his reaction would be. Guilt? No.

Just the same cynical expression I remember from when we were teenagers.

"I have to go." I fled in the direction Babcock had gone. When I found the officer, I looked back to where I'd left Travis. He was gone.

The medic took a look at my wounds and said they didn't appear to be serious. He applied an antibiotic ointment to them and put a bandage on my hand. He checked the cuts on my forehead but didn't think they needed any medical attention. All my real wounds seemed to be inside, but he didn't know that and couldn't have treated them if he had.

It took another fifteen minutes before Officer Babcock finally told me I could leave. He walked me all the way up to my third-floor apartment.

"Detective Ivinson will probably be in touch with you tomorrow," he said. "Be sure to lock your door when you get inside."

Once I put the dead bolt on, I heard his footsteps going down the stairs. This was what I wanted—to be alone—but the silence overwhelmed me.

I tried to pick up Spot for comfort, but he wasn't having any of that. He'd apparently overdosed on chicken. I noticed that the chicken breast on the table was gone. He'd apparently dragged it away to one of his hiding places.

Now I knew what people meant when they said they felt violated. Not by Spot. By the shooter. I didn't want to give in to the feeling. I needed to regain control of my life, and it seemed important right then to keep busy. I knew I'd never be able to sleep unless I wore myself out.

I went to the bathroom and ran a comb through my hair. Tiny shards of glass cascaded to the floor as if they were bits of glitter that I'd sprinkled on my head. I stripped off my clothes and shook them out, then swept up the bits of glass that had fallen. I didn't want either Spot or me to get cut from padding across the floor.

To be sure all the glass was gone, I finally got down on my hands and knees, clad only in my underwear, to wipe up any bits I'd missed with a wet rag.

I bent low to the floor to catch the shine of pieces I'd missed. Suddenly, something hit the back of my head. My forehead banged against the tile. I had a few seconds of sheer panic before I saw Spot, who'd landed in front of me.

He slid across the tile on the rag as if it were some sort of magic carpet. I should have known it was the cat. He'd done this before whenever I got down at his level to find a missing needle or some tiny bit of jetsam that had fallen on the floor. In his younger days, he would have vaulted over my crouching figure as if he were Supercat leaping over a building in a single bound.

This time, he didn't quite make it; plus, he'd never decided to play the game under quite such ridiculous circumstances. There I was in my underwear, crouching in the middle of the bathroom floor and completely unnerved by a cat. I sat up, and despite everything, I couldn't help but laugh.

When I regained some composure, which was hard to do, I finished dragging the wet cloth across the floor, this time with Spot riding on top and trying to grab at the edges as if there was a mouse hiding underneath.

Once I'd calmed down, I was tempted to bypass the shower and give in to my fatigue. Still, I couldn't help feeling that I needed to wash away the memories of what had just happened.

I shooed Spot out of the bathroom, pulled off the rest of my clothes, climbed in the shower stall, and let the warm water run over me. That's when I heard the phone ring. Whoever it was would have to leave a message.

When I finished, I pulled on an extra-large T-shirt and dried my hair. Before I finished, the phone rang again. I dashed toward it and waited for the answering machine to pick up. No one spoke, and the person hadn't left a message on the previous call.

Three more calls came in quick succession. Each time, the party hung up without leaving a message. Fear gripped my stomach again. Was it the shooter trying to see if he'd hit his mark? That meant it couldn't have been Travis, because he knew I was still alive. It didn't make me feel any better.

I turned on the TV, doused the rest of the lights, and sat down on my unopened sofa bed with an afghan around me. The flickering images on the screen gave off a weak light within the room, but I didn't really watch them.

The phone rang again. It was all I could do to keep from answering it. I wanted to yell at the person on the other end of the line to leave me alone, but I didn't.

I should have confronted Travis, as well. I should have asked him why he'd been near the cleaners the day of the open house and why he'd turned up in front of my apartment right after the shooting.

The phone rang four more times. On the fifth ring, I heard heavy breathing. I couldn't stand it anymore. I grabbed the receiver. "Who are you?" I yelled.

All I heard was heavy breathing.

"I want you to leave me alone." I punched the off button on the phone, and for good measure, I yanked the cord out of the wall. There, I felt better. Maybe I was regaining some control.

I returned to the couch, turned the sound up on the remote, and tried to concentrate on what was on TV. I think it was an infomercial. I must have dozed off and been dreaming about the bullet that had almost hit me. A sudden noise sent me diving to the floor, as if the shooter were firing at me again.

I pressed myself against the rug until I realized it wasn't a gunshot that had jerked me awake. Someone was pounding on the door.

Maybe it hadn't been such a good idea to answer the phone. Now someone knew I was in the apartment.

SEVENTEEN

I wasn't about to answer the door. Instead, I plugged in the phone, ready to send another alert to 911.

Fortunately, I didn't have to do that.

The knock came again. "Let me in. It's Mack."

I recognized his deep voice, which always carried to the back of the auditorium when he was acting in one of his amateur theater productions. I pulled on my bathrobe as I went to let him in.

"What are you doing here?" I asked as soon as I opened the door. "It's the middle of the night."

He came inside. "Good Lord, Mandy, I just heard what happened to you. Why didn't you call me?"

"How did you find out?"

"Travis called. Apparently, he'd been calling me all night, but I just got in."

I looked at my watch. It was after one in the morning, and I was puzzled at what Mack had been doing up until this hour. I was even more puzzled about Travis.

"Why did he call you?" I knew Mack had hired him once—against my wishes—so I gathered that Travis had his home phone number.

"He told me someone had taken a shot at you, and he thought I ought to get over here to be with you."

"It was none of his business," I said. "I'm doing fine." Well, that was if you didn't count the attack by my cat and all the hang-up calls on the phone.

Mack went over to my overstuffed chair and sat down before he said anything else. "Travis was worried about you and wanted to know why you were suddenly so cold to him."

"You didn't tell him, did you?"

Mack looked embarrassed. "I guess I shouldn't have, but he sounded really upset. I told him you were uncomfortable because we'd heard he'd been outside the cleaners at the time of the open house."

It wasn't like Mack to violate a confidence, and I was upset with him. "So what did he say to that?"

"He said 'Damn.'"

"That's all?"

"No. I expected he'd deny it or have an explanation, but when I asked him if he'd been there, and if so, why, he said he couldn't talk about it right then."

I didn't like the way that sounded, and I dropped down on the sofa. "Then he had been near the cleaners. I've kept hoping Lucille was wrong."

"I'm sorry I said anything, but I can't believe he was involved in any of this."

"If that's true, why did he show up here right after the shooting? He was supposed to be working undercover, but it was as if he was checking to see if the bullet had killed me."

Mack didn't have an answer for that. "Look, I'm really sorry. I've been coming by every night, and when I'd see your car outside, I figured you were in for the night and that you'd be okay. From now on, I'm going to stick to you like glue."

I wasn't sure I could handle that, and I had to ease his mind. "The more I've thought about it, the more I think that bullet was meant to scare me, not kill me. My car was all lighted up, and the shooter could have killed me if he'd wanted to."

Mack shook his head, and I was doubtful that I'd convinced him, much less myself.

"And there's one good thing about it," I continued, although *good* probably wasn't the best word I could have chosen. "At least it means we can finally narrow down the list. The shooter has to be someone who knew we were interested in the open house—Brett Harrison, Jason Arnell, Cal Ingalls, Mel Sutton, or Betty's grungy guy."

In case Mack had forgotten who they were, I took time to identify them by occupation—the waiter, the model, the engineer, and the policeman. I knew Mack remembered the grungy guy and that he now had doubts himself about Travis.

"I gave their names to the officer who took my statement tonight," I said. "I told him to let Detective Ivinson know."

"But what if it's someone else Ivinson has questioned since you gave him your list of customers?" Mack asked.

Now it was my turn not to have an answer.

Mack changed the subject. "I saw your car here at eight o'clock on my way to meet some of my actor buddies to discuss next season's productions. Why'd you leave after that?"

I explained about Betty's latest escapade, including the ticket I'd gotten for parking in a loading zone, and then I told him about the shooting. I had to admit that Travis had been right about one thing: I'd needed to talk to someone, and I felt better when I finished.

I stifled a yawn and finally told Mack he'd have to go home so I could get some sleep. I had to work the Saturday shift at the cleaners with Ann Marie.

"I'm not going anywhere." Mack put his feet on the coffee table, as if he wasn't about to move for what was left of the night.

"Please, you need to leave and quit feeling guilty about talking to Travis. I should have had the guts to confront him about it myself, but I was too upset."

He leaned his head back on the chair. "I'm staying here, so you might as well try to get some sleep. And for what it's worth, I don't think you should go to work tomorrow."

"Julia won't be there, and I don't dare let Ann Marie handle the morning shift alone."

"Okay, if you're dead set on going, then I'm going to take you there." He closed his eyes.

I was sure I couldn't talk him into leaving, and even though I didn't like his use of the phrase *dead set,* he had a point. The police had hauled my car away, so I needed a ride to work.

I lay down on the sofa, threw the afghan over me, and within minutes, I was gone. It was the best sleep I'd had in days.

By eleven o'clock the next morning, business had slowed down at the cleaners. Remembering what Nadine had said, I was thinking about taking a look in the computer to see if any of my suspects had brought in their jeans to be laundered.

Another thing I needed to do was call Julia and see how she was doing. Just as I reached for the phone, Travis came through the door. He was wearing slacks and an open-necked shirt. No jeans this morning.

Ann Marie was overdue from a break, and even though Mack had finally agreed not to hang around the cleaners on his day off, I half-expected him to be parked around the corner, watching the entrance. I even thought he might come running to my aid when he saw Travis.

"Are you feeling better this morning?" Travis asked.

I stiffened. "Until now." I didn't know why I felt I had to be sarcastic.

Travis clenched his jaws. "I need to talk to you."

I couldn't stop. "Okay, talk."

"Not here. I need you to go over to Tico Taco's with me. It's important."

"I can't." I stopped just short of saying I was alone at the counter, then motioned to the door to the plant so he'd know someone else was there. "Ann Marie is on break."

Unfortunately, she chose that moment to return, and she'd obviously heard the end of our conversation. "Go on," she said. "I can handle things by myself for a while."

I was tempted to refuse to go. At the same time, I didn't particularly want Ann Marie to hear whatever Travis had to say.

"Okay." I led him out the front door and around the side of the building. I didn't feel comfortable walking through the empty back shop with him.

Besides, I wanted to see if Mack might be hovering nearby. He wasn't, and I had to conclude that he'd taken me at my word that I'd be all right until seven o'clock. That's when he'd insisted on coming back to give me a ride home.

Travis seemed almost as tense as I was. He was careful to keep some distance between us. "Mack told me what was bothering you."

"I know, and I'm assuming you have an explanation."

"I do." That's all he said until we got to Tico Taco's.

The restaurant had just opened for the day, and we were the only customers in the place. Travis motioned me to a booth in the back, but once we were there, he said, "We need to wait for Manuel."

"No. I'm not planning to order anything, so let's get this over with."

Travis didn't reply, and I was getting more irritated by the minute. I couldn't look at him. Instead, I glanced around the room at the mementos Manuel must have added in the last few days from his trip to Mexico. There was a huge sombrero and a brightly painted tin parrot on the wall, and a few new piñatas hanging from the ceiling.

I was still inspecting one of the piñatas when Manuel came out of the kitchen. He slid into the booth beside Travis, which definitely wasn't what I expected.

"It's all my fault," Manuel said. "I hired Travis—uh, Señor Kincaid, and he was working for me the day of your open house, but he wouldn't tell you about it until I gave my permission."

"I don't understand."

"I need you to promise you won't tell anyone."

He gave me a pleading look, and I glanced from him to Travis and back again. "Okay, I promise."

"See, I didn't trust my Maria, and so I hired Señor Kincaid to follow her. It turns out that all the time when I thought she was out with some . . . some gringo, she was working at one of those dollar stores to help pay for the trip to Mexico for my birthday."

I didn't know quite how to respond, but he was still looking at me as if he wanted my approval. "Okay, thanks for telling me," I said finally, "and I'm glad it worked out for you and Maria."

He looked relieved. "I wanted to be the one to tell you, and I owe it all to your friend here." He nodded at Travis and gave him a pat on the shoulder. "Thanks to him, I'll never be suspicious of my Maria again."

Travis looked uncomfortable, but he didn't say anything.

"Okay, now that that's over, I'm going to fix you the best fajitas you ever ate. They're on the house."

Travis waited until he disappeared into the kitchen. "Do you believe me now?"

"I guess."

"I remembered the day of your open house as soon as you mentioned it, but I didn't want to tell you, because I'd been hanging around out in the parking lot that afternoon. I was waiting for Maria to leave the restaurant so I could follow her and see what she was up to."

I don't know why I didn't let it go. "I didn't think you took those kind of cases."

"I don't usually." He stopped, but I must have looked at him as if I expected a further explanation. He shrugged. "I figured he was a friend of yours."

I decided to drop it and move on. "About last night—"

"Did it ever occur to you that I finally wrapped up that case at the loading dock, and the first thing I did was stop by your place because I wanted—no, damn it—I needed to see you?"

"Apparently, that never entered my mind."

He shook his head at my apparent obtuseness. "Well, much as I hate to admit that I need you, that's the truth. Now how about going out with me tonight?"

I didn't want to make it too easy for him. "I don't know. I'm really tired. I may need to go home and go to bed."

"That's what I had in mind, too."

I'd left myself wide open for that.

Ann Marie got off work at two, and I couldn't help thinking about how Brett had said something about a date for Saturday night.

"So what are you planning for tonight?" I asked as she started to leave.

"Oh, some of my girlfriends and I are getting together and going to a movie."

I couldn't tell if she was fibbing or not. Too bad she didn't itch when she lied.

"Well, have fun."

"You, too."

I intended to if I could stay awake until eight o'clock, when Travis had said he would call me. I tried to stifle a yawn.

Theresa, who'd arrived to take over for Ann Marie, glanced at me. "You look like you're dead on your feet."

Why did people have to keep using the word *dead* when they talked to me?

"You need to go home and get some sleep," she said. "I can close up for you."

I'd already told her my car was out of commission. "But I need to wait for Mack," I said. I sounded like a child who had orders that her parents would pick her up after school, and I couldn't stand the helplessness in my voice.

I needed to regain control of my life, and there was no reason I couldn't leave early. Although I didn't have a car, I could take the company van. We didn't make deliveries on Saturday, and the van was parked out behind the plant.

I finally told Theresa I'd take her up on her offer. It was 3:30. "If I can't get in touch with Mack, please tell him I've already gone home when he gets here. He'll understand." Of course he wouldn't, but that was beside the point.

When I'd driven the van on another occasion when he'd thought I should keep a low profile, he'd said the Dyer's Cleaners logo on the side was a "moving advertisement" for where I was.

I stopped in my office and tried to call him, just so Theresa wouldn't have to hear him rant, but there was no answer. Maybe I need to give him a cell phone for Christmas, I decided as I drove home.

Once safely inside my apartment, I took off my uniform, pulled on a T-shirt and a pair of jeans, and collapsed on my sofa. Never mind the fact that jeans were the focus of all my thoughts these days. I was almost asleep when I remembered that I'd been planning to check on Julia when Travis had interrupted me.

I didn't bother to get up. I grabbed my cell phone and my address book from my purse on the floor and called her. This time, her husband let me talk to her.

"How're you feeling, Julia?"

"Much better, and by the way, thanks for the flowers."

"You're welcome."

"But I'm not sure if I'll be up to coming back to work on Monday." She must have figured that was the real reason I called.

"Don't worry about it. I just wanted to see how you were and to tell you something I found out."

I told her what Nadine had said about the guy in the jeans

who'd been talking to Ardith at the open house. "Nadine said Ardith appeared to be flirting with him."

I almost fell asleep while we were talking, so I finally excused myself and hung up. I didn't know how long I'd been sleeping when the phone rang. I was still skittish about loud noises, apparently, and I grabbed it before the second ring.

"Oh my God, Mandy, I just remembered something." I could tell it was Julia, and she sounded more animated than she had in days. "It probably isn't important, and it doesn't have anything to do with my seeing Ardith with a man, but I just thought of something she said. She asked if we starched a lot of jeans for our customers."

"You're kidding," I said, but I knew she wasn't. Furthermore, this seemed to fit in with what Nadine had said about the man in the tight jeans. "What did you tell her?" I was on my feet now, my adrenaline pumping.

"I said we did, and I mentioned this one lawyer who wears jeans to work, but he always wants them starched and pressed because he thinks it makes them look dressy."

I knew the guy she was talking about. Too bad he wasn't on my list of suspects.

But "dressy," as in well dressed and so different from the other men Ardith knew. That had to be it.

"And I mentioned that we get a few requests when the National Western Stock Show is in town in January," Julia continued, "but that we're really too far away from the Coliseum to get a lot of rodeo business."

Unfortunately, I couldn't think of a single rodeo performer among my list of suspects, either. We sometimes got requests from other customers, too. I just couldn't remember who they were or why the devil they wanted to starch their jeans to the consistency of a wooden board.

"Damn. Damn. Damn." I thought I said that under my breath, but apparently Julia heard me.

"What did you say?"

"I said 'Thanks.' I got to go."

I didn't tell her I was home and that the expletives had been because I should have called her from work. That way, I could have
checked my computer for any "starched jeans" guys on my list.
Now I'd have to drag myself back to work to check it.

But first, I had a strange feeling that I needed to find out the
"why" of starched jeans, and for that, I knew just the person to call
to get that kind of information.

If anyone could help me, it was Harvey Campbell, with his collectible western shirts and his western-wear store south of Denver,
near Castle Rock. In fact, he could probably provide more information than I'd ever want.

I grabbed the Yellow Pages and looked up the phone number
for Campbell's Western Wear. Please be there, I prayed as I
punched in the numbers. When a woman answered, I asked for
Harvey.

"He's not here right now." My heart sank. "But he'll be back at six
to close up. Then he's going up to his cabin for a few days." She
sounded like a teenager.

"Could you have him call me before he leaves?"

"I can't promise. He's not always good about returning phone
calls right away."

"Okay, I'm coming out there. Tell him this is Mandy Dyer, and
don't let him leave before I get there."

"I'll try."

I guess I felt I needed to emphasize what I'd just said, but I don't
know why I phrased it as if I were a cowgirl in a calf-roping contest.
"Hog-tie him if you have to. I really need to talk to him, because it's
a matter of—" I stopped. "Life or death" might be true, but it
sounded too dramatic. "National security" sounded ridiculous. "It's
really important."

I could tell she was puzzled, and I was afraid she might start
asking questions. "I'll be there as soon as I can."

I glanced at my watch. It was 5:20. Good grief, I thought. I hadn't realized it was that late. I checked the address in the Yellow Pages, grabbed my shoulder bag and a jacket, and was out the door and in the van in a matter of seconds.

I glanced at my watch again. It was probably going to take me half an hour to get to Campbell's. I didn't have time to check out the computer at work, not if I was going to have any hope of talking to Harvey before his store closed.

As soon as I headed for the interstate, I put in the earpiece to my cell phone and speed-dialed the cleaners. Normally, I didn't do that when I was driving, but this was an emergency.

"Will you do a tremendous favor for me, Theresa?" I asked when she answered the phone.

"I thought I already had by offering to close up for you," she said. Fortunately, she was only kidding.

"Would you look up some customers on the computer and see if any of them have had us wash and starch jeans in the last year?" I gave her the names I'd given to Mack the previous night.

Theresa seemed to be whispering, or else we had a bad connection. "Does this have something to do with Ardith?"

"Maybe." I had my fingers crossed. The sooner I could find out and turn the information over to the police, the sooner I could get on with my life.

"Okay, I'll get on it right away. At the moment, I'm with a customer."

That figured. She was probably going to be overwhelmed with business today, even though Saturday afternoons weren't normally that busy. "Good, if you find out anything, call me on my cell phone. Otherwise, I'll call you before you close up."

When we were through talking, I concentrated on driving down South Broadway until I saw a sign to southbound I-25. Fortunately, the entrance was open. Thanks to something called T-Rex, a massive and long-term highway project to widen the interstate and rebuild some overpasses south of downtown, I never could be sure which accesses to the highway were available.

I was in luck. I merged into traffic and moved to the center lane. Since it was Saturday, the road wasn't as jammed with traffic as it would have been during rush hour on a weekday. That's when people poured out of the Denver Tech Center, a huge complex of buildings that housed all kinds of high-tech and other businesses.

The traffic was moving at a steady clip and I had time to think about what, if anything, I knew about starched jeans. A dry cleaner I'd met once at a trade show told me he did a big business starching jeans for rodeo performers up in Montana.

"We call it our bulletproof starching," he'd said. The description had more meaning to me now that someone had taken a shot at my car. Maybe I should start wearing starched jeans and flak jackets to work.

"Those cowboys want their jeans starched until they practically stand alone," the Montana cleaner had said.

The idea of stand-alone jeans seemed downright painful to me. Who in their right mind would want jeans that sounded that uncomfortable to wear?

When we starched jeans, we threw a heavy liquid solution into the final wash. Light, medium, or heavy starch on request. After that, the presser would tug each pants leg into perfect seam alignment before sending the press closed with a hiss of steam. The jeans would come out with a sharp, pressed look that no steam iron at home could do as well.

This meant that the jeans had creases down the front of the legs, just like a pair of dress pants. However, with jeans, the creases were set in place with eventual fade lines that made them permanent.

Why men would want creases in their jeans was beyond me. I tended to agree with George Carlin, who'd once listed types of people who should be "phased out." Two of the people on his list were "guys with creases in their jeans" and "men who wear loafers with jeans—especially if they have creases in their jeans."

You're getting off the subject, Mandy. Forget about George Carlin. Concentrate on Ardith, I told myself. I shook my head to clear my mind and get myself back on track. This had to be what she'd meant when she'd described the sharp creases in her lover's pants. They were sharp all right. No wonder Mack and I had been thrown off by her description at first, but now it all made sense. This had to be the answer.

I couldn't help thinking of something else Nadine had said that first day at the bank. She'd told me Ardith's only living relative was a brother who lived in Texas and hadn't seen her for years. It had made me sad at the time, but maybe it should have been my first clue. What if she'd grown up in the wide-open spaces on a ranch in Texas and that's why she'd had an immediate attraction to a man in jeans—especially starched jeans? She might even have been involved in rodeo. It didn't tell me much about the killer—except maybe that was why he hog-tied his victims—but at least it could explain her interest in someone who seemed so different from her adult persona.

Traffic picked up with Saturday shoppers as I neared Park Meadows, an upscale shopping mall on the southern edge of the Denver area. When I was a child, this had been open space, too, just like the rolling country where I had decided Ardith had grown up.

Now the whole area was covered with sprawling homes in a proliferation of housing developments. They continued almost nonstop to Colorado Springs, eighty miles to the south of Denver, where a big chunk of the land was taken over by the Air Force Academy.

Castle Rock was less than twenty miles away, however, and as I approached, I could see the hill with a rim of rock at the top that gave the town its name. With all the urban sprawl, it was hard to believe there was a cowboy in the vicinity, much less a big western-wear store.

I took a look at my watch, the clock inside the van having quit running long ago. It was 5:50. I wished I knew exactly which exit to take to get to the store. I thought it was before I reached an outlet mall that was one of the attractions that brought people to the area.

Just as I sailed by one off-ramp, I spotted Harvey's store to the west of the highway. I had to go to the next exit and backtrack to the store.

I pulled in the parking lot at a few minutes before closing time and parked the van in front of what looked like an old-fashioned hitching post. However, the only horse in sight was a mechanical pony—not a mechanical bull. It was on a wooden porch leading to the entrance and was for children to ride at a nickel a pop.

The top of the log rail had half a dozen saddles draped over it, and a young woman was hauling one of them off the rail, apparently to take it inside for the night.

I jumped out of the van. "Is Harvey here yet?" I asked. "I'm Mandy Dyer, and I called a little while ago because I need to talk to him."

The woman, about the same age as Ann Marie, was wearing jeans and a short-sleeved shirt, and her blond hair was in two pig-tails that spilled over her shoulders as she bent to put the saddle back on the rail so she could answer me.

"I'm Kelly," she said, "and I'm the one who talked to you." She got another grip on the saddle. "Harvey's not here yet, but he should be coming any minute."

"Maybe I can help you with those." I motioned to the remaining saddles. I slung the strap of my bag over my shoulder and grabbed a hand-tooled saddle, which was heavier than I'd expected. I put it down, got a better grip, and hauled it into the store behind her.

The first thing I noticed when we got inside was the smell. It didn't remind me of horses or other livestock. Far from it. Instead, it was the wonderful scent of leather I'd smelled in brand-new and expensive cars with leather upholstery.

I breathed deeply and commented to Kelly about it.

"You get used to the smell," she said. "I never even notice."

We made two more trips to the hitching post for the rest of the saddles, and when we finished, she gave me a grin that lighted up her face. She had a gap between her front teeth and a bunch of freckles across her sunburned nose. I decided she must spend a lot of time in the outdoors when she wasn't working at the store.

"Thanks for helping me get those saddles inside," she said. "I think that's Harvey's truck now."

I glanced out the front window. A green mud-spattered pickup had just pulled up beside my van. Harvey jumped down from the driver's seat and headed for the door.

Today the heavyset owner was wearing jeans, a shirt with snaps down the front, cowboy boots, and a white straw hat. In fact, he was a walking advertisement for his place of business.

"Well, if it ain't Miss Mandy from the cleaners," he said as soon as he got inside. "What can I do you for?"

"I need to find out something about starched jeans," I said, looking down at his worn denims. I was relieved to see that they didn't have the telltale sign of a whitened crease running down the front. I probably should have had Theresa look him up in our computer, but he didn't actually use our services anymore, since he'd moved his store to this location.

"I'm particularly interested in finding out what kind of man wears them and if you have any idea where he would have been wearing them back in March," I said.

Harvey didn't seem concerned about why I wanted to know. He had an audience, and he was off and running, although Kelly had a puzzled look on her face at the question.

"Well, it all started with rodeo performers," he said. "They're the ones who like starched jeans."

I nodded to indicate that I knew that, but he didn't seem to notice.

"They like 'em because they think their Wranglers look nice if they're starched, and besides, the jeans stay lookin' fresh out on the road for a day or two when they're making the rodeo circuit."

Kelly giggled. "They wear them for way longer than a day or two sometimes."

Harvey remained oblivious to what she'd said. "Personally, I think starched jeans are pretty much for dress, but some ranch hands claim they like them, too, because the jeans last longer. I don't happen to think that's true. They also say the jeans don't get so much dust and dirt on them when the cowboys are working with livestock."

Kelly interrupted again. "I heard that a big rodeo down in Texas even has a 'Starched Jeans' contest where the contestants walk around the center ring of the arena in their extra-long, heavily starched jeans so the audience can pick a winner. I figure the guy with the best-looking butt wins."

She and Nadine were on the same wavelength, but none of this was helping me. Not one of my suspects lived on a ranch, either, as far as I could tell.

"You do know that Wranglers are the jeans of choice by rodeo performers, don't you?" Harvey asked.

"Not Levi's?" I guess I was showing my city-girl upbringing.

He shook his head. "No siree. Levi's may be the most famous clothing label in the world, but it went upscale a long time ago. Levi's are known as *mall* jeans these days."

Apparently, he disdained the concept of selling to the general public, and he didn't give me a chance to get back on the subject of who wore starched jeans and why.

"Nope, Wrangler started to conquer the real cowboy market way back in the forties. It signed on as a sponsor of the Rodeo Cowboys Association, and through some shrewd promotions and giveaways, it became undisputed king of rodeo by the eighties.

"So what did you want to know about them exactly?" Kelly asked.

Bless her. She must have realized her boss had a tendency to ramble.

"I really wanted to know where a guy would wear them around here." I said.

"I'll tell you who wears them," Kelly said. "Guys who go to country bars."

Harvey frowned at her and went on. "One of the things about Wrangler jeans is that they were designed to be longer than Levi's way back when," he said. "The cowboys liked them because they looked good when the cowboys were in the saddle."

Now it was my turn to interrupt. "Excuse me, but what was it you said about country bars, Kelly?" I had a stabbing sensation in the pit of my stomach, like I imagined being gored by a bull would feel. Wasn't that where Brett Harrison had wanted to take Ann Marie? "Do you mean a place like the Last Roundup?"

Kelly nodded, and I knew I needed to call Theresa as soon as I got out of there. If she hadn't had time for anything else, I needed her to look up Brett Harrison's name in our computer.

"There are several country bars around Denver," Kelly said, "and they all have kind of an unofficial dress code about what guys wear when they go there."

"Like what?"

"Oh, you know, starched Wranglers, long-sleeved button-down plaid shirts, and boots. Black felt cowboy hats in the winter and straw hats in the summer."

"Button-down shirts? You mean like oxford dress shirts with buttons in the collar?"

"Yeah." She went over to a rack and showed me one.

I was glad Ardith hadn't mentioned button-down shirts, or it would have thrown Mack and me even further off track. Who would have imagined button-down shirts for cowboys?

"I'm just curious," Kelly said. "Why are you interested in all this?"

I should have been thinking of a good reason on the drive down to Castle Rock. I tried to come up with one off the top of my head. "Uh . . . I'm thinking of trying to develop a sideline by starting to advertise that we starch jeans at my dry cleaners."

"Okay?" The word definitely had a question mark after it. Obviously, she wondered why I would rush out to Harvey's at closing time, saying it was important that I talk to him.

Before she had a chance to ask any more questions, I rushed on. "Do you think I'd get a lot of business if I advertised?"

"Not really," she said. "A lot of guys starch the jeans themselves when they wash them, run an iron over them, and then hang them on a line to air-dry. And some guys just use spray starch when they iron them. At least that's what my boyfriend does."

That was information I hadn't really wanted to hear. It meant I might not be able to track down a starched-jeans wearer in our computer, but I still needed to call Theresa before she closed.

"Hey, thanks for the information," I said, glancing at my watch again. It was already 6:30. "I need to go, and I know it's already past your closing time."

"That's all right," Harvey said. "We got plenty of time." Apparently, he was in no hurry to leave, despite the fact that he was on his way to his cabin. "Don't let Kelly here fool you. A lot of men still favor cowboy shirts with snaps instead of buttons."

Kelly must have been anxious to leave, too. She walked me to the door and said good-bye.

I hurried to the van and got out of the parking lot as fast as I could. I was afraid she might get even more curious about the reason for my visit if I sat outside the store and made phone calls. Besides, I needed to scratch all my itches.

I drove down the road beside the interstate until I saw a restaurant. I pulled into the parking lot and called Theresa from there.

"It's Mandy," I said once I got her on the line. "Did you find out anything?"

"I was just about to call you. Mel Sutton and Cal Ingalls have both brought us jeans to be laundered and starched—Mel a couple of weeks ago, but Cal not since February."

Hmmm. Cal hadn't done it since the open house, when Ardith talked to Julia. That could be significant, except Cal said he hadn't been at the open house.

Frankly, I was hoping no one had brought us their jeans, but thanks to Kelly, I now knew that the information didn't necessarily mean the other people didn't starch their jeans at home. For all I knew, the grungy guy could be a meticulous jeans wearer. All I'd ever seen, though, was his face and his unshaved chin when he'd been sitting in his car.

"What about Brett Harrison?" I asked.

"I couldn't find anything on him."

"Well, thanks." I started to hang up.

"Did that help?"

"I'll let you know." I hit the button to end the call because I had a couple more calls to make.

I rang the Crimes Against Persons division at the Police Administration Building first.

"May I speak to Detective Ivinson?" I asked. Come to think of it, why hadn't he called me earlier in the day? After all, I'd given his name to the officer the previous night, after someone took a shot at me.

"He isn't here now," the man on the other end of the line said. "Do you want to leave a message on his voice mail?"

"No, I need someone to get a message to him right now."

"Okay, shoot."

Not a comforting thought, but I spilled out the complicated story of Ardith's death and my involvement in the case anyway. "I think the killer might have been wearing starched jeans," I said finally.

I got the distinct impression the guy was trying to suppress a laugh.

"Go on," he said finally.

I told him what Julia had remembered about Ardith's comment the day of the open house and how a check of our computer showed that two of my suspects had brought us their jeans to be washed and starched.

I gave him their names, knowing full well that one of them was a cop, and asked for his name in return. I didn't think he was going to tell me for a minute, maybe on the assumption that I was a nutcase.

"I'm Detective Willis, and I'll give Detective Ivinson the message."

"Thanks." I was relieved when the call was over—especially because I hadn't gotten Stan Foster or Jack Reilly on the phone. Both of them thought I was way too involved in police business, although Stan, whom I'd dated for a while, wasn't quite as nasty about it as Reilly. If I weren't careful, I'd soon be running out of detectives to talk to who didn't know me.

I had one more call to make before I headed home. I needed to reassure myself that Ann Marie was okay. Fortunately, I'd brought my address book with me, and I dug it out of my shoulder bag. I looked up her home number. I knew she still lived with her parents, and when an older-sounding woman answered the phone, I asked to speak to Ann Marie.

"She's not here right now, but this is her mother."

"This is Mandy Dyer from work. I need to get in touch with her right away."

"Oh, Miss Dyer. I'm sorry, but she's out for the evening, and she didn't take her cell phone with her."

"Do you know where she went?"

"Yes, she went out with a nice young man she met at the cleaners. You probably know him—Brett Harrison."

I felt as if another bull had gored me in the stomach. Ann Marie had promised me she wouldn't go out with Brett until after this was over. Well, maybe it was more like I'd told her not to, and she'd fibbed earlier this afternoon when she said she was going to hang out with her girlfriends later.

"Do you know where they went, by any chance?"

"Oh, yes. She said they were going to a place called the Last Roundup."

Damn. Damn. Damn. I couldn't go home yet—not until I went to the Last Roundup and corralled Ann Marie.

Before I went rushing off, I made another phone call to Detective Willis. He answered the phone in the Crimes Against Persons section, and I gave my name. I reminded him that I'd just called him a few minutes earlier, but he seemed to remember me without an explanation.

"I found out another person to add to the list I just gave you—Brett Harrison," I said. "I learned he's at the Last Roundup—you know, the country bar—with one of my employees, and she could be in trouble. I'm hoping you can send someone out there and take him in for questioning." I took a big breath when I'd finished.

"Have you starched a pair of jeans for him, too?" Either Willis had just taken a bite of food at his desk or he was trying to choke down a laugh.

"No, I haven't," I said in my most no-nonsense voice, "but I found out that a lot of men starch their own jeans at home. Nevertheless, he *does* have a connection to my business. He's a customer and he's taking a friend of mine to the Last Roundup tonight. I'm hoping Detective Ivinson will want someone to investigate."

"Okay, lady, we'll look into it."

"Thanks." I hung up before he had a chance to ask any ques-

tions to delay my own trip to the country bar or dance hall—
whatever generic name there was for such a place.

I had only a vague idea of how to get there, but fortunately, we
kept a set of phone books in the back of the van in case our deliv-
eryman got lost on his route. I climbed between the seats, found
one of the books, and checked the address.

The Last Roundup was off Interstate 70, in the general vicinity of
the Coliseum. That made sense, because the Coliseum was where the
National Western Stock Show and Rodeo was held each January. The
city was usually overrun with cowboys and ranchers during that
time, and afterward, the prize bull was put on display in the lobby of
the elegant Brown Palace Hotel—which just showed we weren't as
far from our western roots as we sometimes liked to think we were.

I got back on Interstate 25 for the return trip through town. All
the way, I kept thinking how I should simply have talked to Kelly on
the phone. I could have gotten all the information I needed and
maybe done it in time to keep Ann Marie from going out with Brett.

When I got to I-70, I merged into the eastbound lane of traffic. As
soon as I saw the Coliseum, a gigantic rounded version of a Quonset
hut, I started looking for an exit. A few minutes later, I located the
Last Roundup on a side street north of the Stock Show complex.

I guess I'd been expecting a building that looked like Campbell's
Western Wear, only larger. Instead of a rough wooden exterior and a
hitching post out front, it actually looked like a converted warehouse,
a two-story gray building with a few windows up near the roof.

The only evidence that it was a country bar was a sign out by the
street. It said it was the Last Roundup and was surrounded by the
loop of a noose suitable for a hanging. Okay, maybe it was just a lar-
iat and I was reading ominous messages into everything I saw. Near
the main entrance, there was a mural of a bronco rider on a bucking
horse. At least that seemed a little more welcoming to me.

The parking lot was so full that I had trouble finding a place for
the van. Once I had maneuvered into a small space between a
pickup and a Jeep, I surveyed the lot. Not a single police car in evi-

dence. Damn. I wondered if Willis had decided this was all a joke, but I decided to give him the benefit of the doubt. Maybe the cops just hadn't arrived yet. Sure, I said to myself, and if you believe that, you probably believe that the Cartwrights really lived on a ranch called the Ponderosa. I knew darned well the police could have gotten to the bar before I'd made my way from Castle Rock.

I joined the herd of people heading for the entrance like cattle being prodded into a truck for a trip to the slaughterhouse. Perhaps that wasn't a good analogy, but that's the way it felt.

I paid a five-dollar cover charge and was swept along with the crowd trying to get inside. At least the rough-hewn interior was more like what I'd expected, although I still didn't see a mechanical bull. That was a disappointment. However, a split-log railing went around the outside of a huge dance floor, separating the tables from the dancers.

Another railing surrounded a central bar, crowded with people getting drinks, and there seemed to be smaller bars at a number of locations around the darkened exterior walls of the building. And everywhere there were people, so many that it made me feel claustrophobic.

I could tell I was going to have a difficult time spotting Ann Marie, and I looked around for a good vantage point from which to survey the crowd. I finally spotted steps leading to a balcony, where I could see a few spectators looking over the railing at the activities below.

Once I made my way upstairs, I parked myself at a table where I could look over the railing. The dancers were going around the middle bar in a circle. Actually, it was more like a huge oval, and as I soon discovered, if I watched long enough, I would see the same couples come around again like horses on a carousel. And the weirdest thing about it was that the women were always going backward.

"Are you waitin' for someone, or are you here alone?" The voice startled me.

"Excuse me?" I glanced to my right.

"In other words, do you want to dance?" asked a tall, lanky man in his forties. His attire fit the dress code Kelly had described, right down to the creases in his stiff-looking jeans. He was wearing a straw hat, which adhered to the other rule Kelly had mentioned— black hats only in the winter.

"No, I'm just watching," I said.

"If you don't know how to do the two-step, I'd be glad to teach you."

"The two-step. Is that what they're doing?"

The man looked surprised. "Is this your first time here?"

I nodded and turned my attention back to the dance floor, hoping to spot Ann Marie.

"Why don't the women ever get to go forward?" I asked.

"It's just the way you do the two-step."

"Well, it seems pretty discriminatory that we're the only ones who have to go backward," I said, starting to mount my women's rights soapbox. I even thought about asking why the men kept their hats on when they were out on the dance floor, but I let it go.

The music stopped, and the man began to edge away from me, apparently having decided I was too women's lib for him. A deejay I couldn't see from the balcony began to play "Rock Around the Clock" over a too-loud sound system. "We'll now clear the floor for some line dancing," he yelled above the music. "So get out there, girls, and shake your stuff."

I was on a mission now. "Why don't the guys have to shake their stuff, too?" I asked.

"Real cowboys don't line dance," the man said, and I expected him to flex his muscles at any moment.

I cut off the conversation and concentrated on looking for Ann Marie. A bunch of women, all with long, flowing hair, had come out on the dance floor. One of them could have been Ann Marie if she'd decided not to wear her hair in her usual ponytail. Unfortunately, the line was forming at a far corner of the floor, and the participants were facing away from me. They looked like the Rockettes trying to do an Irish jig.

I squinted to get a better look. A bottle blonde with a bouffant hairdo drew my attention. She was more rotund than the other dancers in line. If I didn't know better, I would swear— No, it couldn't be. It was against all odds that it could be my mother. I was having hallucinations because I'd forgotten to call her for Nat after the shooting the previous night. Besides, this woman was wearing jeans. I'd never seen my mother in jeans, although the shiny silver shirt looked like something she might have in her wardrobe.

The cowboy must have decided to give me another chance. "So what about it? After this is over, want me to teach you the two-step?"

I didn't need to learn the two-step. I already felt as if I were falling backward into the Grand Canyon. Never mind Ann Marie. I couldn't take my eyes off the woman with the pouffy hair.

"Sorry," I said. "I have to go." With that, I pounded down the stairs and headed toward the line dancers at the other end of the building.

Good Lord, it was my mother, and even though I had no idea why she'd come, I had a feeling I wouldn't like the reason when I found out.

I charged onto the dance floor as if possessed. "What in the name of—" I sputtered, at a loss for words. I started again. "Would you mind telling me what you're doing here?"

Mom kept dancing. "I might ask you the same question." She sounded slightly out of breath.

I motioned away from the dance floor. "Would you get over here? I need to talk to you."

Reluctantly, Mom dropped her hands from her hips and followed me off the floor.

"I repeat: What are you doing here?"

Mom fluffed her hair, as if the dancing had rearranged her heavily hair-sprayed coiffure. "If you must know, I'm helping out an acquaintance."

The fact that she said acquaintance, not friend, meant it could only be one person.

"I told you not to involve Betty in one of your crazy schemes." My voice shook with irritation.

Mom stuck her nose in the air and went over to a table with a mug of beer on it. "Look," she said, "I was bored. I never could get in touch with Laura all day, and then Betty called. She said she was without transportation tonight because her car was in the garage. She thought we could both help you out by following a man who might have something to do with the murder. So you see, this was *her* idea, not *mine*."

Mom gave a satisfied smile and took a dainty sip of the beer, a drink I'd never seen her order before. This was a whole new side of her personality, but I didn't care to contemplate it at the moment.

"You mean the man came here?"

Mom nodded.

I couldn't believe it. Maybe I was on the completely wrong track.

"So where is your cohort in crime?" I asked, every word dripping with sarcasm.

Mom motioned toward a door on the other side of the building. "She's outside watching the man. She's sure something is going down tonight, but he's just sitting in his car. I got tired of that, so I came inside to watch all the fun. Herb's going to be sorry he didn't come along when I tell him where we wound up. I told you, didn't I, that Herb and I do line dancing at the clubhouse in our condo complex down in Phoenix?"

I stopped just short of saying that real men don't line dance, but that would have been petty. Besides, I needed to find Betty and give her a piece of what was left of my mind.

I'd told Ann Marie not to go out with Brett, and I'd ordered Betty not to follow the grungy guy. Why didn't anyone ever listen to me? Still, I had to admit that it was interesting that Betty's guy had wound up at the same place and at the same time as Brett and Ann Marie. And I couldn't help remembering that the grungy guy had taken off after Brett the previous night. Maybe they got together at the Last Roundup every night. But why?

"Stay here," I ordered Mom before I set off on the crowded cement walkway between the tables and the dance floor. Halfway to the door that led to the parking lot, where Betty was apparently staking out her "perp," I spotted someone who was just as much of a shock as Mom—Cal Ingalls. I might have missed him if he'd been wearing a hat. Besides, he'd told me he was heading for Wyoming right after we talked the previous day, so what was he doing in the bar?

I still didn't believe in coincidences, but this was getting more eerie by the moment. I pretended to bump into his shoulder as he was getting a couple of beers.

"Whoops," I said as some of the beer spilled out of one of the mugs and dribbled down the front of his button-down shirt to the floor. As I looked down at the damage I'd caused, it gave me an opportunity to check for creases in his jeans. Sure enough, they were there. I followed the crease lines to the floor, and that's how I happened to notice his cowboy boots. They looked exactly like the ones Herb had been wearing Thursday night, and I couldn't take my eyes off them for a moment.

"Sorry," I said when I finally glanced back up at his face, pretending to see him for the first time. "Cal, what are you doing here? I thought you were in Wyoming."

He was busy wiping himself off, and he looked irritated at the clumsy stranger who'd done this to him. He stopped when he recognized me, but he still didn't look happy to see me. "Mandy," he said. "Fancy meeting you here."

"Why aren't you in Wyoming?"

He pulled a handkerchief out of his pocket to finish wiping the front of his shirt, and with it, a little plastic Baggie filled with white powder fell to the floor. He swooped it up so fast that I wasn't sure I'd actually seen it.

"I had a change of plans," he said as he put the Baggie back in his pocket. "I've got to go before I spill the rest of my beers."

Just as he started to leave, a woman came up to us and looked me up and down, as if I might be trying to steal her man. "I wondered if you were ever going to come back with our drinks, honey," she said, tossing her reddish brown hair back from her face, the better to give me the once-over.

She looked vaguely familiar, and I extended my hand. "Hi, I'm Mandy Dyer, Cal's dry cleaner," I said, figuring that ought to put her mind at ease.

"I'm Karla Smith—with a *K*—Cal's girlfriend, and—"

Cal didn't let her finish. Maybe he was afraid I'd tell her what I'd seen fall out of his pocket. "Come on, sweetie," he said as he placed both beers in one hand, slopping a little more of the liquid down the front of his shirt, "let's get back to the table before I drop these drinks."

"Nice meeting you," I said as he grabbed her hand and yanked her away.

I would probably never see him again. That's what had happened one time when I'd checked the pockets of a customer's pants before he left the call office and found a similar Baggie with white powder in it. The man grabbed the Baggie and fled the cleaners; he never came back for his pants.

I started toward the door again, but suddenly I stopped. Something was wrong. It was Cal's boots. Something about the boots. They were the same as Herb's, and as Mom had informed me, they were made of ostrich skin and had a strange dotted pattern on them that reminded her of pimples. Herb had called the skin "a full quill," which he said had to do with the tiny puckers where the feathers had been pulled out.

Cal's boots had the same full quill on the pointed toes, and suddenly I knew what was bothering me. Maybe Julia's dog, Rambo, couldn't tell the difference in the boots, either.

Oh my God. Did that mean Rambo's attack on Herb didn't have

anything to do with his hatred of ostriches or a dislike of men, or, as I'd so facetiously thought, that he'd gone ballistic when Herb mentioned that he'd brought me a doggie bag? Maybe it meant that Herb's boots reminded the little dog of the person who'd tried to strangle his mistress. The thought sent a chill ratcheting through my body.

If Cal had been Julia's attacker, it had to mean he'd been afraid she would remember something about that day at the open house. Perhaps he'd even been standing beside Ardith when she'd asked Julia if we laundered and starched jeans, and he was afraid she'd eventually connect the dots, or the "full quills," as it turned out.

I thought about the way he'd yanked back a pair of jeans the day I asked Jason if he'd been at the open house; Cal had said he mistakenly brought them into the cleaners on his way to the coin-op laundry, but maybe he'd wanted us to launder and starch them and then thought better of it.

The chill I'd just felt turned into an icy stab through my heart when I thought about his girlfriend. Was it possible that she seemed familiar because she reminded me of Ardith with her chestnut-colored hair? Yes, she'd definitely had the same general appearance as Ardith, and if he were selecting the same type to kill over and over again, it could mean she was the next victim on his list.

I glanced around the huge room. Cal and his girlfriend had disappeared. I started off in the direction they'd gone, trying to scan both the tables and the dance floor as I went. I didn't see them, and I knew I couldn't waste any more time.

I pulled out my cell phone and tried to call Detective Willis, but the phone wouldn't work inside the building. Besides, I probably couldn't have heard him if I had gotten through to him. I was standing directly under a loudspeaker. All I could hear was Randy Travis blasting out the words to "King of the Road."

I knew I'd have to go outside if I wanted to use the phone. I hurried to the door I'd been heading for when I ran into Cal. It led to a deck above another parking lot at the back of the building, and I was dumbstruck with what I saw when I got outside. Half a dozen police cars and assorted other vehicles had pulled up in a semicircle around a sports car that looked suspiciously like Brett Harrison's.

No, please, I was wrong. Brett Harrison isn't the killer. I wanted to shout this at the cops, but the words stuck in my throat. The police were going to be furious with me after this, and I wondered if I could be charged with causing them to make a false arrest.

Brett was on the ground, being handcuffed by an officer in uniform. Worse yet, Betty in her basic-black cords and sweatshirt was being held back by another cop a few feet away, and she was pointing to an unshaven man in tattered jeans and yelling at the top of her lungs, "No, damn it, you got the wrong guy. It's the grungy guy over there."

TWENTY

For a minute, I thought the police were going to throw Betty to the ground and cuff her the way they'd just done to Brett.

Instead, Grungy Guy, who seemed to be involved in the action, pointed to one of the officers near Betty and yelled, "Get her out of here—now."

That's when I had a comic-strip moment. A lightbulb went on over my head, and I realized he must be an undercover cop, not a killer or even a small-time crook. Was that why I'd been getting mixed messages from the police about his license plate?

The light above my head dimmed and burned out after that. "What's going on?" I asked a bystander.

"They're making a drug bust," the spectator said. "I've seen the guy around here before. Someone said he's been dealing drugs from out here in the parking lot."

Okay, that probably explained Brett's fancy car on a waiter's salary, and maybe it meant I wasn't going to be charged with triggering a false arrest. It also might be the reason Cal had been here tonight and why I'd seen him talking to Brett occasionally outside the cleaners. Brett was probably his supplier, and Grungy Guy had been tailing him because he was dealing drugs.

I still needed to talk to one of the cops about Cal. The one who was in the process of hauling Betty toward me seemed like a good prospect. A tag on his uniform said his name was Blakely.

"She's with me," I said as they approached. "I'll see that she doesn't bother you again."

"Let go of me, copper." She yanked her arm out of the man's grasp.

I cringed. She was going to get herself arrested for sure if she didn't calm down.

"Betty, it's me," I said.

She didn't even seem surprised to see me. Maybe she thought I'd appeared by some sort of magic.

"Tell him, boss lady," she yelled. "Tell him they got the wrong guy."

I leaned over toward her. "Shut up, Betty," I said between clenched teeth. "I know who the killer is, and it isn't him."

That stopped her, and once she quieted down, the policeman started to walk away.

"No, you can't go yet." My voice sounded almost as loud as Betty's had.

The officer turned back to me in surprise. Before he could get away, I blurted out that I knew the name of the killer in the case Detective Ivinson was working on. It took a lot of explanation, but finally someone seemed to believe me, especially when I told him that the man was inside with a date who could be his next victim.

I struggled to remember the woman's name. Oh, yes, Karla "with a K" Smith. I prayed she'd be listed in the phone book, but with a name like Smith, it could be hard to find her. Unless her name was in our computer at work. I shuddered. Why hadn't I thought of that before? No doubt because I was trying to repress the possibility, but maybe that's why I'd thought I recognized her, not because of her resemblance to Ardith. I didn't want to mention it to the police until I was sure. I vowed to go to my office and check in our database the moment I left the Last Roundup.

Blakely said he'd have to consult with his superior and he'd be right back.

"Hurry," I said, "before the man leaves." Of course, Cal was probably long gone, if for no other reason than he knew I'd seen him drop the little Baggie out of his pocket.

Betty was in my face the moment he left. "What about the grungy guy?"

I tried to explain about the drug bust and the fact that her number-one suspect appeared to be a narc or some other type of undercover cop.

"Is that true? Is that a drug bust down there?" she demanded when the officer returned a few minutes later.

He nodded and told her to step away from where we were standing. She did so reluctantly, and once she had moved a few feet away, he said he'd called and informed a homicide detective of what I'd said. He added that he needed to get a statement from me right now.

"But he may be gone if we wait," I said, ignoring my own best guess that Cal had taken off a few seconds after I bumped into him.

The officer wasn't having any of that. "I'm going to go in with you to look for him as soon as we get through out here."

I fidgeted while he wrote down what I said. When we were through and I signed my name to the statement, I motioned to Betty. She dropped her hand from where it had been cupped over her ear, obviously in an attempt to eavesdrop on our conversation.

"Maybe my friend here can help us look for him," I said.

I was well aware that she didn't know what Cal looked like, but it didn't matter. I wanted to keep her in my sight so she wouldn't get into any more trouble. Fortunately, she didn't protest, just stomped along behind us as we circled around the bar several times.

We didn't find Cal or his girlfriend. No surprise. However, I couldn't be sure but what they were still inside. The place had become even more of a mob scene than when I'd arrived.

The person we did find was Ann Marie. Actually, she found us.

She'd been sitting at a table by herself, and when she saw me, she came rushing over to us. She didn't even seem to notice that I was with a cop.

Her eyes filled with tears. "You were right, Mandy. I never should have gone out with Brett. I think he dumped me for someone else. I've been waiting for him for hours and hours, and he hasn't come back."

I didn't think this was the moment to tell her that Brett was a drug dealer and had just been arrested. Instead, I said I'd see that she got home. Mom might as well make herself useful on her "girls' night out" by doing the chauffeuring.

As soon as the officer decided to give up our search, he left, and I set out to find Mom, with Betty and Ann Marie in tow. It was a lot easier than looking for Cal, because I at least knew where she'd been sitting. Only trouble was, she wasn't there. Her beer, hardly touched, was still on the table.

Betty plopped down in a chair, and for a moment, I thought she was going to grab the beer and swig it down. "Whoee, some kind of night, huh?" she said to no one in particular. "Your ma missed out on all the fun."

It wasn't my idea of fun, especially since I still had to explain to Ann Marie about Brett. I asked her to have a seat. "I hate to tell you this, but your date was just arrested outside for dealing drugs."

To her credit, Ann Marie looked appalled. "I'm sorry, Mandy. I should have listened to you," she said finally.

"You don't seem to have a lot of smarts when it comes to men, do you?" Betty offered, which didn't help the situation at all.

Ann Marie began to cry. "What am I going to tell Mom?"

"Just tell her the truth, for criminy sakes," Betty said. Words of wisdom from a former bag lady.

And speaking of mothers, I wondered where the devil mine was. I needed to get out of the bar and go to the office, and I didn't want to have to deal with Betty any more right then.

She must have seen me begin to look around the cavernous interior. If Mom had gone to the restroom, she should be back by now.

"I just saw old Cece go fancy footin' it around out there." Betty motioned toward the dance floor.

"Why didn't you say something?"

"I didn't know you was lookin' for her."

I went to the railing and waited for my two-stepping mother to come by again. Darned if she wasn't dancing with the guy I'd been talking to upstairs. He must have followed me down the stairs and latched onto Mom. "Hey, over here," I yelled when I spotted her. "We need to go."

She waved at me and danced right on by.

On the next go-round, I was ready for her. I went out on the floor, prepared to trip her if necessary. "Mom," I said, tapping her on the shoulder and halting her backward progress—an oxymoron for sure. "We have to leave now."

"So soon," she said as her partner maneuvered them over to the rail. "Well, thank you, Jim Bob." She batted her eyelashes at him, which was second nature to her. "That was fun, but I better go. My daughter always gets so impatient when she wants to leave."

I frowned and waited for her to follow me off the floor, glad she hadn't thought of the fact that we had two separate vehicles. "I need you to do a favor for me and take Ann Marie home," I said.

She glanced over at the table and must have recognized Ann Marie from the cleaners. "What's she doing here?"

"Her date abandoned her." It seemed like the easiest explanation.

"Oh, the poor child." Mom was the complete opposite of Betty when it came to romance, but she was practical, too. "Where does she live?"

That was the hard part. "I think she lives out in Arvada."

Unfortunately, Mom knew that was one of the northwestern suburbs. She glanced at her watch. "I need to get back to the hotel and call Laura. I can only keep that bridesmaid dress until Monday, and she needs to take a look at it. I'm sure she'll love it. It has puffed sleeves and a hooped skirt."

Poor Laura, or actually, poor me, since I was the designated maid of honor and bridesmaid rolled into one.

"Getting back to Ann Marie . . ." I said.

Mom considered my request for a few seconds. "All right. I'll take the poor little thing home, but you have to take Betty."

I should have seen that one coming.

"She was so annoying on the way out here," Mom said. "She kept yelling at me to go faster, slow down, take corners on two wheels. It's a wonder we got here in one piece."

I knew the feeling, and I had three traffic violations to prove it.

"By the way, did the man we were chasing turn out to be the killer?"

"No." I wasn't up to telling her the whole story at the moment, and when I thought about it, maybe it was better that she didn't hear it from Betty. "Okay, I'll take her home, and thanks for looking after Ann Marie."

Once Betty and I got inside the van, she said, "Well, I was right about one thing, wasn't I?"

"What do you mean?" I asked as I grabbed the phone book from behind the driver's seat.

"I got you out here so you could run into that other fella. That's why I had your ma call you and tell you where we were. I knew in my bones somethin' was goin' to happen tonight."

So that explained why Betty hadn't been surprised when she saw me. She didn't know I was already at the bar and unable to get a signal on my cell phone. I decided to let her take credit for it, because I had the headache from hell and didn't feel like trying to explain it.

I could hardly see the names when I ran my flashlight down the

Smith columns in the phone book. Rows and rows of Smiths, and none of them Karla with a *K*.

I tossed the phone book back behind the seat. "Look, I have to stop at the cleaners before I take you home." I started the van.

"Fine with me. Long as I don't have to do no work." She was silent for a moment. "Guess you want to take a look to see if that fella's date was one of our customers, huh?"

She'd obviously heard a lot more than the police officer or I realized when he was taking my statement. I tried to tune her out as she continued her monologue about the killer. It was as if she'd had a bugging device hidden in my purse, instead of a hand cupped over her ear. Talk about acute hearing.

"So what if you're wrong about this guy, the way we were about the grungy guy?" she asked.

I gripped the steering wheel. "Can we just drop the subject right now?"

"Guess you don't want to think about it, huh?"

"No talking. Please."

"Okay. Swell."

Why did Betty have to raise doubts in my mind? Could I be wrong about Cal the way I'd been about Brett? Maybe Rambo hadn't made a connection between Herb's boots and those of the person who'd attacked his owner. What did I know about dogs anyway? And maybe the only reason Cal had acted funny when I'd run into him was because I'd seen the Baggie fall out of his pocket.

The only other clue I had about the killer was what Nat had told me—that the police thought he was a smoker, because he'd left a dirty ashtray or saucer by the side of the bed after he killed each of his victims.

I couldn't help thinking how Julia had always called Cal the Marlboro Man. Was it only because of his appearance, or was there more to it than that?

I pulled over to a side street when we started across Sixth Avenue from the freeway. Betty was already asleep by the time I reached for my cell phone. When it lighted up, I noticed that I had a message. Mom's call, no doubt. I ignored it and dialed Julia's number, which, fortunately, I remembered from all the times I'd called her. She answered it herself, which I took as a sign that she was feeling better.

"I know this sounds like a dumb question, but why did you call Cal the Marlboro Man?" I asked.

"Oh, that," she said. "Well, he used to have a cigarette in his mouth when he came in the cleaners, just like the guy in the billboards. When we changed to a no-smoking call office, I'd always have to remind him to go back outside and get rid of it. One time, he apologized and said he only smoked when he was under a lot of stress."

A trip to the cleaners would hardly seem stressful, I thought, unless you were scoping out customers to be your next victim.

"Why'd you want to know?" Julia asked. "Does it have something to do with the murders?"

"I'll tell you later. I promise. And thanks a lot." I hit the button to end the call. Somehow what she'd said reassured me. I bet he smoked after sex, too, especially when he was planning to kill his lover soon afterward. That sounded like major stress to me.

I pulled back into the lane of traffic. Betty was snoring big-time by then. I thought of letting her sleep when I parked behind the cleaners, but she snorted awake, followed me through the back door of the plant, and waited while I locked the door behind us and attended to the alarm.

When we reached my office, she flopped down on the sofa that was at the side of the room, and I booted up the computer and put in the name Karla Smith. Please don't be there, I prayed. I didn't want to be responsible for Cal meeting another potential victim at the cleaners.

The name flipped up on the screen. A Karla Smith with a *K* had been in several times over the last few months, and she lived not far away. She'd given her address, followed by an apartment number.

I couldn't sit still. I got up and paced. When I finally calmed down, I grabbed my cell phone and placed another call to the police. This time, I got a Sergeant Haggerty. I was tired of having to keep explaining the whole story, but I finally got to the end, went back to my desk, and gave him the woman's address.

"I'm afraid she might be in real danger, so I hope you can send a patrol car over there to check on her right now," I said, and hung up. I was getting good at ending conversations, and in this case, it was my fervent wish that I would never have to talk to the police again—not ever.

Before I could put the phone in my purse, it rang. Well, actually it chirped in one of the many irritating sounds it could be programmed to make.

Betty stirred but didn't wake up.

As soon as I answered, Mom said, "Amanda." It was always a bad sign when she called me by my full name. Besides, she sounded as if she'd been crying. "I have *terrible* news."

My hand began to shake. "Are you and Ann Marie okay?"

"Of course." Mom sounded surprised. "It's about Laura and Nat."

I couldn't help remembering how she'd said she couldn't get in touch with Laura all day, and horrible images flashed through my mind of them crashing Nat's motorcycle in the mountains. "What happened to them?"

"They—" She began to sniffle again. "They called Herb while I was out. They flew to Las Vegas and got m-m-married, and now they're going to Hawaii on their honeymoon."

I was so relieved, I couldn't control myself. "Well, good for them." I could tell immediately that was the wrong thing to say.

"What do you mean? After all the effort I've been making to give them a nice wedding, they eloped." She said the last word as if it were something obscene.

I tried to backtrack. "I'm sorry, but maybe you can plan a nice party for them when they get back."

Mom was never down for long. "Hmmm," she said. "Not that it's going to be easy to forgive them, but I suppose I could. I could use the same western theme I was planning for the wedding, and Herb and I could teach everyone how to line dance. I'll have to think about it." With that, she hung up.

I went over and shook Betty awake. "Come on, Betty. I'll drive you home now."

She staggered to her feet and started to follow me out of the office, or so I thought. My cell phone, still in my hand, rang again as I was en route to the back door.

I punched the button and said hello.

"Thank God I found you." It was Travis. "I've been calling all over looking for you, and your cell phone wasn't working."

I couldn't believe it. I'd really lost it. I'd completely spaced out about the fact that he'd said he was going to call at eight o'clock.

"I'm sorry. Please forgive me. I'll make it up to you. I promise." I was beginning to overapologize, but I couldn't help myself.

"Are you all right?"

I had to make three tries before I was able to reset the alarm system. "Yes, but I have a lot to tell you. Can you meet me at that restaurant on Speer in half an hour?"

I looked back in the direction of my office. Betty wasn't behind me anymore.

"Come on, Betty," I yelled. "We're leaving."

I asked Travis to repeat what he'd just said. He started to answer just as I opened the back door. I didn't hear him this time, either.

Cal blocked the doorway.

Oh, damn. It had never occurred to me that I might be on his list of victims. I didn't even fit the profile.

"I knew if I waited long enough, you'd have to come out." He gave me a stiff-armed shove, sending me backward to the floor. "And hang up that damned phone."

I hit one of the buttons, hoping I wouldn't break the connection. It was the only thing I could think to do.

"Cal Ingalls," I yelled as I slipped the phone into my shoulder bag, speaker side up. "What are you doing here?"

He didn't answer. He pulled a rope taut in his hands. It had a noose on the end.

Y ou killed Ardith, didn't you, Cal?" I scooted away from him as fast as I could.

Maybe it wasn't the smartest thing to do—saying he'd killed Ardith, but I wanted to leave a record for Travis in case Betty and I didn't make it.

Where was Betty anyway? I was tempted to look over toward my office, but I didn't dare take my eyes off Cal or let him know that someone else was with me. Hopefully, she was at my desk and putting a call through to the police at that very moment.

Cal didn't answer, and I hadn't expected that he would. Instead, he flung the rope toward me as if he were going to lasso me, then drew it back and twisted it around his gloved right hand.

I scooted even farther away, dragging my shoulder bag and the cell phone with me. He twirled the rope and sent it toward me again. It barely missed me. My back hit a laundry cart beside one of the presses and I knew I had to get to my feet if I were to have any hope of evading him long enough for the police to arrive.

"Are you going to kill me, too?" I yelled, just so Travis would know I hadn't turned off the phone. I needed him as plan B in case Betty fell back into her "bag lady" paranoia and refused to call the cops because she distrusted them. But between the two of them, surely someone would call 911.

Cal was still standing by the door, and he seemed to be taunting me, showing that he had all the time in the world. "Why are you screaming?" he asked, playing with the rope and making a bigger noose at the end. "You know it won't do any good."

I put my hand back against the underside of the pants press to give me some leverage to get to my feet. My hand landed on something that shouldn't have been there. It was cold and metallic-feeling, and as I scrambled up, I looked away from Cal long enough to see what it was.

A huge pipe wrench lay near the steam pipes that went to the press. Mack or maybe Luis, a new mechanic we'd just hired, must have been working on the equipment and left it there. Mack usually put his tools away, but I blessed whoever had forgotten it.

I had to force myself to look away from the wrench, because I knew I didn't dare make a grab for it then. Maybe it was foolish to think I could use it later, but I knew I had to wait for the right time to try. Besides, if the police didn't show up soon, it was the only fall-back plan I had.

Cal didn't make any attempt to grab me or throw the rope over my head as I stood up, but he did move away from the door. He walked down the aisle on the other side of the press line, still keeping his distance. I edged back toward the laundry department, turning to keep my eyes on him. It was as if he was starting to circle around me, a wild animal waiting for just the right moment to attack his prey.

I had to think of something to say, anything to buy more time. What did I even know about him? Maybe I could ask, How are things up in Wyoming these days? Oh, yes, that would be a real ice-breaker.

What had Travis said about him when he'd run a background check on some of the names on my suspect list? Not much. Only that Cal had gone through a messy divorce a few years ago.

"Is this because of your divorce?" I blurted, my voice trembling.

"Was it so awful that you started killing look-alikes because you couldn't kill your ex-wife?"

Big mistake—or maybe not. I'd hit a nerve. Anger contorted his face, but at least he quit circling around me and stood like a statue across the aisle from me and behind the pants press. "She was a slut," he said. "Just like my momma."

Whoops. This was a whole lot more than I'd expected.

Cal was the one who yelled this time. "She was a rodeo groupie, and she left me for a bull rider."

"Your wife?"

"No, Momma." He slammed his hand down on the press, and there was a high-pitched singsong quality to his voice, almost like a child would have. "She always called me her 'little man' and she told me she loved me until those so-called *uncles*"—he sneered at the word—"would come around. Then she'd lock me in the closet until they left, but one day she took off with one of them and never came back."

Now I needed to try to calm him down. "I was talking about your wife, not your mother. She surely wasn't like that."

"Was, too." He stomped his feet as if he were about to have a temper tantrum.

The horror of watching Cal revert to a tormented child was made even more surreal by the movement of something a dozen feet behind him. There was flash of gray, followed by a dark blob that slithered across the floor near the lunchroom door. It took me a few seconds to realize that it was Betty with her close-cropped hair and the black outfit that she thought made her invisible.

What the devil was she doing crawling toward the front of the plant on her hands and knees? She should have been hanging on the phone with the dispatcher, waiting for the police to arrive.

My heart did a nosedive at the realization that she probably hadn't called the police at all and was on some sort of ill-conceived rescue mission to sneak around so that we could both launch a frontal attack on him. No, that didn't make sense. More likely, she'd decided it was every woman for herself and was on her way to bail on me through the front door.

Travis was the only hope I had left, but if he'd called the police, they should have come by now. Oh dear God, I suddenly realized, I never told Travis where I was.

"If you aren't planning to kill me, why are you here at the cleaners?" I shouted out the question in hopes Travis could still hear me. "At Dyer's Cleaners," I screamed, as if this were some sort of commercial.

I pictured Travis in his car and knew he'd have to get off the phone to call the police. That was assuming he hadn't hung up by now because he'd already called them and sent them to my apartment.

I glanced back at Cal, but he wasn't paying any attention to me. In fact, he seemed to be crying. At least his nose was running, and he grabbed the handkerchief out of the pocket that had had the Baggie in it earlier. Okay, maybe the reason his nose was running was that he'd been snorting the stuff inside the Baggie to build up his courage.

He blew his nose, stuffed the handkerchief back in his pocket, and took a step toward me. He might have fried his brain with drugs, but I was sure his problems had started long before that. He'd probably be able to cop an insanity plea if we ever got out of here alive.

"You haven't told me about your wife yet," I said, stalling for more time and praying that I'd hear a siren before Cal decided he didn't want to talk anymore.

So far, he still did. "You want to know about my wife. Okay, I'll tell you about her—the bitch. She was a barrel racer, and I met her at a rodeo when I was looking for Momma. That was after some people adopted me and I got out of school. Marlene looked just like Momma, only the way Momma used to look before she left me— and she turned out to be just like her, too. She ran off with a calf roper she met rodeoing. Now, does that make you happy?"

Not hardly. I glanced toward the front of the plant, wondering if

Betty had escaped by now. Would she at least run over to Tico Taco's for help?

As I turned back to Cal, I thought I spotted something white being dragged across the floor between the pieces of equipment. I blinked and it was gone.

"What are you staring at?" Cal asked. "Ain't no one here to help you, missy."

I glanced back at him. "I'm not looking at anything. I'm just wondering why you want to hurt me. Maybe Ardith looked like your momma and Marlene, but I don't. Why me?"

He snorted. "I knew you'd figured it out when you followed me to the Last Roundup." Unfortunately, he was giving me a whole lot more credit than I deserved. "Then you spilled beer on me so you could check out my jeans." Okay, that part was true. "Ardith never should have asked that Julia person if you starched jeans there at the cleaners—not with me standing right beside her. I could have killed her for that."

"You *did* kill her!"

"Did not." He was reverting to that chilling childlike voice.

"Did, too."

He stomped his feet again. "Did not. I killed Momma and the bitch. But they wouldn't stay dead, and then I had to kill them over and over again."

I felt as if I were losing all touch with reality along with Cal. "No, you killed Ardith."

Cal blinked. "Okay, I killed Ardith. She was a slut, too, just like all you women."

"But why'd you prey on women at the cleaners?" It was something I really wanted to know.

"Huh?" Cal seemed surprised.

"Lorraine Lovell," I said.

"Oh, yeah. Just lucky, I guess."

It took all my effort to keep standing, much less to think of anything else to say. Besides, I had almost given up hope that the police were coming. Travis must not have heard me once I put the cell phone in my purse, and apparently Betty hadn't called the cops, either.

"You tried to kill Julia, too, didn't you?"

"And I would have done it, too, if it hadn't been for that yapping little dog of hers stirring up the whole neighborhood."

"In case you're interested, she didn't remember you being with Ardith at the open house."

He sneered. "Good, that means you're the only person I have to worry about, you nosy bitch, and now I can finish off the job I started last night." He pointed his index finger toward me as if it were a gun and began to move in my direction. "Ka-boom."

Suddenly a huge blob of white appeared behind him. It was the thing I'd seen being dragged across the floor, and it was moving forward like the Headless Horseman, with no one holding on to it.

It had to be Betty, dressed up like a ghost and hoping to scare him to death. At first, I thought it was a sheet, but as the thing floated toward us, I realized it was a huge panel from a pair of brocade draperies that one of our most fussy customers had brought us to be cleaned.

Suddenly, Betty's head appeared above it, and she waved at me and motioned with an upward and then a downward thrust of her hand that she was going to throw it over his head. Actually, that was just a guess. I didn't know what the devil she planned to do with it, and I wondered if she had any idea how much the drapery weighed.

Whatever she had in mind, I realized it was now or never. I needed to be ready to spring for the wrench the moment she made her move.

The heavy fabric seemed to rustle as she rearranged it in her hands and moved toward us, and I was terrified Cal might hear the sound. I started rattling off words to him—anything to blot out the noise Betty was making.

"So what are you going to do, hog-tie me like they do to . . . uh, hogs . . . or the way you did to those other women?"

"I didn't do that. I tied them up the way a calf roper does, the way Marlene's boyfriend used to do."

Cal had reached my side of the press by now and was just a few feet across the center aisle from me and only inches from the wrench. Betty was just behind him.

"Eeehaw," Betty yelled, and somehow she managed to throw the heavy fabric over his head.

I lunged for the wrench.

"What the hell?" Cal clawed at the material, but Betty had already jumped on his back and grabbed him around the neck. She had her legs around his waist, but I could tell she was never going to be able to wrestle him to the floor. He was bucking like a wild horse.

I ran up to him, held the wrench high in the air, and aimed for his head. He reared back. I stopped. What if I missed him and hit Betty?

"Wallop him, boss lady," Betty yelled. "Whack him to kingdom come."

I sent the wrench down with a mighty blow, but it hit only air.

"Hold him still, Betty." As if she could.

He leaned forward in an attempt to shake her off his back, and I aimed again. This time, I landed a blow directly to his head. He dropped to the floor like a sack of potatoes. Betty fell on top of him.

She lifted her right hand above her head as she clamped the other hand down on his drapery-covered head.

"Eeehaw," she yelled. "It's curtains for the cowboy." She had a big grin on her face.

TWENTY-TWO

I stared at Betty. How could she be acting as if the whole thing were some sort of joke?

Okay, I was even worse. I seemed to be paralyzed by what had just happened. Finally, I came out of my trance and handed her the wrench. "Use this on him if he starts to move." I decided I'd better qualify what I'd just said. "But don't hit him so hard that you kill him."

Actually, I hoped I hadn't landed a fatal blow already. What I wanted was for him to be locked up for the rest of his life and get some serious psychiatric help.

"Don't worry," Betty said. "I'll bop him on the head so gentle, he won't even know what hit him."

That sounded like an oxymoron to me, but rather than contemplate what she meant, I nodded. "I'll call the police."

Betty shook her head. "Better use your cell phone. The cowboy must have cut the damned phone line to the cleaners."

So that's why she'd had to come up with her own harebrained scheme for saving us. I only wished she'd used a sheet instead of half of an expensive set of drapes to throw over Cal's head. Quit being such an ungrateful tightwad, Mandy, I told myself. Instead, I decided I'd spring for new drapes and maybe give Betty a raise besides.

I dragged the phone out of my bag and looked to see if Travis was still on the line. He wasn't, but I couldn't worry about that. I dialed 911 and told a dispatcher that we'd just apprehended a killer at Dyer's Cleaners. Before the police had a chance to arrive, someone banged on the back door. Maybe Travis was here.

I raced over to unlock the door, but I wasn't taking any chances. "Who is it?"

"Police."

I yanked open the door, but as soon as I did, I thought about slamming it shut again. The cop was Mel Sutton, the customer who'd once been on my suspect list, especially after I'd decided he might be in some sort of collusion with the grungy guy. Now I wondered if maybe I'd been right after all, only that he was really working with Cal.

"What are you doing here?" I demanded.

Right then, another cop appeared from the side of the door, where he'd been waiting with gun drawn. Almost simultaneously, several other officers came into view, and I relaxed.

Poor Mel didn't. In fact, he was apologetic. "Sorry to scare you, Mandy. We had orders to run dark because there was a possible hostage situation here."

By that, I decided he meant without lights or sirens, which meant Travis must have heard me and called the police after all. I'd have to give him more than a raise.

"We just got the all clear to come inside," Mel said.

I assumed that was after my own call, but I decided not to puzzle over the workings of the police department or why he'd lied to me about the license plate. Maybe he didn't know what to do when he found out we'd been trailing an undercover cop.

I pointed over to Cal under the canopy of white brocade and explained that we'd just subdued Ardith Brewster's killer.

"He's waking up," Betty yelled, and I was relieved to know he wasn't dead. However, when I looked over at her, still astride his back, she had the wrench pulled back over her head. "Here I go," she said. "Bombs away."

"No." I ran over to her. "We don't have to do that now."

She looked disappointed when I wrestled the wrench out of her hands. By then, I could hear sirens in the distance, and the place began to fill up with cops of both the uniformed and plainclothes variety.

Travis was right behind them, trying to fight his way into the plant. When he finally broke loose, he barged over to me and gave me a hug. "God, I thought you were never going to tell me where you were." That's all he had a chance to say before Detective Ivinson ordered the uniformed cops to take him outside.

At some point, a fire truck and an ambulance had arrived, and eventually Cal was shuttled off to the hospital to see if he had a concussion. It still took hours before the cops were through questioning Betty and me. Ivinson said I needed to go to headquarters the next day to sign a statement. Mel remembered Betty from when we'd followed the grungy guy, and he said he'd take her home.

"How's it gonna look, me bein' dropped off by the pigs?" she whispered, giving me a dirty look just before she left with him.

Travis was waiting for me outside when Ivinson finally told me I could go. I was surprised to see Mack there, too. I could tell he was upset. He said he'd stopped by my place earlier and that my landlady had told him the police had been there to check on me but hadn't found me. He'd immediately headed for the cleaners, and I wondered if he'd been worried about telling Travis why I was suspicious of him and had doubted Travis. This wasn't the time to ask.

"Yeah," Travis said, "I had to find a damned pay phone the first time I called the cops. When you weren't at your place, I tried to get them to come on down here, but I seem to have a credibility problem with them. Luckily, I kept hanging on the cell until you finally said where you were."

Mack insisted on knowing everything that had happened, and I tried to give as brief a summary as possible before I became coma-tose with exhaustion. The more I told him, the more upset he be-came. "You should have called me half a dozen times during the day so I could have helped you."

I could tell I had some serious fence mending to do if he was ever going to forgive me. In desperation, I resorted to a detailed de-scription of Betty's antics.

He remained impassive when I quoted her "curtains for the cowboy" remark. I finally described her, still astride Cal's back, with the wrench high over her head, saying, "Bombs away."

"It reminded me of that all-time favorite scene of yours that you made me watch one time—Slim Pickens riding a nuclear bomb to the ground in *Dr. Strangelove.*"

Mack finally smiled, and I could tell that everything was going to be all right eventually. "See? I knew Travis was okay," he whis-pered as we parted.

I fell asleep as Travis drove me home, and when we got there, I could hardly get up the stairs to my apartment. In fact, I dropped on my unopened sofa bed the moment we got inside, and he shook me awake the next morning to keep my appointment with the cops. He'd spent the night in my overstuffed chair, apparently with Spot on his lap.

I signed my statement at police headquarters, where I was re-lieved to hear that Cal hadn't been seriously injured and Karla with a *K* was all right. I thought about trying to pay my traffic tickets while I was there, but I decided they could wait. I spent the rest of the day explaining to friends and family everything that had hap-pened. I promised a bonus to Julia and a bone for her dog for their help in finding the killer.

When I talked to Mom, she told me that she and Herb were go-ing up to Vail for a few days while they awaited Laura and Nat's re-turn from Hawaii. She said she'd be back in time to host their party.

I was able to reach the newlyweds on Nat's cell phone to extend congratulations and best wishes. When Nat didn't even seem upset that he'd missed out on the big story about the capture of the serial killer, I felt optimistic that the marriage might actually have a chance.

Laura sounded so happy, I didn't have the heart to tell her about Mom, so I asked if she'd put Nat back on the phone. "Uh . . . Mom was really upset about you eloping, and I *might* have suggested the possibility of her planning an announcement party for you and Laura when you get back."

Nat didn't answer, and I tried to point out the advantage of this situation. "At least she can't tell us what to wear. We can pick out our own clothes."

I'm not sure if I convinced him that was a good thing, and when we hung up, it was unclear if he and Laura would ever come home. He said something about trying to get a job at the *Honolulu Advertiser.*

Spot spent that night in the closet, but as long as there wasn't a dog around, he seemed okay with it. And finally, Travis and I were able to spend some quality time together, but to carry on with Betty's "curtain" theme, all I'm going to say about it is that there were several curtain calls and a couple of encore performances.

cLEANiNG TiP

For those pesky buttons that are always coming off in the wash, they can be reinforced by applying colorless nail polish to the thread. If buttons get even harder treatment (see page 142), try sewing them on with dental floss. Or you can always wear a western-style shirt with snaps (page 127) that break away.

For a zipper that gets stuck and won't pull up, rub it with a little soap, paraffin, or even candle wax, which should help it start moving again. If a zipper won't stay closed, add a button, snap, or piece of Velcro at the top. If it gets off track, you may need to replace it, and always zip up the zippers and button the buttons before washing your garments.

F.
John
MYST

Johnson, Dolores.

Pressed to kill.

$23.95

	DATE	
FEB 1 4 2007		JUN 1 3 2007
		JUL 0 9 2007
MAR 0 8 2007		AUG
MAR 1 3 2007		2007
MAR 2 9 2007		DEC 2 6 2007
APR 0 9 2007		JAN 1 6 2008
APR 9 2007		AUG 1 5 2008
MAY 2 5 2007		SEP 3 0 2011

DISCARDED BY THE
LEVI HEYWOOD MEMORIAL LIBRARY

LEVI HEYWOOD MEMORIAL LIBRARY
55 W. LYNDE ST.
GARDNER, MA 01440-3810

JAN 1 9 2007

LEVI HEYWOOD MEMORIAL LIBRARY

3 3945 00259 3306

BAKER & TAYLOR